FOLLOW ME BACK

Nicci Cloke

HOT
KEY
BOOKS

First published in Great Britain in 2016 by
HOT KEY BOOKS
80–81 Wimpole St, London W1G 9RE
www.hotkeybooks.com

A CIP catalogue record for this book is available from the British Library.

ISBN: 978-1-4714-0508-2
also available as an ebook

This book is typeset in 10.5 Berling LT Std using Atomik ePublisher

Printed and bound by Clays Ltd, St Ives Plc

Hot Key Books is an imprint of Bonnier Publishing Fiction,
a Bonnier Publishing company
www.bonnierpublishingfiction.co.uk
www.bonnierpublishing.co.uk

AIDEN

I DON'T HEAR about Lizzie until the police knock on the front door. I'm just in from training, caked in mud, and the shower is running, the bathroom full of steam. I'm about to peel off my soaked shirt when Mum calls up the stairs.

'Aiden, can you come down here?'

There's something weird about her voice – it's sort of restrained and polite, kind of like her phone voice. That wouldn't be that unusual; in the three years since we moved here, I've heard her use her phone voice a lot. Everyone uses phone voices in Abbots Grey. It's a phone voice kind of place.

But this is not her phone voice at all. It's a voice I haven't heard for a long time.

She sounds scared.

I turn off the shower and go down. As I pass the mirror on the stairs, I catch a glimpse of myself – hair crusted with mud, face bruised from a collision last week with Wellsy, our left-back. Rain bats at the window and the October sky is streaked with Halloween orange.

They're in the living room, two of them: a guy and a woman. They're both in suits, and both looking uncomfortable on the edge of the sofa closest to the door. I can't blame them – the sofas aren't very welcoming; big white square things with hardly any cushioning. Kevin, my stepdad, has weird taste in furniture; in fact, the whole house is pretty devoid of soft edges.

Mum is standing by the window, chewing at the edge of one of her nails. She does this when she's nervous and my heart starts to thump. The woman's radio stutters and she flicks the volume right down to off.

'Hi, Aiden,' the guy says. He's tall, blond and big; wide shoulders, massive hands. Eyes small and silverish. He looks at me and he doesn't smile. 'We need to talk to you about a friend of yours.'

'Okay,' I say. I don't feel nervous, only curious. None of my friends are the type to get into trouble with the police – that's why I like them. I look from the policewoman to Mum and back again. I want to sit down but I'm too filthy to go anywhere near the white sofa.

'Aiden, I'm DS Mahama and this is DCI Hunter,' the woman says to me. 'We need to ask you if you've spoken to Lizzie Summersall today? Online or in person?' She has smooth dark brown skin and short black hair tied back in a ponytail. Her eyes have purplish bags underneath them. 'Or yesterday?'

I shake my head. 'Lizzie? No.'

'When was the last time you saw her?'

I have to think about this. 'I think she was in assembly on Thursday.' It's now Sunday. 'Is she okay?'

'Lizzie's missing,' the bloke – Hunter – says. 'We've been looking through her laptop and you two exchanged a lot of messages.'

2

'We used to be close,' I say, but I'm having trouble concentrating. *Lizzie. Missing.*

'Used to be?' Hunter cocks his head at me, like a dog. 'Until when?'

'I don't know.' Suddenly I don't know what to do with my hands. 'We had a lot of lessons together last year.'

'But you're not as friendly now?' Mahama asks.

'No.' *Why am I sweating?* 'We're not in the same lessons any more. Not since we started A Levels.'

'Aiden, do you have any idea where Lizzie might be?' Mahama's voice is soft, friendly. If it's meant to reassure me, it doesn't work.

'No.' My hands are doing weird things of their own accord now. I kind of want to sit on them. 'Like I say, we're not close or anything. It was just –'

'Yes?' Hunter pins me with his stare.

'I don't know,' I say. 'We were just flirting, I guess. For a while.'

'Just *flirting*?' Mahama frowns, like it's not a word she's heard before.

Mum gets up suddenly from her perch on the windowsill. 'Excuse me, but is this an official interview?'

She's still using her phone voice, but she's got her arms folded and she is not smiling. In Abbots Grey, this is pretty much as hostile as it gets. Both the cops know it, and they aren't smiling either.

'Not at all, Mrs Kendrick,' Hunter says. 'We're just making Aiden aware of the situation, is all. We're letting all of Lizzie's friends know, in case anyone's heard anything from her.' His eyes slide to me, and he gives a faint smirk. 'There is a possibility we'll request Aiden's presence at the police station for a more formal chat. Just so we can get all the facts down on tape.'

'Well, please do let us know if that's the case,' Mum says, moving towards the door. 'As you can see, Aiden really needs to get in the shower, and I need to get dinner on.'

It's an expert dismissal, totally polite and totally impossible to refuse, and I feel so grateful to my mum, so protected, like I'm five years old.

That feeling lasts until she shuts the front door behind them. We watch the panda car reversing down the drive. We watch Hunter watching the house the whole way. And then my mum turns to me, her eyes cold and hard.

'What the hell have you got yourself into?' she demands.

I MET LIZZIE on my first day at my new school, St. Agnes's – Aggers as we all call it, and not affectionately. It was a Tuesday in September, but the end of September, which meant term had already started and I had to stand up at the beginning of each class and be introduced, be the New Guy. Nobody spoke to me; everyone was talking about me.

I was sulking, because the way GCSE subjects were grouped at Aggers was different to my old school and I'd ended up with the choice of drama or RE for my final subject, neither of which interested me at all. I went for drama in the end, thinking that if I worked hard enough in the others, my drama grade wouldn't matter anyway.

I guess that's why I wasn't paying all that much attention when I went into that class and the teacher, Mrs Husveld, with her big crazy cloud of red wavy hair, made me stand at the front and introduce myself. Lizzie says she was in my group that first day, and that we had to take a story from a newspaper Husveld (Hussie, as everyone called her, and that *was* affectionately) gave us, and act it out, but I don't remember any of that.

I *do* remember a time a week or maybe two after that, when Hussie gave us all a soliloquy to read. They were all Shakespeare, and she gave Lizzie one that was Ophelia from *Hamlet*. I hadn't paid Lizzie much attention before then; she's small and pale – a bit, you know, mousy, I guess, and pretty quiet in class. But when she stood up and started reading, everyone got really quiet. The drama studio is painted totally black, and with a single spotlight on her she didn't look mousy, she looked… gold. Like she was made of gold. She read, and her voice wasn't loud – Ophelia's not exactly a shouter, I suppose – but it filled up the studio and I swear nobody was even breathing as they listened. I can't remember most of the lines, but I remember the last one, and I remember the way it carried through the room, the sadness in her voice.

'Oh, *woe is me,*
T'have seen what I have seen, see what I see!'

She looked up, and she smiled, and everyone clapped. I clapped too, and I smiled at her, and I thought to myself, *This girl's full of surprises.*

THE POLICE CALL first thing the next morning to 'invite' me to the station for a 'chat' that afternoon. They say three o'clock, which means I have to leave history early. I don't tell anyone why except my teacher, Dr Radclyffe, but someone must overhear because before I've even got down to my car, people are texting me.

Well, *person*, not people: Scobie, my best friend.

Whole class talking about you instead of Hitler, it says. **Hope it goes ok.**

Great. That's just great.

I drive to the station and I remember what Mum's told me. *You've got nothing to hide. Just help if you can.*

I'd prefer it if she was here next to me, saying it in person, now she's calmed down about it all. But after he insisted this morning, it's Kevin who meets me outside, hands in his pockets in a catalogue pose that's supposed to say 'relaxed'.

'Alright, mate,' he says, and I nod. He's always called me 'mate', ever since he first came round to the house to meet me, the third time he took Mum out on a date. It doesn't sound right in his posh accent, but it isn't annoying like it might be from someone else, because it's always been obvious that's exactly what he wants us to be. Friends. 'Don't be nervous,' he says now, and he claps me on the back in a pally way.

'Just want to get it over with,' I say. 'I don't even know why they want to talk to me.'

'Okay. Let's see what they've got to say.' He ushers me towards the door.

The police station is a little building, white stone and black door, an old-fashioned streetlight outside. Just like everything in Abbots Grey, it's charming and fake, dressed up to hide what's underneath.

The man behind the desk has a big, jowly face like a bulldog's. He types something into his computer with one stubby finger, a mug of builder's tea in the other hand. The mug has a blue teddy bear on it and the words 'World's Best Grandpa'.

'Kendrick?' he says, and I nod. 'Take a seat.'

The chairs are blue plastic, the kind we have at school. It's just a small waiting room, with two seats either side and a payphone on one wall. Opposite us is a noticeboard made of cork. There are only two notices on it: one advertising The Policeman's Ball, a fundraiser for the hospital in King's Lyme, the next town over. The other is a poster about Legal Aid. As if anyone in this town can't afford a lawyer.

'How was school?' Kevin asks.

'Weird,' I say, which feels like an understatement. 'Everyone's talking about Lizzie.'

He nods. 'Everyone in town, too.' He looks at me. 'Sorry. You must be worried about her.'

I look at the noticeboard again. 'You think she's okay?'

Kevin looks down at the floor between his pristine Converse. He has about twenty pairs, which he wears with everything: suits, chinos, jeans. It's like his thing. His I'm-young-cool-and-an-internet-millionaire thing. 'I'm sure she is, mate.'

Even though Kevin's a nice guy and he's been good to me, I suddenly want my dad. It's kind of embarrassing, like I'm seven not seventeen, but I do. I want to be back in London with him, not here in this waiting room with its ticking clock and its chemical clean smell.

'Aiden Kendrick,' a voice says. I look up and it's the guy cop from the other day. He smiles like we're old friends.

'Kevin Cooper,' Kevin says, getting up to shake his hand. 'I'm Aiden's stepfather.'

'DCI Hunter. Come this way, please.'

He shows us into an office; a normal, plain office with a desk and chairs and a potted plant in the corner. Not like the interviews you see on *EastEnders* or anything like that; there's no mirror, no steel furniture. There *is* some kind of recording machine on the desk, though.

'You've already met DS Mahama,' Hunter says. 'She'll be sitting in on our conversation today.'

Conversation. Not interview. That's kind of reassuring. Mahama gives us a friendly smile, also reassuring.

'Please, take a seat,' Hunter says. Phone voice.

I sit down, glad now that Kevin is with me. He leans back in his seat, relaxed and professional, like we're here to discuss a new website or app. It makes me relax too.

'So, Aiden.' Hunter laces his fingers and rests his chin on them. It's a weirdly delicate movement; it doesn't suit him – his meaty jaw resting on big, hairy-knuckled hands. 'We want to talk to you about your relationship with Lizzie.'

'It wasn't a relationship,' I say. 'We were friends.'

'Aiden,' Mahama says. Her voice is soft and calm. 'Let me say, before we go any further, that you are not a suspect. We just want to find Lizzie. Any help you can give us would be really great.'

It hits me again. *Lizzie is missing*. 'I want to help,' I say. 'But I don't know anything.'

Hunter looks down at a file in front of him. From my position on the other side of the big desk, I can't see what's in it.

'You and Lizzie talked a lot online, particularly between January and July of last year,' he says, after a while. 'You want to tell us how that came about?'

I think of Lizzie in the drama studio lights, gold and quiet and surprising. 'We had drama together,' I say.

Three pairs of eyes look at me. It's clearly not enough of an answer.

'We worked on the summer show together,' I say. 'Twice. We helped each other learn our lines.'

'They were quite intimate conversations,' Hunter says. He looks as though the only thing he's been intimate with is a bench press. 'Or, as you say, *flirting*.'

I look down at the floor, and I see Kevin's Converse twitch, just a little. Nervous. I don't reply.

'So, why did all the flirting stop after July?' Hunter asks. He looks sideways at Mahama and I feel, for the first time, really afraid. They're reading something into this, something that isn't there, and I don't know what to say to make it go away.

'It was the end of school,' I try. 'We didn't see each other every day, so I guess it fizzled out.'

Hunter looks at me for a long minute, his bloodshot eyes locked on mine. I don't know what he's searching for, and I don't know if he finds it.

It's Mahama who breaks the silence. 'Aiden,' she says, 'have you heard Lizzie mention friends she met online before?'

I shake my head, happy to break away from Hunter's gaze. 'No. Never.'

Now, they're both studying me. 'Has she ever talked about leaving Abbots Grey?' Hunter asks, and I want to say, *Why are you asking me, you've got it all there in front of you*, because it feels so exposed, so private. But instead I just look down at the floor and think.

'She talked about drama school a couple of times,' I say. 'She wanted to be an actress.'

'Like her sister?' Mahama asks, and Kevin scoffs. We all look at him.

'I wouldn't call that acting,' he says, looking a bit embarrassed.

'That's the only time?' Hunter asks, after a beat. 'She just talked about leaving to study after A Levels?'

'Yeah,' I say, and I'm not sure what they're getting at.

'She never talked about running away?' Mahama says. 'Or going to meet someone?'

I shake my head.

'Officers,' Kevin says, still using his It's Business voice, the one I hear him using on the phone to any of his hundreds of employees. 'Is this a case of running away? Or something more serious?'

'I'm afraid,' Hunter says, 'we're not currently at liberty to say.'

THEY MIGHT NOT be at liberty to talk about it, but everyone else is. At school the next day, the hallways and classrooms are buzzing with it. You can't walk anywhere without hearing Lizzie's name, until it's like the whole school is swarming with bees, the z's of her name humming through the walls.

There was no sign of a struggle, they whisper to each other. She took her phone but left her laptop behind.

Apparently she'd met someone online, they write to each other in class, phones buzzing; more bees.

She ran away. She was taken. Nobody seems to know, but that doesn't stop them from being experts.

'Bloody hell,' Scobie says, when the bell rings for break and we're making our way out of the packed main building. 'It's like she's famous.'

It helps, obviously, that her sister actually *is* 'famous'. Inverted commas intentional. Cheska Summersall has been on *Spoilt in the Suburbs*, the reality show our town's become renowned for, for two seasons now, and though she's yet to get a major storyline, her boyfriend cheated on her at the end of the last series and that significantly upped her air-time. I'm sure her little sister going missing has got the producers rubbing their hands together with glee.

'Jeeeez,' Scobie says, glancing around. 'What's everyone's problem?'

Because it seems like the further we get down the hallway, the more people are stopping to stare at us. Even the whispering stops, just for a second, as we pass. 'I don't know,' I say, in a weak attempt at humour. 'It's probably you.'

It's not him. It's me. *Everyone* knows, and everyone is wondering why, out of the 103 people in our year, the police wanted to speak to me about Lizzie's disappearance. Other people have been interviewed too, but obviously that's not as interesting. Abbots Grey is a small town, and even after two and a half years, I'm still the New Guy – and gossiping about the New Guy is far more entertaining.

In the common room, Marnie Daniels sits on her own, crying. She looks up as Scobie and I walk in, and then looks away in a hurry. *Great*. She thinks I've got something to do with it too, then. Lizzie's best friend.

'Yo, Kendrick!'

I glance up. *Brilliant*. Just what I need right now. Deacon Honeycutt, slouched on the bar of the Tuck Shop like it's a throne, a cluster of his adoring fans nearby. I ignore him, following Scobie over to two of the comfy chairs in the corner.

'Yo, Kendrick!' Undeterred, Honeycutt hops down off the bar and lopes over. 'Thought they'd locked you up.'

'It's nothing to do with me, Deacon,' I say warily.

'Sure.' He grins at me. 'Sure.'

14

People are watching. People watch everything Deacon Honeycutt does, and of course, now I'm Murderer Most Wanted, this is viewing gold. Deacon turns, lets the audience in on the show a little. Diamond studs sparkle in his ears. Everything he wears is designer and his light brown skin looks like it's been airbrushed. He looks, basically, like a Premiership footballer, and he thinks he's one too. So did everyone else: he was the school's sports star, the golden boy, the one who'd make it big. Until I came along.

So now he pretty much hates me.

'Always did think you looked a bit rapey,' he says, in a stage voice loud enough to carry across the whole room. He should really do drama.

'Leave it out, Deacon,' Scobie says, and it's pretty convincing except for the fact his pale skin goes instantly pink, right up to the roots of his so-blond-it's-white hair.

'Pipe down, Scabby,' Deacon says, and everyone laughs.

I look around at all the staring faces. *Might as well get it over with.* 'Look,' I say, loud enough for everyone to hear, and not even looking at Deacon. 'I did speak to the police about Lizzie. I told them everything I knew, which is not much, probably about the same as most of you, and they thanked me and let me go. Okay?'

Everyone looks away, embarrassed. 'Yeah, whatever,' Deacon says, but he's bored too, and he wanders off, back to the group of girls waiting eagerly to giggle at his every joke.

'Seriously, though,' Scobie says, when it's just the two of us again. 'That's it? Just a couple of questions?'

I shrug. 'There wasn't much I could tell them.'

15

Scobie looks away and I realise I haven't even asked him how he's feeling. He was at primary school with Lizzie, infants too, I think, although I guess that's not unusual here; there are only a couple of schools in Abbots Grey. He and Lizzie aren't exactly close, and the three of us never hung out together, but still, it must be weird. But he speaks before I can.

'I didn't even know you and Lizzie were still mates.'

'We're not. I haven't spoken to her properly in months.' This is almost, *almost* true.

'They tell you anything about this guy she's meant to have been talking to?'

I shake my head. 'No.'

'Apparently he was some guy in London,' Scobie says, looking thoughtfully at a smudge on his glasses. 'Paedo, you reckon?'

'Hardly,' I say. 'Lizzie's sixteen.'

You wouldn't know it to look at her, though. And the idea of some forty-year-old weirdo messaging her makes my stomach turn.

'Gives me the creeps,' Scobie says, and I nod.

THE FIRST TIME we actually spoke – the first time I remember anyway, because Lizzie always disagreed – was the day after the Ophelia day. It was breaktime and I was heading for the lockers to meet Scobie, so far the only person at Aggers who'd spoken to me about anything other than the subject of a lesson. He's a bit of a loner, I guess, although everyone likes him – he's smart and funny and friendly, but quiet. Keeps his head down. As far as I was concerned, that was perfect.

The lockers are in a place called the 'Locker Room', which might make you think of American high schools and jocks; a big glamorous place with steaming showers and lockers big enough to live in. This is misleading. The Locker Room is a kind of raised area in front of the main block of toilets. It smells like bleach and there's the constant sound of hand-dryers. They're not proper lockers like you'd see in those American films, not even like the skinny bashed up ones we had at my school in Hackney. These are just small and square and a weird greenish-grey colour. Big enough to put a couple of books or your lunch in, but that's about it.

I was meeting Scobie there but I was early; our tech teacher,

Miss Foster, always let us out early. The hallway was pretty deserted as I climbed up the steps to the lockers, which run in two rows. Mine was in the second line, closer to the door to the boys' toilets, and as I went to open it, I glanced down the long row and saw Lizzie by an open locker, a dark-haired girl talking animatedly beside her. Marnie Daniels.

'...total, utter prick!'

I fumbled with my padlock. I'd never spoken to Marnie Daniels before, and the force and fury in her voice was pretty unexpected. Also, it was Lizzie, who had somehow retained some of her Ophelia gold, even in the ugly greenish striplighting of the Locker Room.

'You're maybe overreacting just a tiny bit.' Lizzie was rummaging around in her locker, a jumper and an overstuffed notebook tucked under her arm.

'I'm not!' Marnie said. 'I asked a simple physics question –'

'Not that simple,' Lizzie said, laughing. 'I didn't understand it.'

'– a simple question,' Marnie continued, 'and that sexist pig tells me to just sit there and look pretty.'

'And instead of letting it go, you rose to the bait and now you've got detention!'

'He deserved it,' Marnie said, unrepentantly, and at that moment they both looked up and realised I was there.

'Lyons?' I asked.

Marnie nodded. 'How'd you know?'

'He's my biology teacher. He told a girl in my class not to talk over the boys once,' I said.

'Sounds about right,' Marnie said, but she wasn't raising her voice any more. 'You wait til my father hears about this.'

Lizzie laughed. 'Alright, Draco Malfoy!'

She said it at the same time as I said, 'Malfoy!' and we looked at each other and laughed.

I think it was then that I knew we'd be friends.

AT HOME THAT night, I've only just turned my laptop on when the first message pops up.

Scobie.

Didn't see you after school, you okay?

yeah, fine, I type.

just made a quick exit from all the staring

lol

They'll forget about it by tomorrow

I hope so

How much of the Pure coursework you got left
to do?

err... all of it

lol

No doubt Scobie's already finished his. He's been a good friend to me, but making me look bad just comes naturally to the guy. Before I can reply, another bubble pops up.

Hey

Marnie Daniels. That's… unexpected.

hey

I wanted to talk to you at school today but I felt
weird about it

Marnie
I really hope you don't think I had anything to do
with Lizzie going missing
the police just wanted to talk to me cos we
messaged a bit, that's all
Honestly.

There's a long pause before I see the little '…' that means
she's typing. I hold my breath.

I know

I let the breath go.

she always said you were a nice guy

I don't know what to say to that. It makes me feel really sad.
It makes me realise that this is Lizzie we're talking about. That
Lizzie has gone missing. That Lizzie used to think I was a nice guy.
She …s again, and then stops, like she's deleting what she's
written. There's a long pause and then:

...

I need your help

21

I look at the words for a minute. Four little words, but looking at them makes me feel like I'm on the edge of a cliff. About to step off.

what you mean?

...

I can't say here. meet me tomorrow after
  2nd period?

ok. Where?

Rec. Balcony.

I agree and log off. But my head is spinning. What could Marnie need my help with? I want to log on again and look at Lizzie's profile, see her face, but I can't. I'm too afraid.

Lizzie is a girl who thinks of everyone before herself. She's a girl who loves her family, who tries hard at school, who would never just get up one day and walk away.

Except she has. And nobody knows where, or why. Some guy she met on the internet. I don't believe that. I *can't* believe that.

I try not to think about it. I cross Facebook away. I check my emails. A load of spam, a few notifications. One from Doug, my coach at Norwich. It's the new training schedule, which he's sent to us all, but he's added a message to mine.

Let's meet again end of month and discuss options.

It's not like there are many options. There's his: drop out of school and train full-time as part of the youth team. And there's mine: finish my A Levels and have a back-up, in case

22

football doesn't work out. I know which one makes sense for me, but that hasn't stopped Doug from pushing his plan.

It's not that I don't love football. I *do*. I live, breathe and dream it. Like, seriously. Every night. Matches that go on and on until I wake up. If I'm not bruised and in pain at the end of the week, I haven't trained hard enough and I hate myself. I *want* to be a professional footballer. Having a chance at Norwich is something I pinch myself about on a daily basis.

But something's stopping me. And I can't tell if that *thing* is Mum, giving me her worried eyes, her 'Well, whatever you think is best, love' in a voice that makes it clear what she thinks is best, or Dad, non-committal and hard to read as always, or Kevin with his motivational speeches: 'If they want you now, mate, think how much they'll want you if you make them wait'. Or if it's just because the idea of giving up school and going for it gives me that edge of a cliff feeling again.

So, it's cool. I'll carry on with my A Levels, but in the meantime I'll train harder than anyone else on the squad. I'll need to, to keep up with the guys who've already gone full-time, already committed themselves.

'Aiden?' Mum shouts up the stairs, breaking my train of thought. 'Dinner's ready.'

I head down. When I see myself in the mirror this time, I look weird and pale. It's not just me who notices, either. As soon as I sit down at the table, Mum looks at me, eyes narrowed.

'Are you feeling okay?'

I nod. 'Bit tired.'

'You're training too hard.'

'Maybe.' I look down at my plate. Toad-in-the-Hole. My favourite. Except I really don't have any appetite.

'It's been a stressful couple of days,' Kevin says, sawing off a chunk of sausage. 'Has there been any news about your friend?'

Hang on a second. Kevin eats things like white fish with brown rice and vegetables I've never heard of that are all steamed and green and sad on the expensive white plates. Ever since we moved in with him, he's made it his mission to change our diets; to make everything we eat organic and artisan, stuff grown locally or imported responsibly (and expensively) and not from shrink-wrapped supermarket packs. He's got rid of all the things that used to be our favourites in an attempt to make us as healthy and happy as him. It's all low-carb, low-fat, high-cost. So why are we having Toad-in-the-Hole on a Tuesday?

They're worried about me. The thought makes me feel awful.

'No,' I say. 'Everyone's talking about her running away with someone she met on the internet.'

'That's awful.' My mum takes a sip of wine. She's the only one having a glass – Kevin doesn't drink during the week and, even though they'd happily let me, I'm not supposed to drink during the season. Not that it always stops me. 'Her poor parents.'

'You know, we talked about investing in social media,' Kevin says, reaching to get more peas. 'But this was one of the reasons we didn't. It's so difficult to safeguard, and we just didn't want to take on the responsibility, not without the software to protect young kids from this exact thing.'

Kevin's company was originally an auction site, kind of like eBay, but now it's what he calls a 'global marketplace'. It basically means people can set up their own stores – again, like

24

eBay – but the focus is on ethically-sourced and environmentally friendly products. Lots of vegan chutneys and hemp handbags. People pay a lot of money for that stuff. Advertisers pay a lot of money to be on the site. Kevin owns a load of other businesses now – a web design firm, a security company, a life consultancy (don't even ask) – but he's mostly a silent partner, with investments all over the place. Fingers in many pies, as my dad would – and does – say. As far as I can tell, Kevin's day-to-day work involves checking a lot of emails and giving the occasional keynote speech at technology conventions in random exotic places. He sometimes gets calls from the big newspapers who ask for a quote or an opinion piece if there's a story involving internet trading or responsible consumerism (whatever the hell that means).

'It's so scary,' Mum says. 'I mean, as parents, we have no idea what our kids get up to online.' She sounds like she's being interviewed on a chat show.

I'm pretty sure Kevin could quite easily find out what I get up to online, given that I use his wifi and that he's basically Minister of the Internet, but I don't say that. And, besides, Kevin has always been pretty adamant about treating me as an adult, letting me have privacy. Since I moved in here, I've never had a curfew, never been told I can't go anywhere. Maybe it's because he wants me to like him, maybe it's because he doesn't have kids of his own, but actually I think that's just the kind of guy he is. He trusts people. He believes in them.

'I don't really know if it's true or not,' I say. 'I don't think Lizzie would just go and meet a stranger.'

'Sounded like that was the police's theory, huh?' Kevin says.

'It's just awful,' Mum says again. 'Anything could have happened to her. You just don't know who's out there.'

I stare down at my plate. Has something really happened to Lizzie? Is this actually real?

Kevin must see my face, because he lays a hand over Mum's and briskly changes the subject. 'Have you been in touch with Doug? Have you asked him about taking a couple of weeks off in the summer?'

Mum wants us both to go with Kevin when he gives one of his keynote speeches in Miami next June. Technology convention = not my kind of thing. Miami beaches = very much my kind of thing.

'Yeah, he said it's okay as long as the hotel has a gym.'

'I'll check,' Kevin says, as if he'd stay anywhere that didn't have a gym, a five-star restaurant, a butler service.

We eat quietly for a bit, our cutlery clicking against the plates. Each room in Kevin's house is carefully optimised by various systems that are constantly assessing air quality, temperature, light levels. Occasionally you'll hear a dull beep or a click as the room reaches the perfect level of something and the system goes to sleep. The temperature in the room has clearly reached its ideal degree because it clicks softly off, and then we can hear a faint tapping, the pipes cooling.

'So, Aiden, how's training going at the moment?' Kevin asks, chasing a pea around his plate.

'Good. My leg's getting stronger again.' I was out of action for about six weeks a few months ago, and it really, *really* scared me. One injury can ruin your whole career before it's even started and that's pretty terrifying. I don't get it when guys

26

on the squad go on skiing holidays and stuff. It's like gambling with your whole life.

'And how's school?' Mum asks. She's always careful to mention my A Levels whenever football comes up.

I finish chewing my mouthful and nod. 'Yeah, good. Really enjoying history at the moment.'

'World War Two, wasn't it?' Kevin asks. This is one of my favourite things about him. He *listens*, like really listens, and remembers things people tell him about themselves. His brain is basically like the most efficient computer ever; he's about ninety per cent android. I guess that's why he's done so well for himself.

'Yeah, that's right.'

'You should ask your dad to get some of your granddad's things out for you,' Mum says. 'He has them all in the loft, I think.'

'Cool. I will.'

'Is it next weekend you're going down there?'

'One after,' I say. 'He's at Nanna's this weekend.' My nanna lives in Scotland. She's eighty-six and her husband, my granddad, died five years ago. Since then Dad and his brother take it in turns to go and look after her, because she won't move off their farm. I can't blame her. I love it there. Just hills and more hills, as far as you can see. You could run for miles and still just see hills and sky. It'd be perfect if it wasn't always raining.

Mum's got a dreamy look on her face. She loves it there too. 'We should go and visit her one weekend,' she says. 'She'd like that.'

27

She would. Nanna and Mum were always close, and I know that Mum misses her and my uncle, especially since we moved here, where she doesn't really have any close friends. Don't get me wrong, she's far happier here, but I guess it's hard; when you get divorced from someone there are so many little things you have to leave behind, not just that person.

They told me they were splitting up about a month before they actually did. I was twelve at the time and Mum said they wanted to give me time to get used to the idea. Instead it just made the month the most awkward and uncomfortable period in our whole family life, especially as, instead of bickering constantly like they usually did, they made an effort to be polite to each other. It was weird, like living with a stage family. Rather than being sad, I was just kind of relieved when it was over and Dad moved into his flat.

'I'd better get back to work,' Kevin says, and as he pushes his chair back, he frowns. 'I'll call someone about the heating first thing tomorrow.'

'Oh good,' Mum says, pouring herself another inch or so of wine.

'What's wrong with the heating?' I ask.

'Air in the system, I think,' Kevin says. 'That clicking. Probably a good idea to get it serviced anyway – the news this morning said there's a cold front moving in. Maybe even early snow next week.' He turns to go.

'Do you really have to do more work?' Mum asks, swirling her wine in her glass with a mock sadface.

'I've got a conference call with New York. But I'll see you guys in a while for Movie Night, right?'

Movie Night is something Kevin and Mum do every Tuesday. It's probably something Kevin picked up from the New York office, along with phrases like 'blue sky thinking' and 'idea clouds'. Maybe it's lame, maybe it's cute, but it makes them happy. It makes them even happier if I join in, and hey, today I could probably do with a couple of hours of living in a made-up world.

'Cool,' I say. 'What's on tonight?'

Kevin holds up the DVD and at least has the good grace to look sheepish. '*Gone Girl.*'

Great. That's just great.

I HAVE MATHS with Scobie first period, and then a free, and since I don't want to sit in the common room and listen to everyone talking about Lizzie like she's the latest episode of *Sherlock*, I head over to the Rec even though I've got an hour to kill before Marnie will be there.

Abbots Grey Recreation Centre is probably the bleakest building in the whole town. It must drive them all mad, a big concrete block parked right on the edge of St. Agnes's grounds. Aggers itself isn't that pretty, if you ask me – dark and dingy with narrow, draughty windows – but it's Victorian and apparently that's what counts. It's imposing and grand and showy, and that's pretty much the look of the whole town. It's kind of like their crown jewel, I guess, bang in the centre, and on a bit of a hill, so you can see it from a mile or so away. And yet here it is, sharing a car park with the ugly, grey Rec. I skirt past the edge of the drama studio, which sort of belongs to both, and find my car in the front row. It's still a pretty big thrill to say that – '*my* car'. I turned seventeen at the beginning of September and Kevin just drove up to the house with it that morning, a big bow stuck on the bonnet.

Kind of over-the-top, but unbelievably amazing of him. When Dad heard, he bought me two weeks' intensive driving lessons, which cost way more than he should be spending. I kind of hate it that he feels he has to compete like that when obviously I don't care what he gets me. But at least now I can drive down and see him whenever I want.

I unlock the car and grab a book from the back seat to pass the time before heading for the Rec's automatic doors.

It's just as grim inside as out – sticky beige vinyl floors and those polystyrene ceiling tiles everywhere. But I kind of love it. I love the smell of chlorine from the pool and the muffled squeak of trainers from the squash courts upstairs. I'm just a sucker for sport, I guess. I always have been.

I head up to the second floor, where the café is, and buy a coffee from the miserable-looking guy behind the counter. From here, I can see into the gym: rows and rows of polished Abbots Grey women in designer sportswear, walking and cycling and looking at their phones. From where they are, they can see the menu: fried things and sweet things. It's a pretty neat circle.

I wander back out onto the walkway overlooking the sports hall, where a class, maybe Year 7 or 8, are playing volleyball. I watch the girls whisper to each other, the boys compete for attention. We didn't play volleyball where I grew up. We had a smallish field and a kind of worn-out basketball court and if it was raining hard enough, we played indoor rounders in the damp school hall. Here, as well as Aggers' huge green fields, the kids have the Rec with all its courts and equipment, and they have an athletics track at a centre just up the road. It's just one of the reasons I can see why everyone thinks it's a better life here, but that doesn't stop me sometimes missing London in a way that hurts.

At the end of the walkway there's a set of double doors that leads into the balcony overlooking the pool. I take a seat about halfway down and drink my coffee. I'm the only person up here, and the pool itself is also fairly empty; just a mums-and-babies swim group gathered in the shallows, far enough away that their voices drift over to me in murmurs, no words.

The coffee isn't very warm but it's still okay; surprisingly strong, although nowhere near as strong as I'd make it for myself. I look at the book in my lap but I don't open it. English has always been one of my favourite subjects, especially since I came to Aggers, but I haven't been able to get into it this year. Maybe because it was one of the things that Lizzie and I talked about most, and now that we don't talk about anything at all, it's lost its appeal. Same way I can't imagine taking drama now, even though when we were sorting out our A Level choices last year it took me weeks to decide between that and maths. Suddenly, I'm more glad than ever that I chose maths.

My school in Hackney was bigger than Aggers – in that we had more kids, anyway. It was a bit easier to stay anonymous; at Aggers, everyone knows who everyone is. It gets a bit much, especially at first, and when I got here in Year 10 I spent quite a few lunchtimes on this balcony. The clammy heat and the way sound echoes – it's relaxing somehow. There aren't any windows and it's like being in a bubble, hidden away. I sink lower in my seat and try to at least pretend to read my book.

It's actually a pretty decent book: *Birdsong*. It's about World War One and so it appeals to the history geek in me too. But the warmth of the balcony and the faraway sounds of the mums and the babies in the pool make me feel sleepy and it's hard to keep my eyes open.

I must drift off a bit, because suddenly the door clicks shut above me, and I turn in time to see Marnie making her way down the steps. She looks different today; long dark hair down instead of scraped back like it was the other day, dressed in a bright yellow t-shirt and dark jeans, an expensive-looking leather jacket. She's wearing make-up, too, puffy crying eyes gone.

'Hey,' she says, flopping into the seat beside me. She has a laptop under one arm.

'Hey,' I say. 'How you doing?'

She sighs. 'Not great.'

I nod, and look out at the pool. The mums are climbing out now, babies clinging to them like swollen starfish.

'I guess you've heard the rumours?' she says, and I don't reply.

She puts a hand on mine. 'Aiden, I know we don't really know each other that well, and I know you and Lizzie don't really talk that much any more, but I think you did care about her, didn't you?'

Lizzie. It all seems so long ago now. Lizzie standing up in drama class. Lizzie laughing. 'Of course,' I say.

'So, you'll help me find her?'

I turn to look at her. 'How are you going to do that?' I ask, and she flips open the laptop.

'Look,' she says, and the laptop whirrs awake, the Facebook home page open. I watch her type in Lizzie's email address, and then a password. Her hands move so quickly over the

33

keys I can't make out what it is. She clicks 'log in' and there it is. Lizzie's news feed. Lizzie's profile picture in the corner.

'How did you get her password?' I ask, and Marnie looks at me and rolls her eyes.

'We've been friends since Year 3,' she replies. 'I know her better than I know myself.' Something about the way she says it makes me feel strange, nervous.

She clicks on the speech bubble icon, where Lizzie has new messages waiting. Her inbox unfolds, and it feels so wrong that I hold my breath. It's like watching someone get undressed or sleep without them knowing. It's private.

'We shouldn't be doing this,' I say, thinking suddenly of DCI Hunter and his staring, silver eyes. 'The police have been looking through all her online stuff. They'll think it's her, logging in.'

The colour drains from her face. 'Really?'

'Yeah.'

But neither of us moves to log out. We both look at the screen and the list of names, the list of people who've written to Lizzie. I see Marnie's name, but I don't see mine. I must be pretty far down the list. I see girls I know, a couple of guys. One name sticks out from the rest: Hal Paterson.

As if she's read my mind, Marnie glances sideways at me and clicks on his name. 'This is one of the guys she met online,' she says.

My chest tightens. Lizzie at home, late at night, talking to strangers, flirting with strangers. Trusting strangers.

Marnie moves her fingers on the laptop's trackpad to zoom in on the profile picture. It's of a guy about our age, maybe a bit older. It's just him in the photo, on a beach somewhere, Wayfarer sunglasses covering his eyes. His hair is light brown and longish, falling across his face. *Kind of like mine.*

'His profile's totally weird,' Marnie says. 'There's hardly anything on it.'

I look at the most recent messages, a sick feeling in my stomach.

haha defo

c u soon

bye x

'See you soon,' I say, under my breath.

'Looks like they were talking somewhere else, too – text, I guess, or on another site,' Marnie says briskly, scrolling down the chain. 'I feel like there's stuff missing here. There's nothing really useful anyway.'

I take the laptop from her. 'Who else was she talking to?'

'So you'll help?' she says, obviously relieved, and suddenly, I realise how weird this situation is. Like she said, I don't know Marnie Daniels, not really. And Lizzie and I haven't been close for a long time. *Why* has she singled me out?

'Why are you asking me to help?' I ask, and she looks down, like she's embarrassed.

'I've read the things you said to her,' she says, without looking at me. 'I know I can trust you.'

I look down at my hands. The waves of the pool reflect off the ceiling and cast their blue light over my skin. 'You can,' I say eventually.

'It's him,' she says. 'It's him the police think she went to meet, and I think so too.' And then, after a minute: 'I know it.'

I turn to look at her. 'You *know* it?'

'I can't explain. I just…' She looks at the screen, reaches out to scroll back and forth along the conversation between Lizzie and Hal. I see bits of it flash by.

You're beautiful

lol

so not

big day

always makes me smile

talking to you

like forever

'I just know.'

I stare at the words on the screen. *Like forever.* I move her hand and scroll back to the top of the conversation. *c u soon. haha defo.* 'Did you know she was talking to him?' I say.

'No.' She glances at me and then back at the pool. 'Not exactly. She was online a lot. I could see the people she was talking to weren't people from school.'

'People?' I click back to the inbox. 'So there *were* more?'

'Yeah.' She tugs the laptop back towards her. 'Not so much on here. But she was on *here* all the time.'

I look at the page she's opened. AskMe.com.

'Lizzie had a profile on here?' I wrinkle my face. It's the kind of site twelve-year-olds are obsessed with. They spend hours asking each other questions like 'Top five fittest boys in Year

9?' and 'Top three prettiest girls in your class?' The questions are anonymous. You can say anything you want without anyone knowing who you are. That's why they all like it so much.

Marnie nods. 'I mean, we all had them in like, Year 9 or whatever. But I guess she kept hers.'

I look at the page, and I keep looking, and I can't understand why she would do that. Most of the messages are just abuse about her sister.

Why's your sister such a slag? one of them asks.

Do you think your sister's the stupidest person on tv? writes another.

The thing that gets me is Lizzie's answers. Sometimes she just writes normal things – 'she's not' or 'no' or 'get a life' – but sometimes she writes quotes. In all her most recent answers, she posts lines of poetry and passages of plays or books that I don't even know, and none of it makes any sense.

I look at them.

like a whore, unpack my heart with words

Physical beauty is passing. A transitory possession.
But beauty of the mind and richness of the spirit and
tenderness of the heart – and I have all of those things...
But I have been foolish – casting my pearls before swine!

I am not what I am.

37

All the world's a stage, and all the men and women
merely players

'Marnie, this doesn't make any sense,' I say.

She shakes her head. 'I know.'

'It makes her look –' I don't want to say it. All I can remember is Ophelia singing nonsense songs at the end of the play.

'Yeah.' Marnie glances at me and then back at the screen. 'But Aiden, look –' She leans over and tilts the laptop back towards her, scrolls the page to the top. 'Look at the latest question.'

I look, and my heart stops beating.

Do you love me? it says, and the username underneath it says 'aiden k'.

WHEN I GET home, I log straight on to Facebook and go to my inbox. I scroll down yesterday's messages – Marnie, Scobie, Jake from my English class – and then the messages from the day before, the week before, last month. I go all the way back, way, way back, to last summer, and I find my thread with Lizzie. I look at her profile picture – her and Cheska and their little sister, Evie, at the *Harry Potter* studio tour, all wearing Harry-style glasses and holding wands. Lizzie properly, properly loves Evie. She talked about her all the time, carried a picture Evie drew when she was five in her purse, picked flowers for her on her way home. I wonder what their parents have told Evie about her leaving.

I scroll right down to the end of the conversation, as far back as it will go, and lose myself in the things I said and thought two years ago.

Hey, she writes, after she'd accepted my friend request.

hey, I write and then I use a winking smiley. Smooth, Aiden.

Are you auditioning tomorrow?

yeah, I guess so

The drama department's production of *A Midsummer Night's Dream*. Hollywood eat your heart out.

oh, cool

You sound surprised

lol sorry
How come you do drama anyway?

what, I don't seem the type? ;)

Another winky face. What a sleaze.

not really ☺

Dunno, better than RE I guess?

haha defo

My heart drops like it's made of stone. *Haha defo*.

There's a little jump in the time then, and I wonder why – was Lizzie busy doing something else, or was I? And then she writes again, eight minutes later:

You're good though

You think so?

yeah ☺

haha cheers
you are too ☺

no ☺

                                                           you are

Another gap. Lizzie was never good with taking
compliments.

Do you ever miss London? she asks, five minutes later.

                                                        sometimes
                                              it's pretty different
haha I bet
                                        Do you ever go there much?
yeah sometimes
just shopping and stuff
I wanna go live there
                                                           oh yeah?
yeah
someday
Will you go back?
                                                        yeah maybe
how come you moved here anyway?
                                          my stepdad's from here
oh ok
What's his name?
                                                      Kevin Cooper
Oh I think I know who that is
he's friends with my best friend's parents
nice car right?
                                         haha yeah it's alright

Another gap, and I think maybe we were just playing hard to get. I was probably playing Solitaire, trying to pretend I was away from the screen, too busy to type.

We should hang out sometime, she writes. I can show you around.

That'd be cool

Thanks ☺

Cool ☺
I can show you –

My phone buzzes on the desk. A new text. I feel jumpy, like someone's interrupted me doing something wrong. And there's a part of me that really expects, as I unlock my phone, to see Lizzie's name at the top of the message.

It's Marnie, though.

I found something. Meet me after school tomorrow?

THE POLICE ARE at school the next day. I see the first one outside the main hall around assembly time, a woman talking quietly on a mobile, her eyes fixed on the rows of kids inside the hall. And when it comes to my third period free I go to the Keep, the small building which houses the sixth form, and there she is again, with a bloke this time, waiting outside the Head of Sixth Form's office. I head for the common room and take a seat near the door, where there's a big window looking out at them. I get out my book but I'm not really reading. So not in the mood for *Birdsong* right now.

Mr Selby, the Head of Sixth Form, is the kind of guy who is enthusiastic about *everything*. He practically bounces when he talks, and when he's listening to someone else speak, his hands rub over his thinning hair, or twist together, or tap out a rhythm on the door frame. It's an enthusiasm that is pretty infectious, and I don't know anyone who was in his GCSE history class who didn't get a B or higher. He's pretty much the reason I took it at A Level, but I like Radclyffe just as much. To be honest, all the teachers at Aggers are good. They don't have the war-worn look the teachers at my old school did.

43

Selby comes out of his office and starts talking to the two officers. I can't hear what they're saying – stupid soundproof doors – but Selby's got his most earnest face on, nodding, one arm folded across his chest, the other propping up his chin. He taps at his mouth with a finger as he listens.

It suddenly occurs to me that the police are telling Selby someone has been logging onto Lizzie's Facebook from pretty much this location.

As I think this, his brow furrows and I swear he looks up and through the glass at me. I look down at the book open in my lap, the words just a black smear on the page, and by the time I dare glance back up, Selby is talking, head on one side, his eyes wide.

The policewoman, the one who seems to be doing all the talking, nods and passes Selby a brown cardboard folder, a thin thing, like the kind you find in a filing cabinet. He looks down at it, takes a step back, and ushers them both into his office. I feel a shiver travel through me as I wonder what's in that file.

My phone buzzes in my pocket and I slip it out as the door to Selby's office shuts. It's a Facebook notification: one new message. I unlock the keypad and open my inbox.

Cheska Summersall.

Whoa. Probably the very last name I expected to see.

Hey, she writes. Want to talk to you

She's friend-requested me as well. Despite the fact I think Cheska Summersall is the worst kind of human, I accept. Curious, I guess. And you know what they say about curiosity.

44

Sure, I type, even though the thought fills me with dread. Seeing as I'm pretty sure Cheska Summersall previously had no idea I even existed, I guess she's yet another person to hear about the police interviewing me.

It takes her exactly thirty seconds to reply.

Are you free tomorrow afternoon?
                    I have a free fifth period so after 2.30, yeah
Cool

And that's it. Nothing else. I flick back to my newsfeed and see an update she's posted two minutes ago.

Cheska Summersall is excited about this week's shoot!
It's getting juicyyyyyy!! ;-)

When her sixteen-year-old sister's missing. See what I mean? Worst. Kind. Of. Human.

Spoilt in the Suburbs has been filmed in and around Abbots Grey for two years now. It was meant to be a one-hour documentary about wealthy teenagers in the home counties, but when the producers came here to scout for possible locations, and started interviewing a few of the kids who would eventually become the cast, they quickly decided it had more than enough material to carry a show all by itself. The first series was a smash hit, despite the fact that the 'acting' is really awful (although everyone involved in the show swears it isn't acted or scripted and is all about real people and real lives). It focuses mostly on who's sleeping with who, who's throwing a party that episode, and who will have an argument with who *at* that party. Cheska got a smallish part towards the end of the first series, and she's been working pretty hard to make herself the star ever since.

'Hey,' someone says beside me, and I jump. I've been too busy glaring at Cheska's profile picture (her in a bikini, from a cast promo shoot for *Spoilt in the Suburbs*) to notice Scobie come up beside me.

'Hey,' I say, pulling my bag off the seat next to me so he can sit down.

'Police are about again today,' he says.

I nod. 'They're in with Selby.'

'Birchall reckons they're gonna start interviewing everyone in our year.'

'Really?' Ollie Birchall is the biggest gossip going, but, as the son of one of our deputy heads, he's usually accurate when it comes to school stuff.

'Yeah.' Scobie takes off his glasses and fiddles with them, frowning. 'I dunno, sounds like she's just gone. Without a trace. How is that even possible?'

I shake my head. 'I don't know.' I think about our conversations, the words on my laptop screen. *Without a trace.* It doesn't feel that way to me.

He sighs. 'God. Lizzie. I really hope she's just run away. It could still be that, right? She's off having fun somewhere?'

I nod, because it's the kind thing to do, because it's what I want to hope too. 'Yeah, probably. Maybe she had a row with Cheska or something.'

Scobie gives a half-hearted smile but doesn't say anything, and we sit and watch Selby's closed office door. A few of the girls in our year come in, giggling about something. I notice Lauren Choosken, Deacon Honeycutt's on-again off-again girlfriend, among them and look quickly away.

Scobie picks my book up and looks at it. 'Any good?'

I shrug. 'Yeah, it's alright. Sad.'

He puts it down. 'Done your Pure yet?'

'Nope.'

'Want me to help? Don't want to give poor old Ladlow one of his migraines.'

'You sure?' I'm already taking my book out of my bag.

'No worries.'

I work my way through the questions, picking my way through Scobie's minuscule writing to check I'm doing the working the same way he has. Occasionally he glances over and helps, but mostly he just plays a game on his phone. He gets a bit itchy if he's away from some kind of CGI for more than ten minutes.

I've just finished, feeling a bit of the satisfaction I usually get from looking at pages of completed maths – there's something about the logic of it, the neatness of the numbers – and I'm passing Scobie's book back to him when Selby and the two officers come out of his room. We both watch them as they head down the stairs towards the playground. Scobie looks at his watch.

'Feel like going into town for lunch?'

'Yeah,' I say, stuffing my books back in my bag. 'Let's get out of here.'

After school, Marnie is waiting for me by my car.

'Look at this,' she says, and she flips her phone round to show me Hal Paterson's profile page. It's a locked profile, and she's obviously accessed it from her own account, not Lizzie's, because all that's visible is the public stuff: his profile picture, the number of friends she has in common with him. Which is one: Lizzie. He doesn't have a network so it just says his location, London. There's a little blue box saying 'Friend request sent' where she's tried to add him, and I wonder how long she'll wait for him to accept.

'You friend-requested him?' I ask, my mouth dry.

'Not that,' she says, exasperated, and she scrolls down. Way, way down. There isn't very much to see – he keeps everything locked tight. Just some people he's added as friends, some apps he's used. '*Look*,' she says again, thrusting the phone closer to my face.

But all I see are the same things. Hal Paterson is playing Burger Battle. Hal Paterson scored 30 points on Jungle Fever. Hal Paterson scored Spider-Man on the quiz 'Which Marvel hero are you?'

'I don't see anything, Marnie,' I say. 'So he wastes a lot of time on the internet. Big deal.'

She rolls her eyes and zooms in a bit. 'Look at the location.'

And then I see it. Underneath the post about the quiz, Facebook's location services have added, 'Near Kings Lyme'.

Kings Lyme, as in the town only a couple of miles down the road. Kings Lyme, as in *not London*.

'See?' Marnie says. 'Now do you get it? Maybe she *didn't* meet him online after all.'

INSTEAD OF GOING home, I drive straight to Scobie's, Marnie's words ringing in my ears. I keep thinking of Lizzie, under that spotlight in the drama studio. At home, crouched in front of her laptop. The same confused, desperate four words batting around inside my head: *Where has she gone?*

The Scobies live in a neat little townhouse down by the river. I park my car next to some railings overlooking the riverbank, waiting for an old couple to pass my door before I get out. The water is steel-grey and swift, the ducks huddled into themselves as the current sweeps them along. We're not far from the town centre, which also hugs the river, but it's quiet here, with little traffic. If I glance behind me, I can still see the spires of Aggers rising spitefully over the houses.

I cross the road and head for the Scobies', number seven, in the middle of the little stretch of five identical houses. The front doors are all framed by perfect white pillars, and the windows all have black iron grilles fitted over them, curly and ornate. On the street where I grew up, when we put bars over our windows, we just put bars over them. Here, they have to be a feature.

Scobie's brother answers the door – Liam, the eldest. He's the opposite to Scobie – tall and broad where Scobes is short and skinny – but they have the same white-blond hair, and the same round, pale blue eyes.

'Alright, Aiden,' he says, opening the door wider to invite me in. 'How's that hamstring?'

Liam's studying sports science at uni and has taken much more of an interest in me since he found out I play football. He knows more about my ligaments than I do.

'It's good,' I say. 'Hasn't given me any more trouble.'

'Good stuff.' He loses interest instantly. 'Tom's upstairs.'

On the way up the stairs, I hear thuds coming from one of the rooms, and a computerised voice.

'Right foot two step! Left foot one step! Slide! Sliiiiiiide! You've got the moves!'

'Hey, Frank,' I say, sticking my head into Scobie's little brother's room. Aged six, he is the cutest kid I've ever met – super happy, like, all the time, and really polite. He wears glasses like Scobes but his hair's a darker kind of blond than his brothers' and his face is rounder, softer than theirs. He waves at me from his dance mat where he's puffing away, his cheeks pink, and I carry on down the hall.

Scobie's door is closed as always. It's dark blue, like all the other doors in the house, but Scobie's taken full advantage of this and posted a 'Police Public Call Box' sign across the top to make it look like the Tardis. I really love this kid.

I knock, and from inside I can hear the muted bleeps of Facebook Messenger.

'Yeah?'

I open the door and stick my head in. 'Hey.'

He's at his desk with his back to me, and he swivels round, his face surprised. 'Hey. What's up?'

Scobie's room is tiny; most of the space taken up by his big wooden desk and his giant, glowing Mac, his pride and joy. The walls are bare and dark blue, and the only personal thing he has around is a framed photo on the windowsill of him, Liam and Frank, when Frank was about three or four. I sink down on the narrow bed.

'I kind of need your help,' I say.

He spins the chair properly to face me. 'At your service.'

'It's about Lizzie,' I tell him, and he wrinkles his face as if to say *No surprise there*. 'It's like everyone's saying, she'd met some guy online. Marnie got into her Facebook.'

'Marnie Daniels?' He pulls a face. 'Huh. Impressive.'

'Yeah, well, it didn't get us very far. Reckon you could see what you can dig up on him?'

Scobie nods. 'Sure.' He's practically flexing his fingers with glee. This is Scobie's idea of fun. Information – finding it, storing it, sharing it – is his thing. I haven't met his dad – Scobie never talks about him, so all I know is that he left when he was like six – but I wouldn't be at all surprised to hear he was Steve Jobs. Or Julian Assange maybe – they even kind of look alike.

He's already swung back round to face the extra-large screen. 'What's his name?'

'Hal Paterson. With one t.'

He types it into the search bar and the Facebook profile page comes up as the first entry. He clicks on it and scrolls through.

'Not much here,' he says. 'It's pretty private.' His mouse hovers over the tab that says Friends: 57. 'Hmm,' he says, and shakes his head.

He clicks on the profile picture and we scan through the album. Only four pictures: the sunglasses one, a bright orange sunset, a group of boys in rugby shirts, and a yellow Labrador.

'Hmm.' Scobie clicks through them again.

'What?'

'Dodgy,' he says, right-clicking on the first one, the one in sunglasses. 'Real people have profile pictures. And friends.'

My heart starts to skip. 'So you don't think he's a real person?'

'Nope.' He opens up a search page and clicks on a tab that says 'Images'. He pastes the photo in and hits 'Search'. I watch the little pinwheel spin as it loads, and now my heart feels like it's going ninety miles an hour.

1 match.

'Bingo,' Scobie says, and he clicks on the link.

Another Facebook page. Only this one belongs to a James McArthur (University of Liverpool). James McArthur has 562 friends. James McArthur has at least twenty pictures in his Profile Pictures album.

'Oh,' I say, the wind knocked out of me, but Scobie is already back on Hal Paterson's page. He copies the picture of the rugby boys and puts it through the search engine. This time the pinwheel seems to spin for an eternity.

1 match.

Another Facebook page. Grant Marlowe (Sussex Boys' School). Friends: 712.

'Stolen,' Scobie says triumphantly, and I nod numbly.

He's already back on the 'Hal Paterson' profile, and this time he actually clicks on the Friends tab. He goes through the list, and then turns to me. 'See? All of these people are totally random – they're from the States, Australia, Malaysia. There's no, like, one network where he has loads of friends, like a school or a uni or whatever.'

'He's not real,' I say. I feel shivery, my heart sinking like lead. Scobie is unravelling this profile effortlessly, without even trying. And Lizzie. Lizzie fell for it. *Where is she?* I think again, desperately.

Scobie looks back at the screen, at the photo of the guy – James McArthur – in sunglasses. 'He might be real,' he says, 'but that's not him.'

How was your day?

good thanks ☺

You?

yeah, good ☺

Good ☺

how'd your audition go?

ok, I think!
what about yours?

yeah fine

we find out tomorrow
eeeeek

who'd you want to be?

i don't mind

Bottom it is then

haha
probably!
Can I ask you something?

you just did

lol

Nah, kidding – course, go ahead

54

what do you think of it here?

Here, like abbots grey?

yeah

erm...

it's fine

nice

the people are

...

polite

haha

you hate it

lol

nah

I don't hate it, it's just different to what im used to

I hate it sometimes

so fake

yeah... it is a bit

Did you hear about that tv show they're gonna
   film here?

yeah think so, it's like a reality thing right?

i think so

just saw the audition ad cos Jorgie reposted it

haha fancy it?

god no

that's my actual worst nightmare

not a reality show fan?

they're not even reality

they're scripted

it's so...urgh

tell me about it

all the girls at my old school went mad for that stuff

haha bet you hung out with loads of girls didn't

you...

;)

nah, not exactly

Yeah right

I was dedicated to football i'll have you know

far too busy

lol

suuuuure

haha

So you ready for English tomorrow?

no why???

we're doing the court scene!

omg

I forgot

tut tut Mayella

haha

I wanted to be Scout so bad

I love that book

to kill a mockingbird? yeah it's good

so good

who did you get for tomorrow?

Jem

Oooh big time!

haha I know

pressure

that scene is so sad

56

                                        I know
                                        Dickheads
lol
yeah they are
                        so what are you up to tonight?
learning my lines now!
but also family dinner, it's my mum's birthday
                                        ah nice
not really
my dad's working late so she's upset
also she can't cook
                                        aww that sucks
                                        What's he do?
He's a doctor
at the hospital in kings lyme
                                        oh right
                                        cool
he works a lot
but I guess it's important
                                        yeah
what do your parents do?
                        Dad does bathrooms
            Mum's an architect but she's taking some time off
                                        at the moment
wow that's cool
my little sister wants to be an architect
she's seven though
                                        haha
                when i was seven i wanted to be a vet

57

me too!!!

                                                lol no way

yeah

I used to have a ladybird hospital in our shed

                                 hahaha ahh bless

I don't think many of them made it

it was more like a ladybird prison

                                       evil Lizzie

lol yeah

                   so what happened to the vet plan?

i found out you had to be good at science

                         haha yeah think it helps

and you?

                               I found football

is that really what you want to be? Footballer?

                 yeah... I know it's a kinda crazy career plan

no it's cool

it's amazing you have something you love that
    much

                   yeah I guess. just need a back-up!

that's what my parents keep telling me

anyway I should go

Birthday dinner calls! ☹

                                   have fun!

                       see you at school tomorrow

You will x

'Yo, KENDICK!'

Great. Honeycutt. I haven't even made it out of the car park yet; what a lovely way to start a day. I ignore him and keep walking.

'Talking to you, Rapeface.'

I spin round. 'What's your problem, Deacon?'

He spreads his palms out in a fake gesture of innocence, grinning. 'Haven't got a problem. Just saying hi.'

'Yeah, well I *do* have a problem with being called a rapist.'

He pokes out his bottom lip, like an *Aww, baby* face. 'Just a bit of banter, *mate*.'

I turn back round and keep walking. *Don't lose your temper. Do. Not. Lose. Your. Temper*. I can't do that again. I can't.

'Oi –' he yells after me, but then someone calls him from the basketball court and his attention is instantly and totally diverted. I climb up the concrete steps towards the Keep and my heart starts to slow and I can loosen my hands out of the fists they seem to have formed.

I can't remember the first time I met Deacon Honeycutt, but I do remember the first time I heard he didn't like me and that definitely happened *before* we met. It was just something someone said in passing, in the corridor outside assembly – Ollie Birchall, now I think about it: 'Honeycutt's got it in for you, mate.' I was sure it was a mistake, just mistaken identity. But no. A week later, I happened to pass the famous Deacon Honeycutt on my way across the playground between lessons, and I heard him cough '*Twat*' in a stagey way to the two guys with him.

Later, when I asked Scobie about it, he looked a bit shell-shocked and just muttered, 'Honeycutt hates everyone.' But it was more than that. I'd hear rumours about myself – I'd been caught cheating at my old school, my dad was in prison, I'd had sex with my sister (I don't have a sister) – and whenever I dug a bit, they always led back to Deacon.

I'd heard plenty about him, obviously – he was the captain of the St Agnes's football team, as well as Abbots Grey's Under 16's. He was tipped for big things, always bragging about this team or that team who were on the verge of signing him. I'd already been to camps at Norwich, knew their scouts were keeping an eye on me, but I didn't tell anyone at Aggers that, not even Scobie.

So I guess it was the bad part of me, the part I was supposed to leave in London, that made me try out for the Aggers team when I could've just kept my head down and hoped Deacon Honeycutt would forget about me and move on to the next new kid to come along.

I made the team and became the new favourite of the coach, Mr Connolly, and, inevitably, official enemy number one of Deacon Honeycutt. The rumours started getting more creative – I was a drug addict, I was having an affair with

Connolly – and often, when I was walking through the car park on my way home, a football or an empty drinks bottle would hit me on the head or in the back.

We didn't have our first real run-in, though, until the Year 11 prom – two years after I'd started at Aggers, six months after people had started finding out about me training with the Norwich Youth Squad, and one week before Lizzie and I stopped talking.

That fight, and the fall-out from it, almost meant the end of Aggers for me, and now, with Lizzie gone, thinking of it is even worse; it gives me a sick feeling in the pit of my stomach. I try to squash it back down; try to stop remembering. I push open the door to the Keep, and find myself face to face with a policewoman. Mahama.

'Aiden,' she says, and the fact she remembers my name does not make me feel good.

'Detective,' I say, and I feel like I'm playing a role. One that I haven't read the script for.

'I'd say it's nice to see you,' she says, 'but, given the circumstances –' She spreads her palms wide, as if it's the whole world she finds unfortunate, not just the fact that a classmate of mine has disappeared.

'Is there any news?' I ask, but before she can answer Mahama's phone starts ringing in her pocket, shrill in the otherwise silent hallway. She frowns at me, answers it and then, putting one finger up to me in a *Hold that thought* kind of gesture, she walks away.

I'm ten minutes early for registration, so I take a seat in the almost empty common room and get out my phone. I've got Facebook on there, sports news, games, but something makes me open AskMe.com, and something makes me type in Lizzie's name.

Her profile loads, and my stomach flips when I see the most recent question is still 'Do you love me?' from aiden k. Why would someone write that? *Who* would write that? I wonder what Lizzie thought, reading it. I wonder how she felt.

I scroll down the page, reading the questions and answers more carefully this time.

Why's your sister such a slag? someone asks about two weeks ago, and Lizzie replies:

All the world's a stage, and all the men and women
merely players.

How many people have you slept with? asks another. Lizzie's reply is part of a poem:

What a million filaments.
The peanut-crunching crowd
Shoves in to see

Them unwrap me hand and foot –
The big strip tease.

It's Sylvia Plath – I remember reading it in English last year. I Google it and find the title of the poem: 'Lady Lazarus'. It takes me a minute to remember the story we learnt in RE about Lazarus, and when I do, I feel sick. Lazarus who came back from the dead.

Who u finks fit? another one asks, and to this, she just puts a winking face.

You so pretty babe. That's the only properly nice one I see, and it's the only one that's not a question. Lizzie answers anyway.

I am not what I am.

Soon after, they go back to being abusive. you think you're well fit don't you? someone asks, and I think again how childish this is, how horrible. Lizzie's reply only makes me feel worse.

Physical beauty is passing. A transitory possession.
But beauty of the mind and richness of the spirit and
tenderness of the heart – and I have all of those things…
But I have been foolish – casting my pearls before swine!

They're words I know well. Words I've heard her say aloud. Nearer the top, more recently, someone says haha how can your sister call herself a reality star when she's the fakest bitch on tv? Lizzie's answer is long, and another one I recognise.

I don't want realism. I want magic! Yes, yes, magic! I try to
give that to people. I misrepresent things to them. I don't tell
the truth, I tell what ought to be truth. And if that is sinful,
then let me be damned for it! – don't turn the light on!

That, and the one before it, are from *A Streetcar Named Desire*. And that play will always, always make me think of Lizzie.

r all the Summersall women sluts? bitches be cray someone else puts, and Lizzie puts another long quote, and this one I recognise too.

Oh, what a noble mind is here o'erthrown! –
The courtier's, soldier's, scholar's, eye, tongue, sword,
Th'expectancy and rose of the fair state,
The glass of fashion and the mould of form,
Th'observed of all observers, quite, quite down!
And I, of ladies most deject and wretched,
That sucked the honey of his music vows,
Now see that noble and most sovereign reason
Like sweet bells jangled, out of tune and harsh;
That unmatched form and feature of blown youth
Blasted with ecstasy. Oh, woe is me,
T'have seen what I have seen, see what I see!

Her Ophelia speech. It seems like so long ago that I saw her say it. That I first *saw* her. So much has happened since then.

I glance at the clock in the corner of the screen and realise I've missed the start of registration. I shove my phone in my bag and head for my form room.

Dr Radclyffe is my form tutor as well as my history teacher, and he's just the same in both lessons; soft-spoken, quiet, but alert – his eyes always darting around, always watching, always listening, like really listening, when you're speaking to him. He's a nice guy, and funny, too, although a lot of his jokes are obscure history ones we don't get.

He looks up as I walk in and makes a mark against my name on the register without saying anything about me being late. He waits for me to sit, adjusting his little wire glasses on his long nose before he starts speaking again.

'The police are setting up an interview room in Mr Maclaren's office, and they'll be calling some of you from your lessons throughout the day. They've been given a comprehensive list of your timetables by Mr Selby and they'll try to schedule interviews during your free periods. So please do not leave school grounds during those times.'

He taps his pencil against his desk, long fingers crooked around it. 'It's really nothing to worry about. They're just trying to get a wider picture about Lizzie Summersall's life here, and anything that might shed light on her disappearance.'

Scobie catches my eye from across the room where he's perched on the windowsill. Radclyffe has a pretty slack policy on us sitting at our desks in form room.

There's a couple of groans from people who aren't too happy about being kept on site when such glamorous places as the Rec or the chippy downtown await.

'It's like she's a little kid,' Darnell Hudson, the goalie on our Aggers team, says. 'Get *over* it.'

'Errr, sensitive much?' Jorgie Mitchell, a pretty blonde girl from my English class, says, turning to glare at Darnell. 'Her poor family.'

'Oh what, cos she wanted to get away from her moron sister? No wonder she ditched them,' Darnell says, folding his arms and leaning back against the wall.

I ignore the fact that Scobie is still trying very hard to catch my eye.

'You're such a dick, Darnell,' Jorgie says, and the girls around her tut in agreement.

'Just to be clear,' Radclyffe says, in his usual level, diplomatic voice. 'Lizzie's disappearance is being treated as suspicious. I don't know what the police know, but if they're asking for our help, that's because they want to make sure she's safe. And I'm sure that's something you'll all be more than happy to help with.'

Scobie's eyes are practically boring holes in me by this point. Everyone gets up to head to lessons and I push my way out, not wanting to hang around and listen to all the muttered conversations about Lizzie. I walk slowly so that Scobie can catch up with me as I leave the Keep.

'We have to tell them, Aiden.' He takes off his glasses and polishes them on the bottom of his jumper as we walk, something he always does when he's distracted.

'I know,' I say, the thought of being interviewed about Lizzie again making my stomach turn.

'I mean, you'd hope they'd be able to figure it out for themselves,' he says, pushing his glasses back up his nose. 'It's hardly advanced stuff.'

We push through the double doors of the Keep and onto the playground. We're in maths together first, which is in a draughty old classroom on the top floor of the main building.

We head across the pristine black tarmac towards it, its spires dark against the grey sky.

'I'm worried, Aiden,' Scobie says. 'I've got a really bad feeling about this.'

He isn't the only one.

I'm not called for interview but all day long I hear stories from people who are, hear that the police are asking everything from what Lizzie liked to eat for lunch to whether she talked about the people she slept with. I can't get my head around any of it.

As for the Hal Paterson account, the latest news comes from Scobie at break.

'It's gone,' he tells me, polishing his glasses for the fiftieth time. 'Deleted.'

I double-check. I check several times. It *is* gone. Hal Paterson does not exist, and there's no internet evidence to suggest he ever did.

I'm glad when it's the end of the day and I can get away from Aggers's whisper-filled classrooms, away from the buzzing phones and the knowing looks. Until I remember I've got a date. With the very worst kind of human.

Cheska Summersall has told me to meet her at her salon in town, but what she's neglected to mention is that she's in the middle of shooting a scene there. As I head down one of the cutesy little mews off the high street, I can see a group of teenagers outside, trying to take photos through the windows. They're being occasionally shooed off by a harassed looking member of the production crew, but each time they just regroup a few seconds later.

I push past them and in through the doorway of the salon, Ginger's, which has shiny white counters and floors and walls, and those little potted trees pruned into balls everywhere. It's not actually Cheska's salon, but they kind of make it seem that way on the show. I can't imagine the real owner loves that, although judging by the way the salon is heaving with preening customers, all of them orange-skinned and glossy-nailed, it's good for business.

There's a camera crew huddled around one station – a sound guy with his big fluffy mic, two cameramen and a tall woman with a shiny black bob and headset, a clipboard in her hand, staring intently at a monitor. At the centre of it all, a girl is having her nails examined by Cheska in her pale pink uniform. I stand and watch as she frowns at the girl's hand.

'How are things with you and Thomas Jay?' the customer asks, sounding about as natural as her nails. I glance over at the woman with the clipboard and see she has a list of questions, including that exact one, on a sheet in front of her. As I watch, she checks it off with a pencil. *Her* nails are long and sharp and red, like cartoon claws.

Cheska sighs, a really fake-sounding sigh, and picks up a nail file. 'It's tough,' she says, 'because I keep hearing all these rumours. And it's like it's happening again. But I trust him, you know. I know, *here*,' and she thumps on her chest, roughly where, assuming she has one somewhere in there, her heart would be, 'that he means it. He's changed, you know?'

The girl makes an unconvincing 'Mmm' sound, and then, after a strange stilted pause, she says, in a lower voice, 'Have you heard anything about your sister?'

Cheska looks up, and her eyes fill with tears under her thick false eyelashes. 'No,' she says, in a hoarse whisper. 'We're all so worried. It's all I can think about.' Right on cue, a tear rolls down her face, leaving a pale track mark in her make-up.

'Annnnd cut,' someone says. The woman with the clipboard, who I guess must be the producer, says, crossing off something on another list. 'That's great, thanks, Cheska.'

Cheska instantly lets go of the girl's hand, which flops down to the table with a thud. 'Cool,' she says, standing up and shrugging off her pale pink overall top to reveal a tiny little strappy thing. 'I'm heading out for a bit.'

Even though she hasn't looked up once, hasn't acknowledged me, she heads right for me and slots an arm through mine. 'Let's go,' she says, brightly.

Up close, she smells like coconut and something biscuity. Her perfectly curled long hair doesn't even move in the breeze outside. It's blonde like Lizzie's, except not like Lizzie's – her hair is bright and fake where Lizzie's was soft and darker.

Why do I keep talking about Lizzie in the past tense?

We walk down the high street, Cheska's heels clacking on the cobbled pavement.

'Thanks for coming,' she says.

'No problem.'

'Guess it's kind of exciting to see behind the scenes, right?'

I glance at her. 'Not really.'

She either doesn't hear me or pretends not to, and instead beams and waves at two girls across the street taking photos of her on their phones. 'You're friends with my sister,' she says in a low voice, and it's not a question.

'Yeah,' I say, because it's simpler than saying 'I was' or 'I don't know'.

'I heard the police wanted to talk to you.'

'They're talking to a lot of people,' I say, thinking of the police taking over our headmaster's office. Wondering if they're looking in the right place. *Lizzie*.

'She said things about you.'

These words go through me like sharp stabs of a whispered knife. That Lizzie would talk to Cheska, who she argued with constantly, about anything personal, is a shock. That I was important enough for her to talk about is worse.

'What kind of things?'

Cheska looks sideways at me with a little smirk. 'You had a thing, right?'

'No. Not exactly.'

'Don't be shy…' We've reached the riverfront, the part where all the posh little tearooms and wine bars are. A low, grey wall runs along the edge of the bank, and Cheska perches on it and pats a spot beside her. 'Sit. Tell me everything.'

I stay where I am. 'There's nothing to tell.'

She shrugs and flicks her hair over one shoulder. 'Whatever.'

'Is that all you wanted to meet me for?'

'Aid,' she says, as if we're old pals, and as if 'Aid' is a normal nickname for someone, 'my sister is missing. The least you can do is talk to me.'

This would do a lot more to convince me if it was delivered with even the slightest hint of emotion, but it isn't. We could just be talking about the weather or what she's having for dinner.

She looks at me, eyes narrowed. 'What do you know?'

'I don't know anything,' I say. 'I wish I did.'

She laughs. 'Just checking. No need to get so defensive.'

I don't reply. I'm too shocked. I can't believe she can act so relaxed, can laugh and joke, when Lizzie's out there somewhere. On-camera is one thing, but off…

'Look,' she says after a while, tipping her head back to look at the sky, letting her hair trail prettily behind her. Like this is a photo shoot. 'I know you want to help Lizzie. So let's help each other.'

I sit down beside her. 'And how exactly do you want me to help?'

'I'm still working on that,' she says, airily. 'But I need to know that I can count on you. That *Lizzie* can count on you.'

My mouth feels dry. 'Of course.'

'Good.' She straightens up and looks at her watch. 'Better get back. I'm supposed to be having an argument with Aimee outside the salon.'

She gets up and smooths down her way-too-small top.

'Wait,' I say. 'What do you mean, you're still working on it? Do you know something about Lizzie? Do you know where she is?'

She's already walking away. 'Don't be ridiculous, Aiden. I just wanted to meet you. I want us to be friends.'

'But why me?' I call after her, and she glances back at me.

'Like I said,' she says, flicking her hair again. 'She said things about you.'

And she winks.

Hey ☺

                              hey how's it going?
good thanks! how come you weren't at
   rehearsal tonight?
                        i had training, couldn't get out of it
football?
               yeah... I've been training with Norwich youth
omg!
                              shh don't tell anyone
i won't
that's so cool though, congratulations
                                          thanks ☺
                              So did I miss anything?
not really
Puck and Titania had an argument
                        again? they want each other so bad
i know right
               well i'm glad everyone managed to carry on
                              without 'tree/nymph #5'
haha

you are a crucial part

almost as important as me

shhh you are a great Lady in Waiting 2

it's a challenge but I'm giving it my all

lol

can't believe there's only a month to go til the show

I know

this year has gone so fast

time flies when you're stuck at Aggers huh?

haha it's not been so bad

Are you still going to London for the summer?

yeah

are you excited?

yeah it'll be nice to see my dad and catch up with people but... I think I might actually miss it around here

oh reallllly?

yeah

turns out it has its good parts ☺

well I'm glad to hear it

what are your summer plans?

ummm

...

we're going to spain for two weeks

nice

yeah it'll be ok, except I have to share a room with Cheska

:\

exactly

Then there's a drama club in king's lyme i want
    to join

                                    check you out
I'm so lame aren't i?

                                              no!
                                        it's cool
you think so?

                                      yeah course
            How else you gonna be a big filmstar?
haha hardly

                                      I have faith
☺

            so we should do something after the show

                                              ...
                                    to celebrate
yes let's
what do you want to do?

                                            hmm
                          let me have a think
            need to finish off my first year in Abbots Grey
                                      in style!
☺
yes you do

I TOSS AND turn all night thinking about Lizzie. I manage some sleep at about three, but even then it's full of weird half-dreams, bits of conversations mixed up and repeating themselves in my head. Picturing Lizzie online, alone, late at night, sharing her secrets. I have to do something. I have to find her.

At 5:45am, when I hear Kevin's alarm go off – even on a Saturday, *especially* on a Saturday (yoga is best for your health when you have to sacrifice a lie-in to do it) – I roll onto my stomach and text Marnie.

Meet me at Café Alice at 9.30.

And then I roll onto my back and do something I've never done before. I open a text to Doug and lie my way out of training.

Up all night with food poisoning.

The first half is at least true. And I do feel poisoned. I feel wrong all over, sick and weird. I send the text and stare at my words on the screen.

Now I feel even worse. There's no chance of getting any more sleep, so I slide out of bed and pull some shorts and a t-shirt out of a drawer and shrug them on. I slip the band I use for my iPhone up my arm and stick one bud into my ear as I flick through tracks. Oasis. 'Rock 'N' Roll Star'. They're one of my dad's favourite bands and this song is exactly what I need right now. I click the volume up to full and slide the phone into place. Heading down the stairs before Kevin can emerge in his yoga gear, I retrieve my running shoes from the drawer that pulls out from the lowest step, perfectly concealed. I tug them on, grab a bottle of water from the fridge – I'm still not used to that; what is this, a hotel? – and then I'm out, running.

The air is cool and feels good on my skin, my feet pounding against the pavement. The neighbourhood is deserted at this time in the morning; just me, the birds, and a million 4x4s, parked in their pristine drives like sleeping pet elephants.

I turn the corner of our street and make for the main road, which winds round the edge of town in a curve and heads down past the river. There's a grass verge with a footpath the whole way, the open countryside beyond a pleasant distraction from the big, bloated houses that line the road. I can lose myself in the rhythm of the tracks my iPod lines up, the fields thudding past.

Or I would lose myself, if it wasn't for the fact that every song seems to remind me of Lizzie.

A car drives past me, way too fast, speakers blaring, and I glare after it, a bright yellow little convertible thing. I only notice the licence plate just before it rounds the corner.

CH35K4

Cheska.

It's not even 6:30 on Saturday morning. An early shoot, maybe? That's the only thing I can imagine she'd get out of bed for.

I keep running and even though I try not to, I keep thinking about that first year here, those first conversations with Lizzie. *A Midsummer Night's Dream* and weeks of rehearsals, weeks of hanging around waiting for our scenes; playing Candy Crush on her phone, scribbled rounds of Hangman and Noughts and Crosses in the back of our school books. And that time, a month before the end of term, when I finally got up the nerve to sort of ask her on a date.

I wish we could go back there.

The road drifts a bit further from the houses – or maybe it's just that the gardens get bigger – as I get into the quietest part of town, where most of the properties have huge gates and long driveways. Aimee Burton, one of the original cast members of *Spoilt in the Suburbs* and Cheska's arch-rival, lives in one of these houses. I only know that because sometimes when I've gone for runs after school, I've seen girls waiting outside, wanting to see her or speak to her. Young girls, like twelve or thirteen, acting like she's a movie star. It's all so weird, how someone can become famous just by letting a camera follow them around. How people want to watch other people just doing ordinary things, how they can idolise or hate someone just for their wardrobe, their relationship, their friendships. Like somehow it sets these people apart, just putting that stuff out there. Maybe it does, I don't know. Maybe it's brave, opening yourself up like that. The abuse Lizzie got online about the show was bad enough; I wonder what sort of stuff Cheska gets sent on a daily basis. Is it worth it? Her whole life is a role now, she has to play this character she's created.

But then I guess that's not so different to the rest of us.

The only person I pass in the next ten minutes is another jogger; a woman of about my mum's age, though it's not that easy to tell right away – she's wearing a bright pink tracksuit, with perfect hair and perfect make-up, and a brand new iPhone strapped into the pink holder round her arm. She's jogging slowly, more like a power walk, and as I pass her, she flashes me a Hollywood white smile. Apart from that, the only people I see are the ones who speed past in cars.

Before the road reaches the river, it passes over a little brook, and at this point the footpath splits off and crosses the fields, ending up at the big car park on the outskirts of town. I push myself hard over this stretch, running at my absolute limit, and it feels good, my heart hammering against my chest even as my breathing regulates itself. I love this part of training; my body adapting, my muscles remembering this feeling, this pain. Maybe it's a bit sadistic, but it's a pain that's not really a pain. It's like proof that you've worked, proof that you've *done* something, that you're getting better. Stronger.

I'm so in the zone as I cross the wide, yellowing fields that it's not until I'm about a hundred metres from the car park that I see something *very* yellow. Cheska's car.

I don't know why, but something makes me stop. Something makes me leave the path and work my way around to the side of the car park, to a little straggly copse of trees. And from there, I can see through the driver's side window; the back of

Cheska's head, her mass of blonde fake hair bouncing about, like she's laughing. No – after a few seconds, it's not like laughter. From the way she shakes her head, pauses, bobs it again – it's like she's arguing with someone. I see her hand flare up from the wheel and then slap it. Definitely arguing. But then she stops, like she's listening, and then she leans forward – kind of like... I dare to take a step or two closer and then I'm sure. She's kissing someone. Someone whose hand creeps up into her hair, pulling her closer.

Interesting. And not a camera in sight.

I've turned to make a move – I don't even know why I'm spying on her like this, hiding in the trees like a pervert – when I hear a car door open and close. I glance back at the car, expecting to see Cheska getting out, or Thomas Jay, her on-again off-again boyfriend, and hoping it's not to ask me why I've been watching them get it on.

But it isn't either of them who get out of the car.

It's Deacon Honeycutt.

I have a quick shower at home and head out again in time to meet Marnie at Café Alice. It's a nice little place, quite plain and therefore much quieter than the fancy tearooms along the riverfront that all the yummy mummies and ladies who lunch like to go to. I keep thinking about Deacon and Cheska – are they a thing? I thought he was back with Lauren, but then there are plenty of rumours about what the two of them get up to behind each other's backs. Not that I care about Deacon Honeycutt's lovelife... But I can't stop thinking about how weird it was for Cheska to contact me out of the blue... and how maybe it's Deacon behind it, trying to get at me, or find stuff out, or – I don't know.

Jeez, paranoid much, Aiden?

I'm five minutes early but Marnie's already there, at a table by the window. She looks younger than normal, with no make-up on and pink cheeks like she's fresh from the shower. She smells like it too when I pull up the chair next to her – a nice, soapy smell, vanilla-y.

Err, focus, Aiden.

And stop talking to yourself.

'How are you?' I ask, glancing at the menu; a little laminated sheet on a plastic stand.

'I'm okay.' She glances up at me. 'There's no news.'

The waiter comes over, a tall guy a couple of years older than us who speaks in a voice not much louder than a whisper. I order a pot of tea, Marnie a coffee.

'Want to share a cake or something?' I ask. Her face looks pale and hollow, like she hasn't eaten in days.

'Sure.' She gives another weak smile. 'Why not?'

I order us a toasted teacake and when the waitress has gone, Marnie slides her laptop out of her bag and opens it on the red-checked tablecloth.

'How're you?' she asks as it boots up.

'I'm fine,' I say, but that sounds wrong. 'I mean – I don't… It's weird,' I finish. Lame.

'Yeah,' she says. 'I know.'

'I saw Cheska yesterday.'

Her eyes widen. 'Really? How come?'

'She asked me to meet her.'

'What for?'

The waitress struggles over with our order, and we wait in silence as she unloads my cup, a teapot, the teacake, and then almost spills Marnie's coffee across her soft grey dress. When she's gone, I shrug. 'I honestly don't know. She said she wanted us to be friends. She said something about wanting to know if she could trust me, if Lizzie could trust me.'

Marnie's face darkens. 'What the hell did she mean by that?'

I shake my head. 'I really don't know. You don't think… Lizzie told her something, do you?'

'You mean Lizzie might've told her she was leaving?' Marnie considers it, frowning. 'No. No, I don't. Lizzie hated Cheska, you know that, right? Cheska's the last person she would've told.'

I sigh. 'Yeah, I know. But I don't get why she asked me there.'

'She's just playing games with you! That's what Cheska *does*. I hate her. My dad says she's the worst one of them to work with. A total nightmare.'

It's my turn to frown. 'Your dad works with Cheska?'

She glances away, looking embarrassed. 'He's the executive producer on *Spoilt in the Suburbs*. He hired her.'

'Oh.'

'Yeah.' She looks at me, her eyes hard. 'Obviously I try and keep that quiet. Otherwise everyone would be on at me to get them a part. You know what the girls are like at school.'

'And the boys,' I say, and she actually laughs; just a small, sad laugh, but at least it's something.

'Yeah. And the boys.'

We drink our drinks in silence for a while, rain pattering at the window.

81

'I can't stop thinking about her,' I say, softly.

Her voice is barely more than a whisper. 'I know.'

'There must be something we can do,' I say.

'I just don't know what.' Marnie turns to her laptop and opens a new page. My heart lurches when I realise what it is: Hal and Lizzie's conversation.

'Where did you get this?' I ask. 'I thought the profile had gone?'

'I saved a version of it,' she sighs. 'I had a feeling that might happen.'

'That was smart,' I say, but I'm already looking past her at the screen. I skim through it; all their smalltalk, all their flirting – I can't bring myself to do more than glance at the words as they flash by.

haha defo

                                                    c u soon

bye x

                                                    sleep well x

you ok?

                                                    cant talk

i want to hear your voice
always makes me smile

                                            talking to you makes
                                                    me happy

It's all the same – stuff about their days, their plans for the evening, stuff about things they like and things they don't.

'They never arrange to meet,' I say. 'He always turns her down.'

'On here,' Marnie says, shrugging. 'Maybe they arranged it somewhere else.'

I scroll right down to the bottom, the first message. From him.

> Thanks for accepting my friend request!
> hope you don't think I'm weird, adding a stranger
> just saw your Potter pic on a friend's profile
> and I knew we'd get on, haha

Using Harry Potter to get to her. Of course.

> haha, no problem
> you like HP too then? ☺

It's as easy as that. The conversation starts there, and it goes on and on, with Lizzie revealing more and more about herself as the days go by. So trusting. So happy to chat, so interested in what he has to say.

The more I read, the more 'Hal Paterson' starts to annoy me. He's so over the top, it's sickening. Desperate.

> you're so pretty
> you're so smart
> i love talking to you
> can't wait
> want to kiss you

'Why did she like this stuff?' I ask, my face twisting. Marnie shakes her head.

'I don't know. He's such a sleaze.'

I grit my teeth. I have to force myself to ask the next question. 'You said there were others?'

She nods. 'I'm pretty sure. Maybe she deleted them.'

'Why delete them and not this?' I ask, pushing the laptop away. I don't want to look at the things that were said any more. The things she said to *him*.

'Maybe she *wanted* us to think it was him,' I say. 'Maybe it's, I don't know, like a diversion or something.' The Lizzie I knew would never play games with people like that. But then maybe I never really knew her at all.

Marnie shrugs half-heartedly, like her shoulders are the heaviest thing in the world to lift. 'Maybe.'

I think of the rumours rushing round school, the whispered words quoted from police officers' mouths. *Conquests. Partners.*

'Marnie,' I say, 'is it true what people are saying? That Lizzie…' I don't know how to finish.

She looks up, eyes flashing. 'That Lizzie what? Lizzie got with a few people, got a bit drunk? What difference does it make?'

My stomach drops; a terrible, looping sensation. So it is true. 'That doesn't sound like her,' I say softly.

Marnie's eyes drop to her lap. 'People change.' She starts picking at the edge of the tablecloth, and for a minute she doesn't say anything. I watch her and I think of her by the lockers, I think of Lizzie listening to her, laughing with her, that notebook under her arm.

Just when I think she's not going to carry on, she says, 'It just started in the summer. She wanted to go out all the time. She'd tell me about hooking up with people she didn't even like, blacking out drunk –' She stops suddenly, her eyes filled with tears, and claps her hand over her mouth just as the first sob escapes.

'Hey –' I reach out and put my hand on hers.

'And I just keep thinking,' she says, her voice cracking, 'I should've done something, I should've *known*. All this –' She waves a hand in the direction of the laptop. 'I should've stopped her.'

She starts to cry, her hands covering her face as her hair falls forwards to hide her too.

I edge my chair round the table and put a hand on her shoulder. 'Hey,' I say again. 'Hey, come on.'

And then she sort of lurches towards me and buries her face against my shoulder. I put my arms around her back and I listen to her cry. I keep telling her that it's okay, that it isn't her fault. I smell the nice, soapy vanilla smell of her, and the last of her coffee, the buttery teacake. I think about Lizzie. I think about Lizzie 'hooking up' with random guys. Drinking at parties. Flirting on screens. I reach behind me and close Marnie's laptop.

'It's okay,' I tell her again. 'We'll find her.'

She pulls back and wipes her eyes with the palms of her hands like a little girl. 'God, I hope so.'

'Look,' I say, as she straightens herself out. I really admire how quickly she does it, how efficiently. 'Whatever's happened, you can't blame yourself. You couldn't have stopped her.'

She huffs, like she doesn't agree.

I think of the Lizzie I knew, soft and sweet and caring. I think of the Lizzie I saw later: fierce, eyes flashing. Vulnerable, cheeks tear-stained. 'Lizzie's complicated,' I say, uncomfortable. 'You know that.'

She lets out a small, hard laugh. 'Yeah. You could say that.'

'She might get in touch,' I say, even though the words sound hollow even to me. 'She might contact you. Or me,' I add, even though I'd be last on her list.

'Maybe,' Marnie says, an eyebrow twitching. 'Maybe she will.'

So how you feeling?

better now

It's been horrible

yeah you didn't look the best!

can't believe I missed the last show

did it go well?

it was fine

as good as it could be without the star lady

in waiting

haha

Im so bored

have you been in bed all this time?

yeah

stupid glandular fever

just been watching tv?

yeah and sleeping

sleeping sooooo much

So are you in London now?

yep

at my dad's

                                        weird to be back

aww nice though

                                                    yeah

                        saw some old mates tonight, that was cool

bet they're glad to see you

                                                    yeah

                            When are you off to Spain?

day after tomorrow

                                            excited?

ummm sort of

it'll be nice to get some sun

especially cos ive been in bed for like three weeks!

but two weeks of Cheska

:-s

                                        ahh it'll be ok

                            just hang out with Evie

yeah

bless her she's so excited

                            love to be on a beach right now

yeahhh

that part is good

                my dad's place has got a balcony but we can't fit a

                                    chair on it :/

aww

                        So what's new in old Abs Grey?

ummm

Ok

don't tell anyone

                                    what what what???

cheska got cast in spoilt in the suburbs

...

Say something

...

come on

sorry but

NO WAY

that is

...

Wow

I know

i can't believe she's done it

WHY??

my parents don't even care

they have no idea

they've never seen any of those shows

hey don't worry

she probably won't get much airtime

you don't know her like I do

she *will*

Anyway

whatever! it's up to her isn't it

yeah

You don't fancy it then?! lol

haha no chance

i'm staying right out of it

wise choice

As a serious actress

ha

                    Oh hey, are you still going for that drama club?

yeah I think so!

it's pretty full on, 2 weeks 9-7 every day

                                            wow

                        that's great though, you'll love it

hope so!

weird though, by the time holiday and that are
   done, summer's almost over

                                         yeah

it used to seem so long when we were little

                                    I know

                        like too long to even imagine

I'm kinda looking forward to going back though

                             yeah? how come

i dunno

I've just got a feeling this year is going to be good

;)

I really wish she'd been right.

SUNDAY. ONE WEEK since the police knocked on the door; one week and one day since Lizzie was last seen. And I keep looking back, all the way back, to when we were just getting to know each other, when everything was fun and flirty and full of possibility – and then I have to fast-forward to now, a year and a half later, when Lizzie is just a word whispered round school, a stranger.

And I can't stop thinking about what happened in between.

A conversation bubble pops up at the bottom of my screen: Scobie.

hey
how'd it go with SuperBitch Barbie?

                                                              weird, man
                                    that girl is – I don't even know

Thinking of Cheska makes me think of yesterday morning, seeing her and Deacon... Unexpected. And extremely disturbing. I don't know if two people as self-obsessed as they are can get together without the universe imploding.

91

ha

yeah, she's pretty much the worst kind of human

See? This is why he's my best friend. It's like two guys, one brain, I swear.

how's your weekend?

pretty quiet

Frank's decided he's vegetarian

hahaha really?

This is surprising because for the last three years of his life, Frank Scobie has survived solely on a diet of chicken nuggets, fishfingers, and, weirdly, swordfish steaks. That's Abbots Grey for you.

yeah

as you can imagine, it's left him quite limited

chips it is?

for every meal

lol

occasional bit of toast for variety

dunno what you're on about, sounds like he's got

all the food groups covered

lol

It feels good to be joking, to be talking about normal, everyday stuff; like stretching a limb you haven't realised has gone numb.

you heard anything about Lizzie?

Yeah, thanks, Scobes.

                                        no

my brother said his copper mate Paul was saying
   they've had a sighting

Whoa. My heart just did something I don't think it's done
before.

                                    what?

apparently someone who works at the station says
   she got on a train

                                 where to?

London

London. Where she thinks 'Hal Paterson' lives. *No.* She can't.
She wouldn't.

                                  shit

I know

I feel sick. I click back to my homepage and scan through
the status updates without really reading them. *Cheska
Summersall is excited for the weekend, baby!!!. Jack Ciszewski
is pissed off. Jorgie Mitchell is eating cupcakes with her bestie J.
Cheska Summersall can't wait for tonight's episode… It's a big
one peeps!!!* (Cheska Summersall has Facebook diarrhoea).

93

Scobie's chat bubble bleeps at me.

Shark Week tonight... I'm ready!

He sends a photo of a bag full of Iceland snack platters, samosas and spring rolls and skewers and I have to smile. We did the same last Shark Week, but I know that this time he's making a big deal of it to take my mind off this whole Lizzie thing. It's not going to work, but it's nice of him.

Good work
just what I need

Another bubble pops up. Marnie Daniels.

Hey

hey
you ok

yeah
thanks for yesterday

no worries

I should tell her what Scobie's just told me. I should tell her that it's true; Lizzie did leave by choice, she did run away to meet a stranger without telling anyone. But sitting here staring at the screen, I can't bring myself to type the words.

you ok?

Do it, I tell myself. *Get it over with.*

> Scobie just told me there's a witness who saw L
> getting on a train to London

The seconds until she replies seem like hours.

what?
...
how does he know?

> his brother's friend is a policeman

...
...
oh

> at least it's something
>
> ...
>
> it's a step closer

yeah

And that's true. At least now we have something solid, a place she was. The not-knowing has been worst. And yet I'm so scared to know.

the police came to my house yesterday
they were asking about you

My heart is doing strange things again.

> About me?

yeah, just what i knew about you two

...

...

don't worry, they asked about other
    stuff too

Right. That's fine then.
Not.

what time you coming over dude?

I check the clock. 14:23.

                                     6.30ish?

cool

Marnie's bubble blinks at me.

you ok?

                                        yeah
                               just thinking

Thinking about Lizzie. Boarding a train. Not coming back.

Gotta go, Marnie writes after a while, and even though I feel
bad, I'm relieved.

                               K. I'll call you tomo x

I say goodbye to Scobie too, and I'm about to log out when a little red icon appears at the top of the screen. New friend request. There's a couple there, actually – I'm a bit lazy about checking it, since most people at Aggers think it's normal to add you on Facebook even if they've never spoken to you, or never intend to. I skim through them; a couple of guys from football, a girl from my maths class. The newest is another girl, but I don't recognise the name: Autumn Thomas. I click on her and have a look at her profile. It says she lives in Clapton, so I probably do know her – she must go to my old school. I click 'Accept', and immediately a message pops up from her.

Hey! Wasn't sure you'd remember me ;)

Erm, awkward. Do I admit that I don't?
Apparently, my silence speaks for me, because after a while, she '…'s, and then:

How's Gerber treating you this year?

Oh. Mrs Gerber was my GCSE English teacher – at Aggers. So she's not a London friend. Hmm.

I don't have her this year, I write, playing for time.
Then,
you living in London now?

yeah

97

my dad got a new job at the end of yr10

Looking at her profile photos again, she does look really familiar. Reddish-brown hair, pale skin with freckles. Pretty, but not, like, in-your-face pretty. And then it hits me.

wait – you used to sit two seats behind me, right?

next to

Next to Lizzie.

yeah
its so weird what happened to her
so sad

Nobody seems to really know the right word for the situation. Weird. Sad. No one's sure.

yeah, it's really bad
were you guys still friends?

kind of
we talked on here sometimes
not lately though
☹

Yeah, well, you and me both, Autumn Thomas.

Gotta go. Nice to hear from you.

you too ☺

speak soon x

I log out of chat but not out of my profile. And I click back onto my messages, and carry on living in the past.

hey

You ok?

yeah

SO embarrassing though

everyone's talking about it

it's all over my newsfeed

yeah well let them

it's nothing to do with you

just cos she's your sister doesn't mean you have to

feel embarrassed

i know but i do

and it's school tomorrow and it's all anyone's going

to be talking about

what was she thinking??

Someone else's boyfriend is bad enough, but on tv...

come on, you're the one who said it isn't real...

they probably talked her into it

I'd love to believe that

but...

urgh

SISTERS!

:/

sorry

If it makes you feel any better, i didn't watch it

didn't you?

that does make me feel better

how did you know about it then?

Scobie

ahh I keep forgetting you're back here

yep

back in the hood

how's it feel?

good I think

yeah good

you don't want to stay in London?

nah

not just yet

i can stick it out here :p

☺

so you feeling 100% now

yeah

finally!

Can't believe i was ill all summer ☹

yeah really bad luck

what a waste

at least you made it through drama club

yeah that was the best part

well I look forward to hearing all about it in person

yeah we've got english 4th and drama 5th, right?

you'll be sick of me

                              haha it'll be a novelty for a bit
                                        Been a long time!
i know...
I haven't played Candy Crush all summer

                                        ahh I'm touched
lol
so you ready?
Year 11? Last year? decisions decisions?

                         yeah thanks for that, no pressure!
                                        yeah I'm ready
a-level choices this year
you gonna choose drama?

                                               maybe
                                            not sure
                                            i want to
you should
            well let's see if I get a better part than 'Tree/Nymph
                              #5' in the show this year!
hahaha
you will
I'm sure you will

                                          we'll see

well I better go pack my bag and stuff
i'll see you tomorrow... ☺

                                      yes you will
                                      Sleep tight x

you too x

102

THE GYM IS pretty deserted; Sunday lunchtime, everyone at home eating happily with their families, bitching happily about other people's families. I feel a little bit guilty, actually, because I've left Mum essentially home alone; Kevin's been holed up in his office all weekend working on a new project, door closed. When a new business comes along, we don't see much of him, and when we do, he's totally distracted. You can practically hear the fans whirring in his brain as he processes everything, and even when he's talking to you he's pretty much looking through you half the time. When there's a problem in front of him, that problem is the only thing that exists until it's solved. And given that I'm feeling pretty distracted myself, I can imagine that the two of us aren't exactly the most fun people to share a house with right now.

But being out feels good, and being in the gym, with its purring machines and pumping dance music, feels even better. I run intervals on the treadmill until I feel like I'm about to throw up, pushing the speed up, making myself run an extra hundred metres each time. After the last one, I jump my feet onto the plastic sides of the treadmill, hit the stop button and watch the belt chug to a stop, my breath coming in hard and ragged and hot in my chest.

The main room of the gym is long and thin, with rows of cardio equipment and the windows overlooking the café on one side, a mirrored wall on the other with mats and exercise balls stationed along it. There's only me and three other people in there; two women of about Mum's age, who have cross-trainers next to each other and spend the entire time chatting away, and a girl I recognise from Year 13 power-walking on a treadmill at the opposite end of the row to me. Tucked off to one side is a weights room, and I head for it, rubbing at my face and neck with the rough strip of towel I keep in my kit bag.

The weights room is small and square, packed with equipment. It's darker in there; the windows that look over the car park are tinted so that the light they let in is blueish and dim. The music's quieter in here too, and there's the rhythmic clanking of someone doing reps on the chest press.

I'm still under strict instructions to keep working my injured leg, so I head for the leg curl, where I'll have to sit and do a hundred hamstring stretches. It'll be boring, and I'm already flicking through my phone, looking for a podcast or something to fill the time, when I round a corner in the maze of machines and come face to face with the person at the chest press.

It's Deacon. Of course it is.

He's sweating, his tight grey t-shirt soaked through, lifting a stack of weights far heavier than anything I would attempt. Not because I'm weak; because I'm not an idiot. He's still wearing his diamond earrings, and his long, baggy shorts and neon Air Max look brand new. He looks up and clocks me just as I register that it's him.

We look at each other. We don't say anything.

I find the leg curl and sit at it, and of course, obviously, it's directly opposite Deacon's machine. He begins pulling his reps in earnest, letting out a grunt each time. I start on my stretches, feeling – and hating the fact I'm feeling – kind of self-conscious. Deacon finishes with a clang, and stands up abruptly. I tense, waiting for him to come over, telling myself to keep calm, but instead he heads for one of the abs machines by the window and starts doing rapid crunches. I can't tell if the silent treatment is because it's no fun to pick a fight with me without an audience, or if it's something new he's trying out, but I'll take it. I settle into my stretches and try to forget that he's even in the room.

After a couple of minutes, the girl from Year 13 – Emily, I think her name is – comes in and sits at one of the machines near mine. I see Deacon's eyes flick over her long, tanned legs and up to her face, then he looks away again. I remember him getting out of Cheska's car, the way his hand tangled in her hair, and I smile. I glance up to find him looking at me, eyes narrowed. I look away. I don't let the smirk off my face.

A phone starts ringing somewhere in the room, and Deacon gets off the machine and fishes his iPhone out of his pocket. As he answers, he turns his back to me, but that's okay, because I've already turned my music off to hear him better.

'Oh yeah?' he's saying, and he stretches to look out of the window. 'Cool, babe. Down in a sec.'

He hangs up and stoops to pick up his towel and water bottle from the floor. As he makes his way out, he passes just that bit too close to my machine and makes a quick, almost imperceptible gesture with his hand, one that's meant just for me. *Wanker*.

I count to twenty, rushing through my stretches, and then I get up and head for the window. I look out just in time to see Deacon coming out of the Rec's doors below me, the sweat on his back like a dark bird, its wings outstretched. He pauses to tip water into his mouth, a long, showy stream, like he thinks he's on the pitch, and then he jogs over to a car that's idling in a space at the front of the car park.

If I'm expecting – okay, hoping – to see Cheska's yellow convertible, then I'm disappointed. It's a pale blue Beetle, and although the driver is blonde, it's not Cheska. It's Lauren. So they're back together... if they ever split up in the first place.

I go and collect my stuff, and I'm about to head back to the main room to do some core work, when I notice the girl from Year 13 smiling at me.

'It's Aiden, isn't it?' she says, and I tug one of my earphones out.

'Yeah. Hi.'

'I'm Emily. I'm in the year above you?'

'Yeah, sure.'

'I worked on *A Midsummer Night's Dream* with you.'

So that's where I know her from. 'I'm surprised you remember,' I say. 'I didn't exactly have a big part.'

She laughs. 'Well, I did the set design so I wasn't the star of the show either. I came to see you guys the next year though, you were great.'

I feel like I'm sinking, slowly, my heart heavy. 'Thanks.'

'Do you still act?'

I shake my head. No. I couldn't. Not now.

'That's a shame. You're really talented.'

'I had a good co-star,' I manage to say, and then I turn to go. 'See you around.'

I can feel her watching me all the way out.

By EIGHT THIRTY, Scobie's room is filled with half-empty plates and greasy wrappers. Half a giant pizza sits sweating in its box on the floor, along with a load of shiny bones, which are all that's left to show for the ribs and chicken wings we've also munched our way through. If I didn't play football, I would be clinically obese; I've got no idea how Scobie stays the same skinny shape he's always been.

Scobie has carefully selected and downloaded Shark Week's highlights, and we're halfway through a programme about tiger sharks in Hawaii, with his Mac's screen swivelled round on the desk and a load of pillows lined up against the wall to turn his bed into a sofa. We'd usually be more than welcome to use the actual sofa downstairs, but Frank's still awake and sharks make him cry. Plus Liam's got a girl round, so Jodie, Scobes's mum, is on hyper-hostess alert.

'Tiger vs tiger shark,' Scobes says, through a mouth full of samosa, 'who wins?'

'In water or on land?'

He thinks while he swallows. 'Shallow water.'

'Tiger.'

'Interesting.' He slumps onto one side to look at me. 'Why so?'

'Tigers can swim. And in shallow water, the tiger shark's gonna be all edgy and trapped.'

He shakes his head. 'Tiger sharks love the shallows.' As he says it, the screen shows the silhouette of a tiger shark moving stealthily towards a beach. 'See?'

'Nah, I still say tiger. Cos it can attack from above, like jump out of the water. And it has claws *and* teeth. It's got all bases covered.'

He nods. 'Good points, well made. I still say shark, though.'

'Well, that's up to you, Scobes. You're wrong, but that's up to you.'

He picks up the plate next to him and offers it to me. 'Last chicken skewer?'

'Is it satay or tikka?'

'Hard to tell.'

I take it, even though I feel like at this point I'm at least seventy-five per cent chicken. If Doug could see how far I've deviated from the healthy eating plan Norwich email us all each month, he'd throw one of his purple rages.

'Liam said that sighting of Lizzie's been confirmed. They're going to put the CCTV on the news.'

I nod. 'Hopefully that'll help.'

'Yeah, it might jog people's memories, right?' He looks hopeful. I *feel* hopeful. Maybe it will.

He glances sideways at me from behind his glasses. 'I guess this is all pretty weird for you, isn't it?'

I poke the sharp end of my now empty skewer against one of my fingers, again and again. 'I guess. We were close, and now all of this –' I switch to the next finger, poke a little harder. 'It's kind of like I never really knew her.'

'You guys didn't hang out much this year, did you?'

'No, not really. We kind of fell out.'

He glances at me. 'After prom night, right?'

Suddenly I wish I hadn't eaten so much pizza. 'Kinda, I guess.'

'Was all that something to do with Lizzie?'

'No,' I say, but my heart is really thudding now. 'Nah, that was just Honeycutt being a dick.'

Scobie looks at me and doesn't say anything for a minute, and in that minute I'm sure he's going to challenge me, ask me why I'm lying. But instead he just looks away, back at the screen, where the tiger shark is breaking open the shell of a giant turtle. 'No change there, then,' he says.

I want to tell him that I saw Honeycutt kissing Cheska Summersall but I don't. I don't want to talk about Deacon Honeycutt.

Scobie changes the subject anyway. 'Marnie Daniels still trying to find stuff out about that Facebook guy?' he asks.

You're so cute. My stomach twists. 'Yeah.'

'How come she's got you helping her?'

'She asked me,' I say, even though the question makes me feel funny. 'Could hardly say no, could I?'

He glances at me. 'Have you found anything else?'

I shake my head. 'Not really. Profile's gone, hasn't it?'

He taps his fingers against his plate thoughtfully. 'Maybe not.'

'Huh?'

He sits up suddenly, grabs his mouse and keyboard and clicks away the shark programme. 'It only disappeared this week, right?'

I shrug. 'Yeah.'

'Facebook are pretty slow about deleting data. There'll still be a cached version.' He's busy typing, clicking through windows too fast for me to follow. 'Here we go.'

He sits back so I have a proper view of the screen and, sure enough, there's the Hal Paterson profile, the guy in sunglasses who is not called Hal Paterson staring back at me. I feel a wave of revulsion. How could she fall for it?

'Let's take another look,' Scobie says, and he can hardly disguise the excitement in his voice. He loves technology, loves this step-by-step solving of things. It's like *CSI: Internet* to him. He scans down Hal Paterson's wall, looks at all the app stuff again.

'Red flags,' Scobie says, tutting. 'Total red flags. She should have noticed there was nothing personal on here.'

'Yeah,' I point out, 'but maybe he had it set to private. You can't see the personal stuff on my wall unless you're my friend.'

'You'd be surprised,' Scobie says, but he doesn't elaborate.

'How come you can still see all this?' I ask, suddenly afraid to look at the screen. 'He deleted it.'

'Yeah, well that's the thing about the internet. Hardly anything's ever *really* deleted.'

That's a scary thought.

Scobie's mouse hovers again over the location Marnie noticed on one of the posts. 'So we know he – assuming it's a he – was in or near King's Lyme at the end of the summer. Would Lizzie have been?'

I feel another lurch of nausea. 'Yeah. Her drama summer school thing was there.'

111

'Right –' He points at me, like Kevin does when someone says something smart or interesting in one of his presentations. 'So that's something. That's worth checking out.' He thinks for a minute, scrolling up the page again. 'Hey... Have you tried just Googling him?'

Before I can reply, he pulls up a new search window and types in Hal Paterson.

The computer takes 0.71 seconds to return nearly 700,000 results. Lots about Hals, lots about Patersons, a few Hal Pattersons; none of them what we're looking for. Just that same Facebook profile and nothing else.

"Hal Paterson" London, Scobie types.

Zero results.

"Hal Paterson" Kings Lyme, he tries.

Nothing.

'Thought he might be using the name on other sites,' Scobie says, after a minute. 'Guess it was just that profile.'

He turns and sees the expression on my face. I'm guessing it looks pretty bad.

'They'll find something,' he says. 'Liam reckons the police have got computer forensics guys in. They can do all kinds with signatures and IP addresses and stuff.'

'Can Facebook find out who set up the profile?' I ask, my fingers bunching themselves inwards to form fists.

'He could have set up a fake email account to use,' Scobie says, 'but yeah, they'll have stuff that'll be useful. It's tricky, though. Privacy laws and data protection and all that. They'll have to go through the courts.'

'Even with something like this?'

He shrugs. 'It's complicated.'

Isn't everything?

I look again at the face in the photo, the eyes hidden behind those mirrored sunglasses. *Talking to you. Always makes me smile.*

'We're assuming she went to meet him, but there's nothing that says that anywhere. Can you honestly imagine Lizzie – *Lizzie* – doing that?'

Scobie considers this. 'It's just weird, isn't it? The guy says he's from London, Lizzie boards a train to London.'

I suddenly feel close to tears. I think of Marnie, sitting in Café Alice, her head in her hands. *I should've done something.* I think of Lizzie, smiling at me across the drama studio, the *Midsummer's* set going up around us. 'I should've done something,' I say, quietly.

Scobie turns round to look at me. 'Hey. What could you have done? Nobody knew. Nobody knew any of this stuff about her.'

I stare at the screen. Hal Paterson stares back. I feel a twist of hatred in my gut. 'There must be something we can do,' I say. 'Somebody knows where she is.'

Scobie considers this, and then he briskly clicks away from Hal's profile page and onto his own newsfeed. With a couple more clicks, he's opened a new window: Create Page.

FIND LIZZIE SUMMERSALL, he types in the title box, and then he pauses over the description. HAVE YOU SEEN THIS GIRL? he tries, and we both look at this and shake our heads. MISSING, he puts instead, and then he stops. 'I'm no good at this,' he says. 'Words, you know – not really my thing.'

I've read enough of Scobie's history coursework to know that that's not exactly true, but I know what he means – when

113

something's this important, this personal, the words just seem to dry up. I take the keyboard from him and I picture Lizzie catching my eye across the playground, her hair blown back by the wind. I start typing.

MISSING — Can you help?

Lizzie Summersall has been missing from her home in Abbots Grey, Hertfordshire, since Saturday 8ᵗʰ October. The last known sighting of her is of her boarding a train to London Kings Cross in neighbouring town, Kings Lyme.

Lizzie is a much loved sister, daughter and friend. She loves Harry Potter, roast potatoes, and every kind of sweet except orange ones. She is 5'5", with long, blondeish hair, and green eyes.

If you have any information, please, please share!

Scobie reads over my shoulder and when I'm done, he nods. 'That's good,' he says. 'That's perfect.'

He takes the mouse and keyboard back from me and clicks 'Create'. 'Now we need to find a good photo of her,' he says. 'Do you have one?'

I shake my head.

'That's okay, we'll just get one off her profile.'

He finds Lizzie's Facebook, and I look at her beaming at me from the corner. He clicks through her profile pictures until he finds one of just her, close-up, a shot of her at the fair that came to Kings Lyme last autumn. The sky is purple behind her and she's holding a huge stick of candyfloss. Her hair is down and shining in the bright lights of the waltzers beside her, and I can almost hear her laughing.

'That one,' I say, but he's already saving it.

After he's uploaded the photo to our page, we both sit and look at Lizzie, at the word MISSING that we've typed beside her.

'Someone must know something,' I say, and my voice is small and hopeless.

He gives me a sympathetic smile and an awkward kind of man-pat on the only part of me in reach: my socked foot. 'Fingers crossed,' he says. After a couple of minutes' silence, he tries: 'Distracting shark attack documentary?'

Somehow, I manage a smile. 'Always.'

'It's got actual footage, not just reconstructions.'

'Good times.'

He hits play and slides back into his own space.

'Scobes?'

'Yeah?'

'Thanks.'

We sit and watch in comfortable silence. After a bit, we hear Jodie bring Frank to bed, even though he keeps telling her, in between yawns, that he's 'not tired yet!' Near the end of the programme we hear two sets of footsteps going into Liam's room, the door closing quietly. I feel a sudden pang of jealousy.

'Who goes swimming near a seal colony anyway?' Scobie says, sitting up to grab some of the cold leftover party food. He considers the guy being interviewed on screen, the scarred outline of a shark's jaw right across his side. 'Idiot.'

But I'm not really listening; too busy idly flipping through my phone. Trying to resist the urge to look at my messages with Lizzie again. 'Hey, do you remember a girl called Autumn Thomas who was in our year for a bit?'

He thinks about it, tapping a spring roll against his plate. 'Yeah, think so… redhead?'

'Yeah.'

'Never really spoke to her.'

'She was in my English class. She friend-requested me the other day.'

He pushes his glasses up his nose. 'Oh right.'

'She seems nice enough.'

He shrugs and takes a bite of the spring roll, attention returned to the grainy camcorder footage of a fin cutting through the water towards a canoe.

But then he frowns. 'Are you sure –' he starts, but before he can ask me whether it's really a good idea to be talking to some new girl when all I'm *really* thinking about is Lizzie, the lights – and Scobie's Mac – go out.

'Liam!' Jodie yells from her room, at the same time as Liam calls out 'Sorry!' sheepishly.

'Well, if they'd just *listen* to me and get the fuses actually fixed properly,' Scobie says in a huff, getting up and heading downstairs.

'I'll take that as my cue to leave,' I say, following him. 'See you at school tomorrow, mate. Good luck with the electrics.'

'Yeah, thanks.' His hand finds my shoulder in the dark. 'And look, don't worry. This Lizzie thing. It's all going to be okay. They'll find her.'

I just wish I could be as certain.

I GET HOME from Scobie's around ten, and realise I need to finish a history essay for Radclyffe that's due in tomorrow. Mum and Kevin are already in bed, so I make myself a coffee, grab one of Kevin's weird healthy oat and seed bar things – because, yep, unbelievably, I'm still hungry – and head for my room. I put the TV on low and flip open my laptop. I've only got the conclusion to finish, so I'm hoping it won't take too long. I feel drained, like I could sleep forever. The last week hasn't exactly been restful.

I've just started checking through the last paragraph I wrote, when Facebook flashes at me from another tab. Autumn's sent me a new message.

hey, how you doing?

Hey

not bad thanks

how are you?

good thanks

...

While she's typing, I try to work out if I've ever really spoken to her properly. I'm pretty sure it was just English we had together. I try to remember the projects Gerber gave us that year, if Autumn and I were ever grouped together. I think I remember her being Miss Maudie when we did our read-through of *To Kill a Mockingbird*, and us reading a scene together, me as Jem, with another girl, Katie Jupe, narrating as Scout. I try to picture Lizzie there too, head bent over her book, hair tumbling forwards.

how's your weekend?

She *does* seems nice enough. But maybe I shouldn't really be talking to some random girl right now, especially when there's every chance she's just fishing for gossip about Lizzie.

yeah, good thanks, I write, and I don't add anything else.

I click onto her profile. She has 302 friends, most of them from her school in Clapton. I look at the little box which says we're friends with each other, and the one next to it, with a tick and the word 'Following', and a chill runs through me. It's such a creepy word, especially now, especially with Lizzie... It was so easy for her to let strangers follow her, to let them look at everything she did and thought. Just like I've done with this girl, even though I barely remember her.

There are loads of photos of her; some from a beach holiday somewhere, a few parties. Lots of her horse-riding. I flick through them and start to relax a little bit. Seems like Autumn has a nice enough life; friends, a happy family, potentially her own horse – which is not that unusual for a girl from Aggers. She's always smiling, never doing that annoying pout girls like Lauren and Cheska do every time they see a camera. She seems sweet. Friendly. Like the kind of person who maybe *would* add someone just because they went to school with them once.

I have to go quite far back to find any of her in Abbots Grey, and I'm shocked when I do at how young everybody looks. Funny how much people can change in two years. Scary, really.

The photos from Aggers are mostly just normal stuff; lots of girls from our year hanging around by the basketball courts, one of them on a bus on a school trip somewhere. There's a couple of her and Lizzie, and my heart stalls in my chest. Lizzie, in her school blazer, beaming, her arm round Autumn. Lizzie, in her shirt and tie at their desk in English, and there, in the corner of the photo, just the edge of my face, caught in shadow. I click away quickly, look through more of the boring school trip ones.

But then I find one of Autumn and Lauren Choosken, arms linked as they grin at the camera. And then another, both of them in pyjamas on someone's sofa. And another, the two of them on a skiing trip somewhere, pink-cheeked and laughing, their jackets zipped up high. Suddenly I'm suspicious. So she's friends with Lauren, the girlfriend of the person who hates me most in this town. That *can't* be a good sign.

I go back to Autumn's profile page and scan down it. Lots of messages from a couple of girls – friends from her school, I guess – posting funny links or saying hi, or commenting on her photos. Her status updates are the same as most of the girls in our year: *Autumn Thomas is soooo bored. Autumn Thomas is looking forward to the weekend.* One about a week ago catches my eye: *Autumn Thomas is worried about an old friend* ☹

She must have meant Lizzie. I look at it for a while. It's weirdly touching, that little sad face, and the fact that she doesn't mention Lizzie by name. So many of the girls at school are desperate to pretend that they were best friends with Lizzie, just to get attention. Maybe Autumn really *is* just worried about an old friend. And maybe she really *is* just talking to me because we went to school together, not because she wants the gossip on Lizzie, or because Deacon Honeycutt is somehow trying to get at me through one of Lauren's friends – and thinking that through, it *does* sound totally ridiculous.

So how's life in Abbots Grey? she writes, and I think you know what – why not? Why not talk to someone who doesn't want to ask me about Lizzie (yet, anyway), someone who doesn't know anything about me past what happened in Year 10, that first year at Aggers. The good year.

Oh the same, I type

You miss it?

Ha no

Not at all

Too many fake people

Yep well that's still true

I haven't been paying attention to the telly, but at the sound of a familiar voice, I look up and see Cheska's face. Of course.

120

It's Sunday night, and the newest episode of *Spoilt in the Suburbs* is on. I roll my chair round to watch it properly.

Cheska is in one of the cafés in town, sitting at a table by the counter with Ricky Dean, another member of the cast who's tall, tanned and impossibly good-looking – and the biggest bitch of the lot of them. They're both clutching hot chocolates with huge towers of whipped cream and the staff behind the counter are trying to pretend they haven't noticed the cameras. They aren't doing a very good job.

Cheska is wearing a grey hoody, her hair pulled back in a ponytail. It's a very different look for her, and I guess she's too worried to care – or that's what we're *supposed* to think, anyway. She isn't too worried not to bother with make-up, though – her face is loaded with it as usual. Big fake eyelashes and shiny lips, just to drink hot chocolate in a café?

'…the police,' she's saying. 'Going through all her things.'

Ricky is doing his serious face, nodding, his perfectly plucked eyebrows drawn into a fake-looking frown. 'Oh, babe. How are your parents doing?'

'Terrible.' Cheska looks down at her cup. 'I'm just trying to protect Evie from it all, you know? She's too young to understand.'

'You're being so brave, babe,' Ricky says, reaching out a hand to stroke her sleeve. 'You're amazing.'

Yeah, right. So busy being brave and looking after her little sister that she's got time to sit in cafés drinking hot chocolate and being filmed.

The scene changes to one of Thomas Jay, Cheska's boyfriend, with his thinks-he's-David-Beckham tattoos and greasy man-bun. He's playing golf with Marlon, one of 'the lads' who bulk up each episode with parties, pub crawls and cheating on their girlfriends.

'How's Cheska?' Marlon asks, leaning against the golf cart and drinking from a bottle of beer.

Thomas Jay takes a swing at a ball and watches it sail up into the sky. 'She's doing okay. It's tough.'

Right, so Lizzie is the focus of the whole episode. Great. I knew Cheska was pretty shameless about using her life for publicity, but this is too far.

are you watching this? Autumn writes.

                                    unfortunately yes

what is with that bitch?
shes so fake
i cant believe shes talking about it on tv

                                              i can

lizzie always used to say she was fake
even before s in the suburbs
I never met her though

On the screen the scene switches back to the café, where Cheska and Ricky are leaving, their hot chocolates untouched.

'Coming to Marlon's party later?' Ricky asks Cheska, linking his arm through hers as they step onto the street.

'Yeah. Just what I need to take my mind off everything,' she says, leaning her head against his shoulder.

Urgh. I reach over and turn the TV off.

going to bed

night

k

sweet dreams x

'AUTUMN THOMAS'

THIS IS EASIER than I thought it would be. He's clearly lonely. Clearly wants someone to talk to.

I'm sure he looked through my photos. Trying to see what he could find out about me. Trying to see what kind of girl I am. Some people think you can judge something like that from the things someone posts about, from the people they hang around with. Unfortunately he's one of them.

He probably didn't remember me. I didn't expect him to. Just the girl who sat behind him in English. Not important enough to pay much attention to.

But then Aiden doesn't really pay attention to anything much that goes on around him. All he *really* cares about is himself.

If he cared about anyone but himself, then maybe this wouldn't be happening to him. Then again, maybe none of this would be happening at all.

If he *did* care about anyone but himself, he'd probably remember that the redheaded girl who sat behind him in Year 10 English was called October Thomas, not Autumn.

AIDEN

LYING AWAKE, ALL I can think of is an English lesson, a weirdly sunny February morning last year. Mock exams are coming up, and we're looking through a past paper, talking through the questions. We've got held up halfway through, on the question about *An Inspector Calls*:

> *How successfully is the idea of collective responsibility explored in this play?*

'Isn't that the point?' Katie Jupe says. 'That's the whole point of the play? They're all to blame?' Everything Katie Jupe says is a question.

'Yeah,' Harry Yates chimes in, looking down at a page in his book where he's clearly scrawled everything Mrs Gerber has ever said about *An Inspector Calls*. '"We're all responsible for each other"'.

'No man is an island,' Ollie Birchall says. Smugly.

And it is. It is the point. A girl is killed. A girl kills herself. A girl is gone, forever. And each and every person has played a part.

'Well, yes,' Mrs Gerber says. 'But how successful is it? Do

you agree that they're all to blame? And how has Priestley presented each character, their language, their directions, their reactions, to make you feel that way?'

This sets off little pools of conversation, which Gerber loves. *An Inspector Calls* was the text we all liked the most, really, or the one that started the most discussions, anyway.

Probably, nine times out of ten, nobody would've heard what Lizzie said. But it just happens to be one of those moments when, as if by magic, there's a gap in everyone's conversations and everything goes quiet.

'Gerald,' she says, quietly but fiercely. 'Gerald's to blame.'

'Whaaaat.' Kieron Decker, from the back. Not really like Kieron to volunteer an opinion on literature, but what Lizzie's said *is* controversial. Gerald's part in the play is pretty small, over early. He's not even part of the Birling family, the ones who have all, without realising, contributed to the girl's suicide. Even if you don't buy into the idea that everyone is equally responsible for the welfare of the people they come across in the world, however small that meeting might seem to them – and that is the point of the play, Katie Jupe's right – even if you do think some of the cast are more responsible than others, Gerald's probably the last person you'd accuse.

'Interesting, Lizzie,' Gerber says, her face neutral. 'What makes you say that?'

Everyone is listening now, and the sun comes through the greasy old window and makes Lizzie look gold again, just like her Ophelia moment.

'He made her love him,' she says. 'And that's where it all went wrong.'

I KNOW SOMETHING is up as soon as I get into our form room. I'm not late for once, which is especially rare on a Monday, but when Radclyffe looks up and sees me, his face changes from its usual confused owl smile to something harder, something that looks almost… anxious. There's still a couple of minutes until the bell for registration, and there's only Jorgie Mitchell and Kirsty Allison in the room. They're both pretty wrapped up in their phones, perched on the windowsill, and Radclyffe beckons me over to his desk.

'This is for you,' he says, sliding a slip of paper to me.

I look at him before I look at it.

'Nothing to worry about,' he says, but if he convinces himself, he definitely doesn't convince me. I look down at the slip. It's typed, and at the top is the school logo. Beside it is a crest which, when I look closer, reads 'Hertfordshire Constabulary'. It says that I'm required for an interview today during first period in the headmaster's office. And it says that my mother has been invited to be present, but that if she is unable to, Mr Selby will be present on my behalf. It's very formal and it makes my stomach turn in loops. I take it and

127

turn away without meeting Radclyffe's gaze.

I look at the note again as the rest of my form drift in, trying to read between the lines. I don't think anyone else who's been talked to in the temporary interview room the police have set up got a note like this. I don't think anyone else's parents were asked to attend. Or maybe they were, and I haven't heard about it. Maybe it's just the law, because most of us are under eighteen. Or maybe… No. Stop. No maybes.

I hardly even notice when Scobie sits down beside me. 'Alright?' he asks.

I push the sheet of paper across to him. His eyes flick back and forth across it at high speed. 'Oh,' he says.

'Do you think that's weird? That they've asked my mum to be here?'

He shrugs. 'Nah. I'm sure it's nothing. We're minors, aren't we?'

'Has everyone else had their parents around?'

He looks away. 'Maybe. I think Selby sat in on most of them.'

This does not make me feel better. Neither does the fact that Jorgie and Kirsty have started talking about how last night's episode of *Spoilt in the Suburbs* was 'so sad' and how Cheska is being 'so brave' and 'so sweet'. I'm pretty sure that they, like everyone else in our year, spent the whole of the last series telling Lizzie what a slag her sister was for stealing Thomas Jay from Aimee, and then, later, what an idiot she was for taking back him after she'd found out he was cheating on *her*, too. But now Cheska's brave, and sweet, and the star of the show.

'Want me to come with you?' Scobie asks as the bell goes for first period. 'I've got a free.'

I shake my head. 'Thanks, Scobes. I'll be alright.'

'You've got nothing to hide, right? So don't worry.'

Yeah, sure. Nothing to worry about.

The headmaster's office is in the north wing of the school, also known as Nightingale. It houses a couple of classrooms, which are hardly ever used, the school nurse, a conference room, and the offices of the two deputy heads and the school governors. There's a reception desk where you're supposed to sign in if you're late or a visitor, and the walls are covered in work Aggers wants to show off. Artwork, presentations and, in the main corridor, a 'Wall of Fame', with past students who've gone on to be actresses or writers or scientists. Because students only ever come here if they're ill or in trouble, it's deathly quiet. I smile at the receptionist, who's a skinny guy in his twenties and has, in the past, seen me about to sign in as late and waved me away. 'I'll pretend I didn't see you,' he said to me that time, and maybe I'm being paranoid, but it seems like the same goes for today.

The offices are through a set of double doors just behind the reception. A long, narrow corridor, dimly lit; the doors all closed. The head's office is right at the end, and the corridor seems to stretch ahead of me, impossibly long. I've only been here once in my time at Aggers, but I remember it horribly well.

The current headmaster of St. Agnes's, Martin Maclaren, is relatively new. He started just a bit before me, so I guess maybe three years ago now, and at first he wasn't very popular with either the parents or the governors. He's reasonably young – in their eyes, anyway – at fortyish, and he's got a lot of new ideas about how to run the school. Aggers is not the kind of school that uses *new* ideas. It's all about tradition. They make the pupils wear blazers and ties and even the sixth-formers are supposed to follow a dress code, although hardly anyone does.

Most people only see Maclaren when he does his full school assembly once a week, and since the sixth-formers don't attend that – we have our own, in the Keep, with Selby – I haven't really seen much of him since term started. He does stalk around the school occasionally, in his perfect suit and his stiff shoes, his thin curls flapping in the breeze, but apart from that, he keeps himself to himself. I've been glad of that. The last time I saw him was the day after prom, and that isn't a meeting I want to repeat. Even the idea of being in his office makes the hairs on the back of my neck stand up.

It's less of an office, more of a, I don't know, suite. The main door is open, but I knock anyway. Inside, at a small dark wood desk, Maclaren's secretary is on the phone. There's also a female police officer sitting in a chair to one side with a laptop open on her lap. She looks up.

'Interview?'

I nod.

'What's your name?'

'Aiden Kendrick.'

She glances down at an iPad on the seat next to hers. 'Right.' Am I imagining it, or does the tone of her voice change? 'We just need to wait for your mum to arrive. Take a seat.'

'My mum's coming?'

'Well, she said she was when I called her half an hour ago, so I assume so, yes.'

I don't know if that makes me feel better or worse.

The police officer takes the iPad off the chair so I can sit down. She also shifts her chair round, ever so slightly, so that I can't see her laptop screen.

Maclaren's secretary finishes her phone call and smiles at me before returning to her computer. Then there's just silence, broken occasionally by the click of a mouse or soft tapping on keyboards. Behind the secretary's desk is another door. It's also made of dark wood, a glass panel in the centre. The glass is frosted so you can't see through, but occasionally I think I see a shadow move behind it, like a shark deep below the surface of the sea.

I listen to the tap tap of typing, and I wonder if Lizzie ever got sent to this office. It seems unlikely but then everything I'm hearing about her these days does. I remember how upset she was last year, coming back to start Year 11 with everyone talking about Cheska and *Spoilt in the Suburbs*, and I wonder what she'd think about Cheska talking about her on TV, or the way everyone's suddenly feeling sorry for her sweet, brave big sister.

The double doors out in the corridor creak open and I hear footsteps coming down the hall. Someone wearing heels. I hope against hope that it's Mum, although I'm dreading seeing her. Just like me, she's only been in this office once; the last thing I want to do is remind her of it. I try to think of other times she's visited the school, and I remember our shows. She came to see our shows; me and Lizzie on stage together. The thought makes my stomach lurch.

Mum knocks on the half-open door just like I did. Maybe a bit less nervously.

The WPC rises. 'Mrs Cooper?'

It's still weird to hear her called that. They got married two years ago, but it's still strange to think she has a different name to me. She was going to keep Kendrick at one point; she said it felt like hers, now; that it was a part of her. But Kevin persuaded her that it was better to have a new start.

'Hi.' Mum is in the room, relaxed smile, hand extended, as if the policewoman is someone she's interviewing for a job.

'I'm WPC Gilligan. Thanks so much for coming.'

'Not a problem.' My mum glances at me. 'Okay, Aiden?'

I nod.

'Are you missing any classes?' Her voice is pointed. I hear it, and Gilligan hears it too.

'Sports studies.'

'Let's see if we can get started,' Gilligan says hurriedly, and heads for the inner office. 'Get you off before the end of the lesson.'

I move closer to Mum. She leans towards me as we stand. 'I thought they'd asked you everything.'

I shrug. I can feel her studying my face.

'Is there more?'

'No,' I hiss.

When Gilligan knocks on the frosted door, I hear Hunter's voice.

'Yeah?'

She opens the door a crack. 'Aiden Kendrick and mum, ready for you.'

'Great.'

She holds the door open for us and I follow Mum in. It's *almost* the same as I remember it: a big wooden desk dominates the room and there's a long bookcase against one wall. There's all Maclaren's stuff – a brand new Mac, some framed photos – but then there's two laptops and a load of cardboard files spread messily over the desk. Police stuff. Mahama and Hunter are both sitting behind the desk. I notice that Hunter has Maclaren's leather desk chair while Mahama has to make do with one of the plastic ones we have in class. They both get up when we enter.

'Mrs Kendrick, nice to see you,' Hunter says, coming round the desk.

'It's Cooper,' she reminds him, in a not very friendly voice. She shakes his hand quickly and sits down, leaving him to make his way awkwardly back to his seat.

'And this is DS Mahama, as you'll remember, Aiden.'

'Good to see you again, Aiden,' Mahama says, watching me as I sit too.

'We're a little confused as to *why* you're seeing him again,' Mum says, pulling her chair a bit closer to the desk.

'We're asking many students for second interviews,' Mahama says. 'It's not something to worry about.'

'It's not an interview,' Hunter says, shooting Mahama a look I can't read. 'It's an informal conversation. A *chat*. Not something to worry about.' The way he says it is different to the way Mahama did. His way implies a silent *Yet* after it. 'We've been learning new things about Lizzie. We're wondering if you can help us with that.'

I am very aware of my heart drumming against my ribs. But the fact that Mum is next to me gives me some confidence.

'I'm learning stuff too,' I say. 'So I don't know how I'll be able to help. I don't think I knew Lizzie very well after all.'

'Yes, well.' Hunter looks down at a file in front of him. 'You said before that you and Lizzie had a falling out at the beginning of the summer.'

Mum is straight in there. '*Did* you say that?'

I shake my head. 'We just didn't really talk much after that. It was summer.'

'Right, fine, okay. Did you hear anything about what she might have been up to during the summer?' Hunter slides a file closer to him but doesn't open it.

'No.' I glance at Mum. 'Well, not until recently.'

'And what did you hear recently?' Mahama asks.

I look from her to Hunter and back again. 'People have been saying she… started seeing guys. More than usual.'

Hunter nods, his mouth turned down. 'Mmm. We've been hearing that too. Do you think it's true?'

I shrug. 'I really don't know.'

'Does that sound like something Lizzie would do?'

'No.' I look down at my hands. 'I don't know.'

'Any idea who these "guys" could be?'

I shake my head. The thought makes me feel sick.

'You think they were local guys, or people she met online?' Mahama asks.

'He just said he doesn't know,' Mum says, although a little of the sharpness has gone out of her voice. She's obviously decided I'm not in any immediate danger of being arrested.

'What do you know about Lizzie's activities online?' Hunter asks, even though I haven't answered Mahama's question yet.

My palms begin to sweat. 'Nothing. I mean, not much. Just what everyone's been saying.'

'So you wouldn't know anything about a Hal Paterson?'

The name makes me want to throw up. 'I think I've heard that name. I think people are saying it's someone she met on Facebook?'

Hunter cocks his head, one eyebrow raised. He almost looks as if he's about to smile.

'We know you've been accessing Lizzie's Facebook, Aiden. Marnie told us.'

My heart starts to really thud. My mouth has become instantly, impossibly dry. 'We just wanted to help,' I say, swallowing a couple of times.

'What you consider "helping", we consider tampering with evidence.'

'We didn't delete anything,' I say quickly, panicky. 'I swear. We just looked.'

'And what did you see?' Hunter asks. His voice is cold, sarcastic. Mahama looks earnestly at me, waiting for my answer.

'She was talking a lot to that guy on there, but the profile's a fake,' I say carefully.

'Which is quite concerning, given that we believe Lizzie set out to meet him, isn't it?' Hunter's voice is low, the words sinking across the room.

'She doesn't say she's going to meet him,' I say, but my voice sounds small and hopelessly hopeful.

'Mmm,' Hunter says, noncommittally. 'Aiden, I want to show you something we found in Lizzie's locker.' He lifts out a clear plastic bag from underneath the desk and puts it on the table in front of me. 'Can you tell me what that is?'

I can. I recognise it well.

'It's a note from me.'

'Can you read the note for us?'

My voice sounds hollow as I read the words. 'Don't do this. Talk to me.'

I hear Mum draw in her breath sharply beside me.

Hunter looks at me over his knuckles, elbows propped on the table again. 'Don't do what, Aiden? What was Lizzie doing?'

There's a thudding in my ears. 'It's not what you think – it's old, the note's old. It's from weeks ago.'

'It's not what I think? What do I think?' Hunter asks, and we look at each other across the desk. Mahama clears her throat and leans back in her chair. Mum's hands are gripping the edge of her chair, her knuckles turning white.

'Okay,' Hunter says after a minute, still fixing me with his steel stare. 'I'll tell you what I think. I think maybe you and Lizzie *are* still close. And maybe she told you she was going to leave. And maybe you're trying to protect her. Or yourself. Probably yourself, now you realise the profile's a fake and she could be in serious danger here.'

I'm starting to feel like the room's getting smaller. Like the walls are closing in. 'You're wrong,' I blurt out. 'She hasn't spoken to me in months.'

Both of them look at me. Mum looks at me. Nobody says anything.

'The note's old,' I say, looking from my mum to Mahama. 'I – we – she wouldn't speak to me. I missed her. But I don't know anything about this. I swear.'

Mahama leans forward in her chair again. 'Aiden, anything you can tell us is very important,' she says. 'Time really is of the essence here.'

'I know!' I say, frustration making me sound panicked, angry. I check myself, try to keep calm. 'I don't know where she went, or why. I *wish* I did.'

The silence seems to stretch on forever before Hunter finally leans back and folds his arms. 'Okay. I think we're done here.' Mum stands up straight away, gathering up her bag and coat. I can tell, without looking at her, that she's upset.

'Keep in touch,' Hunter says, sliding a business card across the desk to me. 'You know, if anything jogs your memory. That thing DS Mahama said, about the time. She's not kidding.'

I don't ask why.

I find out by the end of the day, anyway. I don't know who hears first, but by fifth period it's all anyone's talking about, and by six o'clock, it makes the national news.

Someone in London has found Lizzie's clothes.

LIZZIE

WHEN I FIRST met him, it was like the perfect story. He was the boy and I was the girl, and there was a happy-ever-after written just for us from the very first line.

And then it all went wrong. Things didn't go according to the script; they went their own way.

He broke my heart.

He hurt me.

I trusted him. I trusted them all. That's where I went wrong, because not everyone can be trusted. I know that now.

But now is too late.

AIDEN

I DRIVE TO training that evening without paying any attention to the road. Lizzie's clothes. Found on a bench in Victoria Park. I can't think about what that means. I can't. I can't.

Police are searching through CCTV of the area, trying to find an image of her at some point in the last week. I hope against hope that they find one. I'd do anything to see her again, even in some grainy black-and-white shot. Something to prove she was there. Something to prove she exists.

I've left Mum at home, silent and tense. When I got in from school, she was sitting in the kitchen, the paper unopened in front of her. She watched me take off my shoes. She didn't say hi.

We've always been close, Mum and me. We joke around with each other a lot: I ruffle her hair, she teases me about my parking. She's quick and witty, full of one-liners, always the first to pull me up on something funny I've said without meaning to. Over the years, but especially in the six months between the divorce and Mum meeting Kevin, we've become more like friends.

So it's only really now that I realise I can still be just as scared of upsetting her, of making her angry, as I was when I was nine and I broke the dining room window with a football.

In the kitchen, I pulled out the stool opposite hers and we both looked down at the picture of Lizzie – a school photo from Year 11 – on the front page.

'I'm telling the truth, Mum,' I said.

She looked at me for a long time. 'This is really serious, Aiden. If she told you *anything* –'

'Mum, I swear she didn't. She wouldn't. We aren't friends any more.'

She sighed and looked at the picture again. We both did. After a while, she got up and started taking things out of the fridge for dinner.

'I'm going to get ready for training,' I said, and just as I got to the door, Mum spoke.

'I keep thinking about the two of you on stage.' She reached for an onion and started chopping; the last four words were almost lost under the tapping of the knife. 'You were good together.'

That's what I keep thinking now. Things I should have done, things I wish I'd done. How I wish that Lizzie and I were still good together, how I wish we were still close enough for her to trust me, to tell me her secrets. To tell me where she was going, to tell me how I could follow her.

I pull up in the deserted car park of the training ground, the sky already dark. Hefting my kit bag off the back seat, I try to switch off thoughts of Lizzie, try to get my head in the game. For probably the first time ever in my life, it doesn't work.

It starts to drizzle as soon as we're all out on the pitch, the floodlights trapping swarms of tiny droplets in their beams.

Doug sets us off running laps, moving us quickly through our warm-up as our shirts get slowly sodden. The balls make hushing noises as we pass them over the slick grass, and I'm glad of the silence, glad of having one focus, just one thing to think about and nothing else. The stands are in shadow, seats clapped closed.

Halfway through, Doug tosses out coloured bibs and splits us into teams to play five-a-side. As he throws mine to me, he pauses. 'Alright, Kendrick?'

I nod.

'You look a bit peaky. That better not be a hangover.'

Farid Jarrar, one of the other centre-forwards, elbows me as Doug turns away. 'Bet it is.'

I shake my head. 'Nah.'

Farid claps his hand to his head. 'Aw, mate, I should've thought. You're mates with that Lizzie girl, aren't you?'

Farid isn't from Aggers; he goes to school in Norwich. All he knows about Lizzie is what he's seen on the news. He's a nice guy – probably one of the people I like best on the squad – but I really don't feel like talking to him right now. So I shrug. 'Sort of. Not really.'

He frowns. 'She came to see us, though, right? Last Christmas, that charity match down by you? Thought I recognised her.'

'Maybe. Can't remember, mate.' I pick up the ball at my feet, speckled with grass and mud, and pass it to him, harder than I mean to. He catches it against his chest with a thud. 'Let's go,' I say. 'I'm freezing here.'

I do remember. I remember her, front row of the stands, cheeks pink, a pale blue beanie pulled down over her hair.

Taking off her mittens to clap, cupping her hands round her mouth to cheer.

But it's only later, on the drive home, the mud drying chalky on my legs, that I remember something else about that day. Something she said to me, after the match, her breath warm against my frozen cheek. 'Thanks for inviting me. I like to see you play.'

And then she leaned in closer, hat in her hand, and she whispered, 'It makes me want to play with you.'

I SAW THE news, Autumn writes, when I'm just out of the shower, my microwaved dinner in front of me.

> her clothes
> you ok?

But after my interview today, the note in its plastic bag, I just want to put space between Lizzie and me.

>> i'm ok
>> pretty grim right
>> feel bad for her family

Casual, like I didn't really know Lizzie. But hey, that's how it feels now, isn't it?

> yeah me too
> did you see deacon's post
>> about it?

An alarm bell rings. Deacon: that's the first time she's mentioned him.

> no
> we're not friends on facebook

lucky you
he's a dick

Maybe I should feel relieved, but the fact she's brought Deacon up at all has got me suspicious again. Like she's *trying* to get me to slag him off. Trying to get me to badmouth him so she can report back, maybe? But then what do I care, anyway? It's not exactly like he'd be surprised that I only had bad things to say about him.

I settle for:

> yeah
> can't say we get on the best

She doesn't reply straight away and after a while, I look back at the messages. Deacon posting about Lizzie?

A sensible voice in my head tells me not to ask. But it's pretty small, and easy to ignore – as the sensible voices in my head usually are – so I ask anyway.

> what did he write?

...
doesnt matter
a stupid joke

he's a dick

                                                          yeah

                                                          he is

but you're better at football than him, right?

                                                          haha

                                          I don't know about that

Not to be a gossip but I heard you were
    signing with Norwich

Okay, now I really *am* suspicious. Why is she asking me
about that?

                                                  Not exactly
                          I've been training with them for a couple of
                                                    years now

Wow that's so cool

                                                  um thanks

So you think that's what you'll do?

                                                  Maybe

I look at her profile picture in the corner of the screen.
She's changed it today, to one of her sitting in a deckchair in
a garden somewhere, a copy of *Catcher in the Rye* in her lap.
It's a great book, one of my favourites. She's smiling up at the
camera, or the person behind it, and it's a wide, genuine smile,
like they've just told a joke and she's about to start laughing.
It's the kind of smile that makes you want to smile back.

Maybe I'm being paranoid, and she's just being nice, just
interested. It's stupid to think that Deacon would be interested

enough in me to ask some girl who used to go to our school to stalk me. Right?

I still change the subject, though. Just to be on the safe side.

> What about you, what do you want to do?

Erm

Nursing i think

> cool, what kind of nursing?

I want to be a paediatric nurse
So just hoping to get really good grades and go
    to college

I feel myself relaxing again. She's only making conversation, like normal people do. Some people *are* just friendly. Not everyone has another motive.

And, okay, yeah – maybe, when I read the conversation back, it does feel a bit like she might be flirting with me. And maybe that does feel kind of nice, after everything. Is that so bad?

> In London?

Yeah there's a really good one here
I thought about going to one in Cambridge but if I
    go here I can live at home and it won't cost so
    much

> Ok cool, that makes sense

Yep

Just got to study now!

Yeah. Studying. Not something I've been doing a lot of lately.

                                                            I know

                    Crazy to think we've got a year left and that's it

I know

I'm not ready to be a grown-up yet!

                                                    Haha me neither!

...

Hang on, just got to go help my mum with
    something

brb

                                                            k cool

But she doesn't come back. I sit and watch the conversation
window but it goes to idle, and then to offline. And even though
she's a random girl I don't really know, I've missed conversations
like this; just talking for the fun of talking, getting to know
someone. And so, when Autumn doesn't come back, I do the
next best thing, and I go back to a conversation from the past.

Hey

hey

long time no speak

i know

sorry

haven't seen you around much this week

You ok?

yeah

Im just kinda sick of people talking about
   Cheska all the time

trying to keep a low profile

yeah

people are dicks

ignore them

i know

just easier to stay out of the way

How are you?

i'm good

that's good ☺

Hey auditions next month

148

                                        I know
                        we better get good parts this time!
or there'll be trouble...

                                        haha
                        we can start a protest

don't worry, Hussy loves you

                        not as much as she loves you
                Hey that scene you guys did last week was
                                        really good

you think so?
ahh thanks
did you do your english homework yet?

                        the 12th Night thing? Shit no
                        what was the question again?

erm
...
...
"Disguises and changes of clothing are central
to the plot of Twelfth Night. Which characters in
the play spend time in disguise, and how is this
thematically important?"

                                        urgh
                                  sounds long

haha yeah
I like the play though

                                yeah it's been fun

gerber's a really good teacher

                                yep she's alright
                        right cheeky little minx

haha!

she's like 60

                                              :p

                                       bless her

lol

                      you want to catch up tomorrow?

                      we could go get a coffee at the rec

yeah cool

breaktime?

                                       It's a date

150

On Tuesday morning I'm leaving the gym, still wet from the shower, when my phone rings; a number I don't recognise. I've got five minutes before first period starts so I answer it jogging through the car park to chuck my kit bag in my boot.

'Hello?'

'Aiden, it's Cheska.'

I pause, the boot lid halfway up.

'Hi,' I say slowly. Cautiously.

'Can we meet today?' She sounds so casual, so relaxed, so in charge. Like I'm an employee of hers.

'Erm…' I look around the car park, and then into the boot. 'Today's not great,' I say decisively. I do *not* feel like seeing Cheska Summersall today. I heave my bag into the boot.

'Please, Aiden.' She drops a little of the casual cheer in her voice, does a reasonable job of sounding a bit sadder. 'I really need to speak to you.'

I look up at the sky. I don't say anything.

'Please,' she says again, capitalising on my silence. 'Please. If you won't do it for me, do it for Lizzie.'

I sigh. I know she's playing me. But…

'Fine.' I say. 'I'm going into town at lunchtime. You can meet me then.'

'Great,' she says. 'Wherever you want. Thank you.'

I hang up. And when I slam the boot shut, I slam it just that extra bit harder.

I meet her outside Waitrose in town, after I've picked up some dry-cleaning for Mum and grabbed myself some lunch. She's dressed in the hoody again, with a pair of jeans and towering high heels. I guess that's what counts as dressed down for her, but it looks too thought-through, too much like a costume. Like she stood in front of her wardrobe this morning and thought *What would a person who feels sad wear?* I want to tell her that she's got the shoes wrong.

'Has something happened?' I ask instead, because I don't feel much like making small-talk.

'Not exactly.' She glances around. 'Here, come this way.'

There's a war memorial in the middle of the road, the sides carved into sort of sheltered seats. Cheska leads me over to one and when we sit down, we're out of sight of most of the street.

'I don't have much time,' I tell her, checking my watch. I want to try and find Marnie before lunch is finished. I haven't heard from her in a couple of days and I'm worried about her, especially after the news about Lizzie's clothes.

When I glance back at Cheska, she's smiling. 'You don't like me much, do you?' she says.

'Not really.'

'You don't like the show.'

'No.'

152

'You think I should keep my personal life private and not use it to get on TV.'

It's so bang on that I'm shocked. I may as well be honest. 'Pretty much.'

'Did you ever think that maybe someone watching the show might come forward with information? That it might stop people from forgetting about Lizzie?'

I don't reply. There *is* a kind of twisted logic to that, I guess.

'Aiden, 300,000 people follow me on Twitter, and that number gets bigger every day. That's 300,000 people who see everything I write about Lizzie, who'll be looking out for her. That can't be a bad thing, can it?'

'I guess not,' I say, even though I can feel her leading me somewhere and I don't like it.

'I'm glad you think so,' she says, 'because that's kind of what I wanted to talk to you about.'

There's something about the way she's talking that isn't right. It's posher than her usual fake-dumb twang, and she's speaking carefully, like she's trying to get it right, even though she's trying to sound casual. It's like… I don't know –

'You want to help find Lizzie, right?' she asks, leaning a bit closer to me.

'Of course –'

'Do you know that Sunday's show had the second highest audience share? That's of *all* the channels. That's huge!'

'Okay…' I still don't see where she's going with this.

'All of those people were reminded of Lizzie. That means they went to work on Monday with her story fresh in their minds.'

153

Suddenly I realise what's wrong. These words aren't hers. It's like someone's feeding her lines. Like someone's given her a script.

'So people know Lizzie has a family who love her waiting for her at home. Don't you think it would be even better if they could see she had a boyfriend who loves her, too?'

I jerk round to stare at her. 'Cheska, I'm *not* –'

She waves the rest of the sentence away. '*I* know you're not her boyfriend. But you sort of were once, right? And what does it matter, really? It's constructed reality. You know, like real life *made better*.'

I'm too disgusted to even reply.

'Look,' she says, 'you wouldn't have to do much. Just a scene, maybe two – me and you, talking like we are now. We'd just talk about Lizzie and how worried we are. And then she might see –'

I jump up. 'She might see us talking about her on a TV show she hated! And you know what, she hated you, too, Cheska. She hated you, and she hated me, and she would really, *really* hate all of this –'

It's at this point that I look up and see the camera crew setting up on the other side of the road. The producer is back with her clipboard, and all of them are watching us like we're animals at the zoo.

'*What* the –'

'Aiden.' Cheska's voice is still calm but I can see she's starting to get twitchy. 'It wouldn't take very long. It would help, honestly.'

I look from her to the crew and back again. *Would* it help? Is there any chance that Lizzie might be watching? And what would she think if she saw me?

Cheska stands up next to me. 'They'd pay you,' she whispers.

'Go to hell, Cheska,' I say, and I walk away. As I pass the crew they all goggle at me, like they can't believe what they're seeing. The producer scowls down at her clipboard and starts scratching something out with her pen. I'm almost out of earshot when I hear one of her assistants say plaintively, 'But she *promised*.'

'It's fine,' the producer says. 'We'll do a scene with Aimee instead.'

I feel a vicious stab of satisfaction that I've just cost Cheska airtime, but it's only temporary. My bad mood lasts the rest of the day.

ON THE DAY of the auditions for our Year 11 production, we waited in the drama studio's back room. It's all brown and beige, instead of the studio's black – plain beige brick walls, prickly brown carpet. It serves as backstage a lot of the time, so there's empty rails for costume changes, a couple of plastic chairs and not much else. The room was full of people; all of our drama class, the other Year 11 drama class, the Year 10s and a couple of randoms who wanted to take part. Lizzie and I sat on the floor at the edge, our backs against the wall, feet stretched out in front of us.

It was good to sit with her, to be next to her. It was still February, cold and icy, and the second season of *Spoilt in the Suburbs* had just started. Cheska had found out at the end of the first series that Thomas Jay had been cheating on her with various girls who'd made themselves known on Twitter. People had felt sorry for her, and the constant taunts that had followed Lizzie everywhere around Aggers had pretty much died down. In this season though, Cheska had decided to take Thomas Jay back, and now she wasn't just a 'homewrecker' (despite the fact Aimee and TJ never lived together) or a 'slut', she was also an idiot. Lizzie had got really quiet. Like she was trying to melt into the shadows whenever she was walking between lessons. The only times I really saw her animated were when she was performing in drama, or in English when we were reading aloud.

'Eat the orange ones,' she said to me then, holding out a pack of Jelly Tots. 'I hate the orange ones.'

'Oh, right, so I get landed with them? Cheers!'

She leaned against me, just for a second, and smiled. 'You have your uses.'

We went back to studying the page on our laps, a photocopied double-spread from the play, which had been handed out to everyone when they arrived.

'Seems pretty straightforward,' I said.

'Yep, we got this.' She leaned her head back against the wall. Her feet were small next to mine, just in pale blue socks, her boots kicked off next to her. This was something she always did. She always performed without shoes if she could. Even in other lessons, you'd see her foot sliding out of a shoe, as if she hadn't even noticed she was doing it. I turned to look at her, her face side-on to mine, eyes closed like she was running through the lines in her head, and I thought how easy it would be to lean over and kiss her. I wondered why I hadn't done it yet, why she hadn't either. I almost leaned in, because suddenly it seemed like time, like the exact right time, like it couldn't wait any longer.

And then Hussy came into the room and called Lizzie's name.

'Wish me luck.' She stood up.

'Go get 'em,' I told her, and she smiled and picked up her boots.

'See you on the other side,' she said.

I'M JUST ABOUT to sit down to my dinner for one when the doorbell rings. I consider ignoring it, but seeing as my microwaved lasagne isn't at all appealing, I leave it on the coffee table and head for the door.

Marnie is standing on the doorstep in just a t-shirt and jeans, even though the wind is howling round the houses and it's starting to rain. She looks like she's been crying.

'Can I come in?' she asks.

I stand aside and let her pass. She kicks her shoes off – Kevin would like her – and then looks at me questioningly.

'This way.' I show her into the lounge. The weird white leather sofas are as uninviting as ever, but Marnie immediately flops down in one and curls her legs up under her as if she's been waiting to sit down all day.

'Is anyone else in?' she asks.

'Nope. Just me.' It's as good as true, anyway. Kevin's holed up in his office again on a conference call, which I've got strict instructions not to interrupt, and he's arranged for Mum to have a fancy meal out with one of her old London friends. Sounds awful but I'm glad I don't have to sit down to dinner with them right now. I don't feel like answering questions about my day.

'I looked for you today,' I say. 'You okay?'

'I couldn't face school,' she says. 'The clothes thing...' Her eyes fill with tears.

I sink down beside her. 'I know.'

'It doesn't make any sense,' she says. 'You know, her mum told me that they were folded. All neat. Left on a park bench. Why? Why would they be there? I mean if... If –' She can't bring herself to finish, but I know what she's trying to say. If Lizzie was attacked, or her clothes had been thrown away because they were evidence, you wouldn't expect to find them left right out where anyone could find them.

'You went to see her mum?' I ask.

Marnie nods and looks down at her hands.

'How is she?' I ask, though I don't think I want to know.

'Not good.' She starts fiddling with the skin around one nail. 'She looked like she hadn't slept in days.'

'I saw Cheska again today,' I say, and she looks up. 'She asked me to be on *Spoilt in the Suburbs*.' Saying it aloud I almost want to laugh. Almost.

Marnie's face drops, and her voice instantly jumps up by about a million decibels. 'Doesn't she have any limits?! Just when you think she can't go any lower!'

'I know,' I say, trying to be soothing. 'I know. It's twisted.'

Her cheeks flush. 'That show! I *hate* that my dad's involved in it. I hate that they're making *money* out of this. I could hear him on the phone the other day, bragging about the advertising rates they can charge now.'

'Here.' I get up and go to Kevin's booze cabinet in the corner, a tall, silverish thing that looks like a sculpture until you push just the right part of it – click – and a door swings open to reveal bottles and bottles of expensive alcohol. I grab the first bottle I see and pour some into one of the fancy tumblers that are stacked into the circular rack at the top of the cabinet. After some thought, I pour one for myself, too.

I pass Marnie her drink. 'Breathe,' I say.

She lets out a long, puffing breath that blows her fringe off her face, and takes a big swig. She pulls a face at the same time I do. 'Bleurgh.'

'Yeah.' I put the rest of my glass down on the table.

Marnie drinks hers, and slides her empty glass next to mine.

'She's still out there,' she says quietly. 'I can feel it.'

'I know,' I say, and I mean it.

She glances sideways at me. 'You know, she never really told me what happened with you guys.'

I fidget with the remote, even though the TV isn't on. 'I don't know if there was much to say.'

'But you liked each other, right?'

'Yeah. No. I don't know.' I look away, trying not to think about the days when all I thought about was whether Lizzie liked me. 'It just didn't happen. With me training, and her at that drama school thing…'

She nods. 'We drifted apart a bit too this summer.'

'How come?'

'I didn't see much of her after prom. I felt like she pushed me away, I don't know. And then she'd always be online but sometimes she wouldn't reply to me. And I'd see pictures of her at parties *I* wasn't invited to.'

'Parties?' When Lizzie was still talking to me, she didn't go to Aggers' parties. She hated them. Boys getting drunk in back gardens, girls bitching in kitchens and bathrooms, everyone gossiping about who'd ended up with who in the dark bedrooms.

'Yeah. Every weekend. The kind of parties she used to hate.'

'Who with?'

'Some of the girls from school. Lauren Choosken and that lot.'

Lauren. Once again, things lead back to Deacon.

'She was hanging out with Lauren?'

Marnie shrugs. 'They just started inviting her places.'

Yeah, I bet they did.

'I think she thought it was funny at first,' Marnie says, kind of thoughtful. 'I mean, Lauren's wanted to be on *SITS* since it started, everyone knows that. Lizzie just thought she wanted to get closer to Cheska.'

I don't want to ask the next part. 'And there were guys?'

She looks at me. 'Well, yeah. I mean, there were rumours, I'm not sure –'

I don't say anything.

'Aiden, do you think it could be someone like that who set up the Hal profile? Someone she met over summer?'

I look at her, the faint tapping of the pipes and the rain lashing against the window the only sounds in the room. 'No,' I say eventually. 'Why would someone she'd already slept with –' the words feel sticky and sickly in my mouth – 'go to all that trouble? I don't think the kind of people who hang out with Lauren and Deacon would think of something like that.'

She picks up my fork and begins idly twirling it between her fingers. 'I just don't understand – last year she was all about school and studying and her acting. And then, in the space of a summer, she starts drinking, partying, talking to strange guys on the internet. How can someone just change like that?'

I look away. 'I don't know.'

Marnie gets up and goes to the window. She looks out at the neighbourhood I've got used to looking at but I don't think will ever feel like home; at the perfect, polished houses, and their empty, dark windows staring out at the street.

'Something happened to her this summer,' she says. 'I know it.'

AFTER MARNIE LEAVES, I log into Facebook. The lasagne's gone cold and cement-like, and I'm not hungry any more. I scan through the updates, but there's nothing interesting. For once, it seems like Cheska isn't clogging up everyone's newsfeeds, but when I get past about an hour ago, I see why.

Cheska Summersall is off to shoot!!! ☺ #partyscene #drinkdrinkdrama #comingsoon

Urgh. I scroll back up through all the updates about people's weekend plans and people's homework and people's best or worst days ever.

I've got a new message from Farid, asking if I'm going to the match on Sunday and want to meet up with a group of them. I'm relieved he doesn't seem offended after I brushed him off at training the other day, and I should be excited about Sunday, our derby against Ipswich, so I write straight back and say yes.

My computer bleeps and another conversation window pops up. I'm glad to see Autumn's name at the top of it. We spent this morning's lessons chatting, my phone hidden under my desk, and after my run-in with Cheska I could've used the distraction this afternoon, too. I feel stupid for being suspicious of her before; all we talk about is normal stuff – our days, our teachers, funny videos that are doing the rounds online. Normal stuff is what I want right now, what I need. And Autumn's funny, too. It feels like forever since the last time I laughed.

How was maths?

> Alright actually
> stats today
> prob my favourite

Errr totally over my head I'm afraid
:p

> Sorry
> maths bore!
> how was the rest of your day?

it was good thanks ☺
went shopping in my free
Bought new shoes yaaaaay

> haha
> Erm exciting?

Sorry that was such a girly thing to say!
wrong audience

> I like shoes lol
> so long as they have studs in them

ooh sexy

> haha! FOOTBALL STUDS

I know im kidding
you don't strike me as a kinky dresser :p

yeah sorry 50 shades of trainers over here

lol

I click back onto my other conversation. Farid says we're all meeting at a pub outside the ground at twelve-thirty on Saturday, and suggests that me and Jody, a defender who lives in Kings Lyme, get a lift together. Then he logs off.

Farid and Jody both left school at sixteen and are already getting some games with the reserve team. Sometimes I wonder what it would be like to be with them. What it would be like if I'd never gone back to Aggers after this summer.

It almost happened that way, actually. But not out of choice. Autumn's window blinks again.

im guessing not, but are you watching SITS?

no, I'm not

A feeling of inevitable dread seeps through me.

Is it bad?

umm
Kinda

The sensible me knows I shouldn't. But, like I've said, the sensible me is not very persuasive. I reach over and turn on the TV.

The camera's on Cheska, up close so we can see the tears filling her eyes. Her mascara is leaving sticky little rings underneath her eyelashes, but her hair's down and done now,

165

not in the serious ponytail she's been trying out for the last couple of episodes.

'We've just got to be strong,' she's saying. 'We've got to carry on as normal, and hope that she'll come home. She knows we love her. She knows we're waiting, doesn't she? We'll be here when she gets back.'

The show shoots a couple of days before each episode airs, so I reckon this was before Lizzie's clothes were found. I can at least give Cheska the benefit of the doubt on that one, although as I look at her fake-worried face, I remember the status update I've just seen her post. Then the camera swivels round to show who she's talking to and I almost spit out the mouthful of drink I've taken.

Lauren Choosken, orange tan glowing, tiny white see-through t-shirt showing her pink bra. She's leaning across the table to hold Cheska's hand, and she's nodding.

'You're right,' she says. To the left of her face a caption says 'Lauren' and underneath that 'Lizzie's best friend'.

that bitch

I know!

did Lizzie even like her?

No, I type, but then I realise I don't know if that's true.

Well supposedly they went out together over the summer

Really??

that's weird

I know

not friends with Lauren then?

no

I went to primary school with her

she's a total bitchface from hell

even when she was 5

        not surprised

Can't believe they've got her on there

         I can

        they asked me too

Omg really?

          yeah

       don't tell anyone that

     They wanted me to pretend to be her boyfriend

omg

it's pretty sick, isn't it

         yeah it is

I look at the screen. Cheska is giving Lauren a hug. 'Come on,' she says. 'Let's go and get a real drink.'

Turn off your tv immediately

       lol, is that an order?

yes it is

It's a health warning

         haha

        it's off, it's off

Good

So what do you like to watch when you're not

 catching up on Spoilt in the Suburbs?! ☺

      Well obviously nothing compares

167

but i like sports stuff

and 24, Game of Thrones, that kind of stuff

Action stuff

me too

Also some trashy stuff

like what

REVENGE

it's amazing

Haven't seen it

whispers and I do watch some reality shows

Better ones than SITS though!

you're saying there's a show better?! :p

haha believe it or not...

i'm not sure i do

I've just flicked the TV over to the news instead of turning it all the way off, and I lean back in my chair to watch the sports headlines. The presenters on all the sports shows are so familiar to me that hearing them is kind of soothing. They remind me of Saturday afternoons on the sofa with my dad, listening to *Final Score* and feeling sleepy, usually full of junk food because he always liked treating me.

Autumn's window blinks again.

So when will you next be in London?

erm

weekend after next

to see my dad

do you still have a lot of friends here?

                                        yeah
                        i mean, i don't see them much
                but still speak to them on here and stuff
cool
☺
                you must've met lots of cool new people?
yeah
everyone's really nice
and there's a lot more stuff to do
after school i mean
                                Oh yeah, like what?
I do an art class at the local community centre
And there's a drama school that runs weekend
    courses that sound fun

Lizzie, Lizzie, Lizzie. Why does it always come back to you?
Suddenly I don't feel much like talking any more.

WE WERE THE leads. Me and Lizzie, in the drama department's production of *A Streetcar Named Desire*. I never expected to get Stanley, and when I saw my name on the cast sheet pinned up outside the studio, I wasn't that excited, to be honest. The rehearsals plus football training plus revision time meant a lot of hours I didn't really have. And, well, he isn't the nicest character to play. He's cruel and a bully and the person who gets the brunt of that for the whole play is the other main character, his sister-in-law, Blanche. Lizzie. I didn't know if I could be convincingly horrible to Lizzie for an entire play.

But Lizzie. Oh my god, Lizzie. She was all anyone could talk about. At school she was practically invisible, or at least she tried to be, trying to avoid the latest Cheska storm. She kept quiet, kept her hand down in class, and the only person who could bring her out of it was Mrs Gerber. We were still doing *Twelfth Night* in English, and Gerber always asked Lizzie to read Viola. Viola suited her; she's young and smart and witty. But Blanche DuBois… I didn't think she could do it. Blanche is broken and manic and a fantasist; nothing at all like Lizzie. I didn't see how she could play her.

But she did. In rehearsals and on the night, on all three nights, Lizzie *was* Blanche. She was perfect. She said the lines in this high, haughty, quivering Southern Belle voice and the audience hung off every single one. She moved around the stage and even her steps were different, the way she moved her hands, the way she sighed. She had become someone else, she had gone somewhere else, and it was horrible and haunting and incredible.

And the, I don't know, the energy between us – it was crazy. She made me feel like I *was* Stanley. She stood in front of me and she stuck her chin in the air, defiant, and I grabbed her wrist and I could feel everyone believe it. Because of her. Because she was so good.

She *was* Blanche. She was broken and she was manic and she was perfect. Lizzie was Blanche and I was Stanley, and she was afraid of me.

That's the part I remember most, now.

I MAKE MYSELF invisible on chat, because I don't want to talk to Autumn or Marnie or Cheska or even Scobie right now. What I *really* want is to talk to some of my old friends from London, but none of them are online, and every time I start to draft a text or a message, I can't find the right words.

Instead, I find myself clicking idly through the bookmarks at the top of my screen. The football homepage on the BBC. The Norwich City message boards. My email inbox; my other email inbox – both full of junk mail and things I haven't bothered unsubscribing from. Facebook. An article about core strength exercises. An essay about *A Streetcar Named Desire* I bookmarked during the rehearsals. That role was everything to me for those few months. I might've bitched about the rehearsal times, but something changed each time I got on that stage. I realised that I was *good* at it; that, like my mum said, Lizzie and I were good together. I realised the play could actually really work, and I saw how much Lizzie cared about it so I spent hours online, reading reviews of different productions, watching clips of different actors playing Stanley. I said my lines to myself in the mirror. I said them to Lizzie in the warm blue light of the balcony over the pool.

It meant something to me, and then it scared me. And even the thought of being on stage now, of not having Lizzie to rehearse lines with, not having Lizzie's face to look into while the audience disappears, makes me feel sick. I delete the article.

The next couple of tabs are more random links – a boxset I wanted to buy Mum for her birthday, a *Doctor Who* t-shirt I wanted to get for Scobie. My Twitter account, which I never use. Then my Instagram profile.

I glance through the photos – I haven't updated it in a while. I find the whole site kind of annoying, because it's mostly just pictures people take of their own faces or their dinner. And it's covered in hashtags, which are kind of my pet hate. Why not just have a photo of a sunset, without screaming '#sunset #beach #holidays #yes' all over it? The photos on mine are mainly of the crowds at matches I've gone to watch, and, yeah, even I'm guilty of it, a couple of dinner shots from a fancy restaurant that Kevin took us to for Mum's birthday. But here, right at the bottom of the page, is a photo of Lizzie, backstage in her Blanche costume. She's dressed in white with her hair in old-fashioned curls tucked behind her ears, which have pearl studs in them. And she's looking right at me, her phone held up in front of her face, the camera flashing. I've tagged it with her username, @lizbethsums and, for once, I've used a hashtag: #blancheandstan. I click on it, and there are only two photos that come up. One is mine, and the other is the counterpart, the one Lizzie was taking on her phone. It's me, in my Stanley costume: a shirt with the sleeves rolled up, braces, my hair slicked back. And half my face is covered by my phone, its camera flashing too. The half you can see is smiling.

I miss that smile.

I click on Lizzie's username and her profile loads. It's much fuller than mine, rows and rows of photos, right up until a couple of weeks ago. I look at the most recent ones and it's a shock to see Lizzie like that, to actually see her face. They're all selfies, mostly her phone outstretched to take a picture of her face, one or two of her in her bedroom mirror. This isn't the Lizzie I know. This is Lizzie in lipstick, pouting; Lizzie with her hand on one hip. Lizzie in the toilets at a club in town, one that's pretty famous for letting underage kids in. All from a month or so ago.

I look further back, even though I've got a crawling feeling in my stomach. There are pictures of the summer: Lizzie's feet in flipflops on bright green grass; one of a cloudless blue sky. They feel more authentic, they feel more like *her*, and I'm relieved. But then there are more of the selfies, more pouts, more tight, small dresses. There's a picture of her and Lauren, faces pressed together to fit in the frame, both blowing kisses. And one of Lizzie with a group of guys I recognise from the Abbots Grey football team, all holding cans and jeering at the camera. It's dark and they're in someone's back garden. Lizzie looks drunk. I don't know who's taking the picture. She's hashtagged all of these photos with '#goodtimes' and I wonder if they were. I wonder if Lizzie was happy, if she enjoyed letting loose and getting drunk and having boys flirt with her, finally, instead of Cheska getting all the attention.

I wonder if she thought about me.

I flick back, and this time, I notice that under some of the photos there are more quotes.

On the one of her in the club toilets, her hair all hairsprayed and big, her pouting lips red, she's written:

'who in the world cares for you? or who will be injured by what you do?'

And on the following one, posing in her bedroom mirror in a pair of tiny shorts and a vest top:

'i care for MYSELF'

Under another, the one with her flip-flopped feet against the green grass:

'you never really understand a person until u consider things from his point of view… until u climb into his skin and walk around in it'

I recognise that one. It's from *To Kill a Mockingbird*, and it makes me feel like yelling at her: *We're all trying to understand! Why are you making it so hard?* But the next photo takes my anger away instantly. It's another pouty one, but underneath, she's written:

'I want to kiss you, just once, softly and sweetly on your mouth!'

That's a Blanche line. I can remember her saying it in that strange, other voice, her eyes bright and soft.

I flick through the rest and there are a few more selfies she's hashtagged as '#icareformyself', and one – one of the most recent ones – where she's used another quote I recognise: 'I am not what I am.' It takes me a minute to realise that I've seen it on her AskMe profile, but this time, I remember where the line's *originally* from. It's one of Viola's, from *Twelfth Night*. Ophelia, Viola, Blanche. The women Lizzie's been, the parts she's played. I wonder which one she feels closest too. I see the photo of myself as Stanley again, and a chill runs through me.

My Facebook bleeps at me, and I see I've got a new message. It's Autumn, writing to me even though I'm supposedly offline.

So... how long are we going to play this game for?

I sit up straighter. *Game?*

huh?

come on... you must be dying to talk about it
to someone

My heart is suddenly beating faster.

what do you mean?

Oh come on, Aiden, she writes. The truth about you and Lizzie

What??

I know, Aiden

176

all of it
the meadow
the leavers ball
I know what really happened

And I believe her.

OKAY, SO I haven't been totally honest. I haven't told the whole truth, or anything like the truth. When I say that Lizzie and I were just friends, that isn't true.

When I say nothing really happened between us, that isn't true either.

But I guess you already knew that.

Our last exam was English, and after it, we met outside the Rec. We grinned at each other and then we hugged, her hair hot from the patch of sunlight she'd been sitting in for the whole exam. She smelled clean; like sun cream and, faintly, strawberry. Fake strawberry, like strawberry sweets.

'Let's go,' I said, and I shouldered my backpack.

We cut through the car park and into the Grove, the tree-lined footpath that follows the river. The trees are overgrown and the path was shaded, just occasional spirals of sunlight breaking through. Everywhere smelled hot and green and we could hear the quiet shhhh of the river. After our other exams we'd analysed the questions, worried about our answers. But after this one we didn't talk about it once. We didn't talk much at all, actually, but it was a comfortable silence. We were so used to being with each other after *Streetcar* and all its rehearsals, after the many afternoons we'd spent in the common room or in the Rec café revising together, that we just fitted with each other, without needing to talk.

About halfway down the Grove, the river narrows and there's an ancient lock. We pushed through the trees, long grass scratching at Lizzie's bare legs, and we climbed across the lock and into the meadow.

The meadow is actually rows and rows of fields and it goes for miles; on one side is the river and beyond that Abbots Grey and then Kings Lyme, on the other are a few farms and, hidden from view, the motorway.

We walked along for a while, staying close to the riverbank where the grass was short, Lizzie trailing her hand through the long blades that bobbed alongside us. There wasn't a sound coming from anywhere, and a faraway plane cut a single white line through the bright blue sky.

Eventually we got to the perfect patch: a little flat circle that still had enough tall grass around it to hide us from view, no cows or sheep in the field, the sun in front of us and the river wide again. We sat down and I opened my backpack, which had two biros, one pencil and six bottles of cider inside. The purple, berry-flavoured cider that was Lizzie's favourite. Usually too sickly sweet for me, but that day? That day it seemed like the perfect thing.

'We did it,' Lizzie said, and I smiled.

'I guess we did.'

'It feels weird.'

'I know.'

'Like we've been working towards this for so long and now we're here.'

And I knew what she meant but I wasn't sure we were talking about exams any more. I leaned closer to her, nudged her a little. 'That's a good thing, right?'

She looked up and smiled at me, and it was one of her full-beam smiles, the kind that dazzled you when you least expected it. 'Definitely,' she said.

We opened the ciders with a fridge magnet bottle opener that Lizzie had taken from her parents' kitchen. It was warm but not too warm and it fizzed inside my mouth like static.

'Cheska asked me about you,' she said, looking mischievous.

I lay back and raised an eyebrow. 'What about me?'

'She asked who I kept talking to all night. She could hear my laptop bleeping.'

I laughed. 'Why don't you turn the sound off?'

She looked down at her lap. She was wearing a pair of jeans she'd cut off into shorts and a pale blue t-shirt with the sleeves rolled up. 'In case I fall asleep,' she said, and the words went through me warm and clear like the day. She wanted to stay awake to talk to me. She was afraid she'd miss a message, didn't want the conversation to end. She felt the way I did.

I would've kissed her then – I was already moving closer to her, to the sun-warmed, strawberry smell of her – if it wasn't for the dog that bounded into her lap; literally into her lap, a little thing, long curly ears, white with reddish-gold patches. It was off the lead and its tail was wagging like mad, face turned up to Lizzie's.

'Hello!' she said, ruffling its ears with both hands. 'Hello, gorgeous.'

'Sorry –' A woman staggered up to us, red in the face, a lead in her hand. 'He just loves people.'

'That's okay.' Lizzie was still fussing over the dog, her face close to his. 'He's just friendly, aren't you, poppet?'

'He likes you,' the woman said, as the dog carried on licking Lizzie's face and hands, his tail beating at the grass. She looked down at our bottles of cider and smiled. 'Just finished exams?'

'Yeah.' We both grinned at her. She was nice. A lot of people in Abbots Grey would've had something to say about teenagers drinking in public in the middle of the day, but she just told us 'Well done' and let Lizzie stroke the dog, who was lying on his back now with his paws up in the air, for a while longer, before she clipped his lead on and said goodbye. We watched them head off up the meadow and Lizzie said, 'I wish I had a dog.'

'Get one.'

She shook her head. 'Not allowed.'

'Parents don't like them?'

'Cheska's allergic.'

'All the more reason,' I said, and she laughed and elbowed me.

'Oh, the sun's so nice,' she said, sighing, leaning back on her hands and turning her face up to it.

'We can do this all day now.'

She looked over and grinned at me. 'Until drama school starts.'

'*I* can do this all day now,' I corrected myself. 'Jealous?'

She closed her eyes again. 'Totally.'

'What's on the menu at drama camp again?'

'*A Winter's Tale*, I think. And *The Crucible*.'

'Can totally see you as a Puritan,' I said. 'You burn those witches.'

'I *am* a witch,' she said. 'Didn't you know?'

'Talk about stating the obvious.'

'Speaking of witches and/or words that rhyme with them.' Lizzie sat up a little, drank some more of her cider. 'Did I tell you about Lauren Choosken messaging me?'

'Again?'

'She's so obvious, it's ridiculous. Every time she speaks to me at school, it's like she's looking round for the cameras.'

'Yeah, well, I heard a rumour that her and Deacon have been using cameras for something *very* different,' I said, laughing.

'You did *not*! Did you see it?'

'Oh, yeah.' I took another long pull of my cider. 'Deacon showed it to me on one of our boys' nights in. And then we hugged and played Xbox and had a sleepover.'

She gave me a *ha ha* smile. 'You know, sarcasm is the lowest form of wit.'

'And yet you keep coming back for more.'

We sat like that for a long time, talking, the sun sinking slowly but always on us. And then, without really thinking, I did it; I leaned over and kissed her. It was a soft kiss, slow and long, and I let my hands get tangled in her hair. Her mouth was sticky with cider; I guess mine was too.

I pulled back and she looked up at me and she smiled, a really small, soft smile, and I could see every detail of her face;

the way her eyelashes got lighter near the top, the way the sun brought out freckles across her nose. I could smell the strawberry sweets smell of her and the green smell of the grass, and before I had time to think anything more, she leant back up and kissed me, harder this time, much harder, her hands on my face holding me there, more insistent.

We ended up in the grass, Lizzie on her back, me half next to her, half over her. I ran my hands over her skin, let my fingers trail over her thighs. Her hands moved over my back, pushing my t-shirt up and tugging it over my head. There was no sound apart from the hardness of our breathing and the soft rushing of the river. She pulled her own t-shirt off and I stopped and looked at her, at the way the sun made her skin glow. Her bra was white and plain and it just made her more golden. I kissed her shoulders, moved across her chest. I pushed the straps of her bra down and kissed the soft skin under them and I heard her moan.

When it happened, it was perfect. I'd like to say that it was my first time, but it wasn't. That had been the week before I moved to Abbots Grey, just after I turned fifteen, with a girl I hardly knew, at a party with some people I hardly knew either. That was what London Aiden was like. But if he could have known about Lizzie, and the river, and the last day of term, I think he would have waited. Waiting would have been so worth it.

I'd like to say it was my first time, and maybe I do, maybe it is – because it felt like it. It felt like nothing else, in the green grass, the sun above us, looking down at Lizzie, Lizzie looking up at me, and everything glowing.

I don't say it was my first time because I don't say anything about it to anyone. It's a secret, perfect moment that I've kept from my friends, and now from the police. It's something that only we know happened; me and Lizzie.

Me and Lizzie and Autumn.

At school the next day, my mouth tastes sour and of berries, no matter what I do. I check my phone but no more messages come from Autumn. I look again and again at the one she sent last night. *I know the truth. I know what really happened.* I feel like throwing up.

I skip registration because I'm late and I can't face walking into a full form room. Instead I loiter outside Ladlow's classroom, ready for first period maths.

Outside the draughty, iron-framed window, the sky is grey and looks like rain. But all I can think of is blue sky over a meadow, gold hair in my hand. All I can think of is the smell of summer grass and sun cream and strawberry sweets. I can hear Lizzie's breath in my ear, feel it on my skin. I've lied, I've lied, I've lied. And someone *knows*.

I try to rationalise it. What difference does it make if Autumn Thomas knows that Lizzie and I were, for a few short weeks last summer, more than just friends? What difference does it make if anyone knows that?

How does she know that?

'You're keen.'

I've been too wrapped up in my thoughts to notice Scobie coming along the corridor. I manage to give him a weak smile.

'Was late. Thought I'd come straight here.'

'Me too.' He leans up against the wall beside me. 'You okay?'

'Yeah. Just a bit of a late night.' I hate lying to Scobie, especially as right now I can tell I'm not doing a very good job of it.

He doesn't call me on it, though; he's too polite. He just nods and changes the subject. 'You had a look at the chapter he asked us to do?'

I haven't. I totally forgot. And this is the second time I've forgotten work Ladlow's set us. He's not going to be happy. Scobie takes one look at my face and immediately pulls his folder out of his bag.

'Have a look at my notes now. It's easy, you'll pick it straight up.'

Scobie's idea of 'easy' tends to be vastly different from the rest of the world's, but this time he's right. It's a straightforward chapter on algorithms and it's nice to lose myself in it for a while; Scobie's small, neat handwriting, the precise wording and formulas. It calms me and for at least three whole minutes I don't think about Autumn's message. *I know what really happened.*

It's just us at first; me reading, Scobie playing a game on his phone which, judging by the sounds and the way he keeps tipping himself from side to side without realising it, involves flying a fighter jet. But then the bell goes for first period and people start coming out of classrooms, heading for their lessons. It's all Year 7s and 8s in this part of the school, and they are loud. They surge around us like a river. Me and Scobie raise our eyebrows at each other.

'We weren't that small, were we?' Scobie asks.

'I wasn't here, don't forget,' I say. 'You might well have been.'

'I'm sure we weren't.'

'Give it here!' one kid yells at another one, and they have a little scuffle over the phone he's clutching. They look like kittens playing. It almost makes me laugh.

And then I remember.

I know what really happened.

The Year 7s disappear off down the stairs, their voices fading into the distance. I turn my attention back to the last page of Scobie's notes, trying to make as much of it go in as possible.

Two girls come along the corridor; we hear the clacking of their heels before they've even rounded the corner. But it's not until they're walking past us and I hear someone say 'Lizzie' that I look up and see that it's Lauren Choosken and Maisie Diggins, one of her hangers-on. They're whispering, but I can't help thinking that Lizzie's name was said just that bit louder for my benefit. Lauren meets my eyes as she strolls past, totally shamelessly staring at me while Maisie looks away and giggles.

It comes out before I realise I've said it.

'What's your problem?'

Lauren stops in her tracks, blinking at me, all wide-eyed and innocent. 'Problem?'

The blood is thumping in my temples. 'If you've got something to say to me, say it to my face.'

Lauren spreads her hands wide, like, *Who, me?* 'I haven't got a problem with you, Aiden.'

187

I can feel Scobie move closer to me, like he's trying to get me to back down, ready to tug me away. I can practically hear his thoughts: *It's not worth it.* But it's too late. I remember seeing her stupid fake tears on *Spoilt in the Suburbs* last night and I see red.

'You're disgusting!' I yell at her. 'Pretending to care about her just to get on telly!'

Lauren raises a pencilled-on eyebrow while Maisie half sniggers, half shrinks away. 'I'm not sure what you're talking about, Aiden,' Lauren says calmly. 'Lizzie and I were friends. Can you say the same?'

There's something in the way she says it; just a little edge, an almost-smile tugging at the corners of her mouth, that turns me hot with rage and yet makes my blood run cold. And as she spins on her heel, I lose it totally.

'You're a bitch, Lauren! You're a slag!'

'*Aiden*,' Scobie says, tugging me back, and I wheel around just in time to see Ladlow appear at his classroom door with a face like thunder.

'Are you finished, Kendrick?' he asks, and without waiting for a reply, he thrusts the door further open. '*Get in here.*'

Uh-oh.

Mr Ladlow is famously bad-tempered and although he can be good fun, his lessons fast-moving and full of jokes, nobody wants to get on his bad side. Everyone's far more careful about teasing Ladlow than they are Selby or Radclyffe. He's younger than them, but more old-fashioned, too.

He's probably the worst person who could have seen that.

He stalks over to his desk, and I follow, the rage that just a second ago burned through me quickly shrivelling.

'Want to tell me what that was all about?' His voice is calm again, his dark hair in place, but I can hear the anger beneath the surface. I've always liked Ladlow and worked hard in his class, and before today, I might've hoped he had a pretty decent opinion of me. Now I feel about six inches tall.

'Sorry, sir. I lost my temper.'

'You don't say. Unfortunately, Kendrick, that's no excuse for speaking to *any* of your classmates in that way, male or female.'

I turn away, stare out of the window. Ladlow's classroom looks out over the school playing field and the greenhouses that back onto the science block. Grey clouds creep in, low and heavy. 'Sorry,' I say again.

Ladlow's quiet for a minute too, both of us just looking out at the rain rolling in. 'Are you friends with the Summersall girl?'

I look levelly back at him. 'I knew her.'

'You were in the play together,' he says. 'I remember now.'

I nod.

'Has that got anything to do with what happened just now?' he asks, but before I can answer the door opens and a couple of girls from my class walk in. Scobie hovers in the doorway looking uncertain. Ladlow looks from them to me, and says, reluctantly, 'Sit down, Kendrick. I don't want to see you behaving like that again.'

'I'm really sorry, sir,' I say, and I make for my desk, relieved to be off the hook. The anger's still there, small and tight like a knot, somewhere deep down, but I've got it under control again. Scobie pulls out the chair next to mine.

'Mate,' he says. '*What* is going on with you?'

I shake my head. 'Lauren. She just winds me up.'

'Look, I get that you're mad about the show –'

I look up at him in surprise. Scobie's the last person you'd expect to watch *Spoilt in the Suburbs*.

'My mum,' he says, apologetically. 'She's got really into it.'

Most of the class is in now and Ladlow has started prowling round, tossing handouts onto the end of each row of tables. 'Take one, pass them along,' he says. He's even brisker than usual, not making his little teasing asides to people, and I guess I've put him in a bad mood.

'I just hate that she's using it to get famous.'

Scobie nods. 'Yeah, it's pretty shitty. But it's Lauren, Aiden. You can't be surprised.'

'I know, but then when she walked past… She was doing it on purpose. She probably knows I turned them down.'

'Turned who down?'

'*Spoilt in the Suburbs*.'

Scobie's eyebrows shoot up. 'No way.'

'Right,' Ladlow says, closing the door. 'Let's get started. Who can fill us in on the chapter I asked you to read?'

'Yes way,' I hiss at Scobie. 'Obviously I said no.'

'Well, they're scraping the barrel with Lauren,' Scobie says, and as he sees Ladlow's eyes sweep across the classroom and lock on me, he raises his hand.

'The function of x is greater than zero for all real values of x, and the function of x increases at an accelerated rate as x increases,' he says, and Ladlow gives his weird, painful-looking smile and turns to the board.

'Excellent work, dear Thomas,' he says. He starts writing on the whiteboard, the pen squeaking as his hand flies back and forth.

'Look, this Lizzie stuff… The way you've been acting… Is there something I don't know?' Scobie's giving me one of his earnest looks, his eyes scanning my face.

I almost, *almost*, tell him. But even as the words bubble up, I remember. I remember Lizzie in the grass, Lizzie's hands on my face, and I can't. I can't share it because it's so perfect and private. So perfect and private and ours.

'Has anything happened with the Facebook page?' I ask instead. 'Has anyone posted anything?'

He looks awkward. 'Not anything useful,' he says. 'Mostly, just… People messing around.'

I get out my phone under the desk and look for myself. Our page has thirteen followers. There are three posts. One from Kieron Decker, one of Deacon's mates. **Last seen in my bed!** he's put, and I want to smash his face in. Another from a girl whose name I don't recognise. She's just written **So sad** ☹**.** The last one is a kid writing in Japanese, so I have no idea what it says.

The sponsored ads down the side are equally depressing. One for some kind of online dating service – ARE YOU LOOKING TO MAKE FRIENDS IN YOUR AREA? 1000s OF COOL SINGLES WAITING! – and one for some kind of security app for Facebook – DO YOU KNOW WHO YOU'RE REALLY TALKING TO? TRUEFACE CAN TELL YOU!

I grimace. 'Brilliant.'

'Aiden,' Scobie says, looking at me over his glasses now, his most serious face. 'You don't have to tell me. But is there something I can do to help?'

I shake my head. I wish talking to Scobie *would* help, but there's only one person I need to talk to now.

And unfortunately she isn't around to ask.

I MAKE IT through maths and then English, but by breaktime I know I can't take this any more. Too many thoughts, too many memories, and still everybody talking about Lizzie, Lizzie, Lizzie. Clothes folded on a bench. Lying beside me in a field. And Autumn's last message beating behind it all like a horrible drum beat. *I know what really happened.*

I've got a free third period, and then sports studies in the afternoon. Connolly won't check up on me if I don't show, he trusts me. I just need to get out of here – I can't cope with the claustrophobia of Aggers right now.

I get to the bottom of the steps to the Rec, checking my phone – no new messages – when a hand hits me hard in the chest. I look up, stupidly expecting to see Connolly waiting to catch me out even though his lesson isn't for another two hours. Instead I see Deacon blocking the bottom of the steps. His arms are folded and he does not look happy.

Which makes two of us.

'I hear you've got a problem with Lauren,' he says, and that's when I notice all his hangers-on crowding round behind him. Someone comes down the steps behind me and I turn to see

Kieron Decker, super sidekick. He's obviously followed me from English and let them know where I am.

'No idea what you're talking about,' I say, but I don't give him the satisfaction of trying to push past.

Instead, he takes a step closer to me, until he's right in front of me, toe to toe, and when he speaks, he jabs at my chest with two fingers after each word. 'You – call – my – girlfriend – a – bitch – again – and – I – will – kill – you.'

I shouldn't rise to it, but I do. 'Oh, you mean Lauren?' I say. 'Is she still your girlfriend? Hard to keep track of who she's sleeping with.'

His top lip lifts into a snarl and I can practically feel his fists twitching at his sides. 'Watch your mouth.'

It's childish and lame but all I want is to goad him and so I say it anyway. 'What you gonna do about it?'

He pulls back a little and laughs; a half laugh, a sarcastic one. 'Give me a reason, Kendrick. Make my day.'

'Oi!' A girl's voice, shrill with anger. We both look round to see Marnie pushing through the crowd. 'Pack it in! Leave him alone.'

Deacon sniggers again. 'Aww, look. His little girlfriend's come to protect him.' He turns to look at me. 'Kind of sick, though, don't you think? Her best mate?'

The anger is pumping back through me properly now, my face twisting with it. 'Shut up.'

'Aww, don't like it when we talk about Lizzie, do you?'

The words come out of my mouth in a hiss this time. 'Shut *up*.'

'You heard him!' Marnie yells. She's right up next to Deacon now, having shoved her way past his goons. 'Come on, Aiden. Let's go.'

'Yeah, *come on, Aiden*,' Deacon says, mocking her voice.

'Stay out of it, Marnie,' I mutter, and she looks at me like I've slapped her. I look at her and then I look away. She melts back into the crowd.

'Oh, don't feel bad,' Deacon says to her, putting on a fake-friendly voice. 'He's just scared of what I might say –'

I hit him. My hand flies out, the fist so tight it hurts, and it connects squarely with his jaw, knocking his head backwards. There's a moment of total silence and then there is a roar.

We launch ourselves at each other, animal noises forced out of us as we hit the ground. I aim punches at him blindly, feeling his skin turn wet under my fists. His blows land on my neck, my head, my ribs, but I don't feel pain, just the thumps as they travel through me like shots. We hit each other, again and again, and we've only hit each other like this once before –

He catches me in the throat with one of his swings and the pain is bright and white and for a minute I can't breathe. I flop away from him, onto my elbows on the gravel, and try to draw air into the tiny pinhole my throat has shrunk to.

Just as oxygen starts returning to my lungs the buzzing in my ears fades, and I'm vaguely aware of Deacon scrabbling to his feet beside me.

'You see that?' he's yelling to everyone who's gathered to watch the show. 'You see that? He's crazy, man. He's a psycho.'

I pull myself onto my hands and knees and spit onto the playground. There's a spool of red unfolding in the saliva. I hope it's just my lip or tongue and not a tooth come loose.

'Psycho.' Deacon aims a last kick at my ribs, but it's just for show; or at least I can't feel it any more.

I heave myself to my feet and spit again, this time within a centimetre of Deacon's box-fresh Jordans. 'Stay away from me.'

He lets out a harsh laugh and I notice for the first time his split lip, the way his eye is starting to swell. 'You hear that? He wants *me* to stay away from *him*. With pleasure, psycho.'

As he says it I see Marnie in the crowd, white-faced. When her eyes meet mine, she looks away. She looks horrified. Terrified.

Terrified of *me*.

'Just... stay away,' I say, staggering a few steps back.

'I'll stay away after I've reported you,' Deacon says, but most of the fight has gone out of his voice. I feel lightheaded and I turn, start to head for my car. There's a path clear for me now – most people heading for lessons now the bell's gone, and those who are left only too keen to get out of my way.

'Have fun getting kicked out!' Deacon yells after me. I turn back to look at him. He says the next part a little quieter as he turns to follow the dispersing crowd up to the school, but I still hear it.

'Just like you did at your last school.'

I NEVER WANT to hear from Autumn Thomas again. So, naturally, the first thing I do when I get in my car, face and fists throbbing, is pull out my phone and send her a Facebook message.

When did she tell you? I write.

I sit, waiting for her to reply, watching for the little words at the bottom of the screen to change from 'Sent 11:07' to 'Seen'. The throbbing in my face becomes an actual pain, and there's a horrible ache in one of my ribs. Each second on the dashboard clock seems to take an age to tick over, but still the words on my screen stay the same. Where is she? She usually writes straight back.

After another five minutes, I can't take it any more. I start the car and drive without really caring where I'm going. I don't slow down for the speed bumps in the car park and I bounce in my seat, all my bones jolting painfully.

Out on the road that leads through town, I try to focus on driving. Stop at the red light, clutch up at amber, go at green.

Slow for the corner, remember to check the crossing. Give way to the old lady trying to turn out of one of the tiny little side streets. Indicate and turn onto the busier main road, where I can put my foot down and try to get some kind of distance between me and Abbots Grey.

I didn't know Deacon knew about what happened in London. Looks like everyone knows all of my secrets, these days.

I glance down just in time to see the petrol light click on. Perfect timing. Right now I'd like to keep driving and never stop.

Great, run away. Suddenly, and furiously, I'm not angry at Deacon, or Lauren, or Cheska, or Autumn. I'm angry at myself. I've lied, and I've hidden, and now I'm trying to hide again. I'm a coward.

I turn into the next petrol station. It's a big one, eight pumps across a spotless forecourt, and I head for the furthest, not in the mood to bump into anyone I might know.

The smell of petrol always reminds me of my dad – weekends driving to watch football, or him taking me to training camps. A couple of family holidays, when I was much younger, before the arguments started. That's not to say *oh, poor me* – my parents are good friends now, they're both happy, I had a nice and not neglected childhood. But, you know, they still fought.

I fill my car with petrol, thinking about how much I really want to call my dad. The thought calms me a bit and I decide that, instead of spending the rest of the day driving around like a freak, I'm heading home. Kevin's at a meeting in London, and Mum's visiting her friend Eleanor in Bridgington, a biggish village the other side of King's Lyme. She won't be back till dinner, which we've agreed to order in from the new Thai place that's opened up by the river. I'll go back, read up on the sports science stuff I'm missing today, catch up on my English reading, call Dad and then hit the gym before Mum gets back. Possibly gym first; I could do with working some of this tension out.

I shift to put the petrol pump back and there's a painful twinge in my rib. Hmm. Maybe not gym. I look at my face in the window. It's starting to swell, around one eye and across the opposite cheekbone, too. I poke a finger against it and wonder if it's fractured. How am I going to explain that to Mum? The thought sends a new wave of anxiety through me. Mum has had to see my face like this way too often. Why am I putting her through it again?

I head inside to pay, belatedly checking I've actually got my wallet on me. Outside the shop are the usual half-wilted bouquets of flowers and the grey plastic display cases of newspapers behind their finger-smeared lids. It's one of those times that the knowledge something is bad for you and the fact that you're going to do it anyway occur to your brain almost simultaneously. I know I'm going to see Lizzie. I look anyway.

She's not on every cover; not even close. A Cabinet Minister has been caught taking drugs and another has been recorded accepting a bribe and those stories are taking up a lot of the broadsheets' reporting time. Lizzie makes it onto the cover of one, but even then only in a tiny box at the bottom of the page, no photo.

But the local paper's a different story. That's Lizzie, A3, a photo taken I don't know when, although a sick voice inside me says it was that week, the week of the last exam and the meadow. It's summer and she's wearing a dress I recognise, a pale yellow one with skinny straps and lots of tiny hearts over it. She's smiling, but not really at the camera, and I wonder who or what she can see.

The headline reads LIZZIE LIVED SECRET LIFE ONLINE, and though I try to stop them, my hands reach out and lift the lid and take a copy.

There's just a paragraph of text underneath the huge photo:

Police are uncovering new leads in the case of missing teenager, Lizzie Summersall, with the help of computer forensics experts. By studying the laptop and tablet belonging to Lizzie, 16, DCI Hunter, heading up the investigation locally, said they had discovered that Lizzie spent 'a large chunk of her life online', and that she had conducted 'longstanding' friendships with strangers on the internet. Hunter said that 'a considerable' percentage of these friendships could be considered 'flirtatious'. For full story, see page 4.

It makes me feel ill, and the throbbing in my ribs increases. This is bad news. They're trying to portray her in a certain way, trying to – what's the word? – *smear* her. A week ago, she was a lovely, well brought-up schoolgirl who'd been tricked by some sicko on the internet. Now she's some stupid girl who flirts with strangers online, a girl who's asking for trouble. As if anyone would ask for this.

I want to turn to page 4 but one of the attendants comes out and pointedly starts rearranging the newspapers. So I take the paper with me and pay for it with my petrol. The guy who serves me looks familiar somehow; tall and skinny, longish dark hair, a tattoo of a mermaid – an old school, retro kind – over his forearm. He's looking at me funny, like he recognises me too. Or maybe he's just wondering what the hell I've done to my face.

'Aiden, right?' he asks, handing me my card back.

I nod.

'Luke,' he says. 'I met you at a game once. You're friends with Farid, right?'

'Oh, yeah,' I say. 'How you doing, man?'

He nods. 'Yeah, good. Same old.' His eyes run over my face again. 'You doing okay?'

'Yeah. You know.' I keep looking at him, though, because the match, that isn't it. That isn't why he looks familiar. It's something else.

'Have you got a brother my age?' I ask, thinking maybe it's someone from school, or training.

He shakes his head. 'Nah, older. You probably know him, though. He's on *Spoilt in the Suburbs*. Dick.'

That's it. He looks just like Thomas Jay, Cheska's boyfriend.

'TJ,' he says. 'You watch it?'

I shake my head. 'I know who you mean, though. He's going out with Cheska Summersall, right?'

He shrugs. 'He was. Dunno now.'

'They broke up?'

He gestures at my newspaper. Lizzie's face. 'All that stuff going on, they just film her mostly. Guess she doesn't need him

200

any more.' He smirks as he says it, like Thomas Jay's getting what he deserves.

'Harsh.' I fold the newspaper. I don't like Lizzie's face looking out at us. I don't like looking at hers.

A guy comes up behind us, waiting to pay for his petrol. 'Cool, man,' Luke says, as I edge out of the way. 'We should get a drink sometime.'

I nod. 'Yeah, for sure.'

He taps at the till, tells the man, 'Forty-five sixty', and then, to me, he says, 'Add me on Facebook.'

I nod and wave, and as I leave, I think that I'm never going on Facebook again.

Just as I pull into Kevin's – still, after three years, it takes a bit of doublethink to say *my* – driveway, my phone buzzes. Facebook notification. A new message.

It's from Autumn, and when I read it, I forget about things like turning off the ignition or taking my foot off the clutch. I just sit in my car and I read the message and I read the message and I read the message.

She told me a lot of things, she writes.

And underneath that, she posts a photo of a baby's clothes.

'AUTUMN THOMAS'

I PICTURE HIM getting that message. I see it turn from 'Sent' to 'Seen', and I imagine him sitting there, his phone in his hand. I imagine his eyes getting wide, his face turning pale.

What's that supposed to be, he writes, as if he doesn't know.

I don't get it, he puts when I don't reply.

Is this some kind of joke, he writes, and that's when I know he's really panicking.

And that really makes me happy.

AIDEN

SHE DOESN'T REPLY. I wait and I wait, the engine running, my heart pounding, and she doesn't reply.

I turn off the engine, my hand sweaty. I try to tell myself to be calm. I try to tell myself that she's just a girl who used to go to my school. She doesn't know anything about me. Autumn sat next to Lizzie in one lesson two years ago and then she moved to London. She's just playing a joke – a really, really sick joke. I try and laugh. As if Lizzie would tell some girl who used to go to school with us. The laugh falls flat.

I have no idea what Lizzie would do.

Eventually I go into the house and close the door behind me. Out there, it feels as though there are a million eyes on me, as if suddenly everyone in Abbots Grey can see right inside me, inside my head, inside my memories, inside my past.

'Aiden?'

Kevin appears in the kitchen doorway, his hands pushed into his pockets, and I nearly jump out of my skin.

'Hi –'

'Why aren't you at college?'

I keep my face turned away from him as I hang up my

jacket. I don't want him to know about the fight. 'Sports studies got cancelled,' I say. 'Connolly's off sick. I'll get more work done here.'

I don't expect to get away with that for one second, but all Kevin says is, 'So you're not going in this afternoon?'

I sit down on the bottom step to take my shoes off, keeping the most swollen side of my face turned to the wall. 'No lessons. I thought you were in London all day?'

'Just on my way now.' He grabs a laptop case from the kitchen counter behind him and shoves something inside. His Converse squeak past me on the tiles, and he pauses at the door. 'You sure you're okay? Want to talk?'

I shake my head, keeping it lowered over an imaginary knot in my laces. 'I just need some space. Too much –' I trail off. There isn't an end to that sentence that can explain what I'm feeling right now.

I expect him to push me further, to sit down next to me or something. But instead he just puts a hand on my shoulder and squeezes. 'I'll see you later.'

But at the door, he turns back. 'It's all going to be okay,' he says softly. And then he's gone. I hear the roar of his car starting up, the silky purr of it pulling away.

I sit on the bottom step for a long time. The house is quiet and cool, and I close my eyes and try and calm my heart. I close my eyes and try not to picture those tiny little baby clothes.

I close my eyes, and I remember.

I REMEMBER THE night of the Year 11 prom. We didn't have dates. Nobody was doing dates.

Lizzie was my date.

I got ready at Scobie's – both of us in our tuxes, drinking cheap fizzy wine in fancy glasses with his mum. Scobie had a white bow tie, I had a gold waistcoat. The wine went to my head and made me giggly.

The wine went to my head and made me different.

We took a taxi, which Jodie gave us a tenner for, and in it we drank the four cans of lager Liam had bought us in secret the night before. We looked out of the windows and watched Abbots Grey roll by, everything just slightly different, even as it was the same. The end of school, and even though we'd be back to the same place in September, it felt big. It felt like the end of something or the start of something. I was happy. There was Scobie, there was Lizzie, and I was happy. I'd finally left London behind. I'd started again.

I was drunk.

The prom was held in the Burford Hall, the events space that joins the Rec and the drama studio. The place where we'd been in *Midsummer's Night Dream*. The place where Lizzie had been Blanche. And now the car park was filled with limos and sports cars, full of Abbots Grey parents with their fancy cameras and their expensive outfits, cooing their kids into the frame. Boys in tuxes, some with tails, some with all the trimmings – cummerbunds, braces, the works. Girls squeezed into long and puffy dresses, so many sequins that in the late evening sunshine it made you dizzy. The air was hot and full of perfume and hairspray. And money. Everywhere in Abbots Grey smells of money.

The theme – decided by the Year 11 Prom Committee, who had been elected by a vote that we all had the right to take part in and which about twenty people actually did – was 'A Whole New World', and so there were *Aladdin*-themed things everywhere: silk scarves swooping across the ceiling, ornate pots and lanterns on the tables, incense burning somewhere so that the air smelled smoky and strange. Inflatable palm trees and the occasional toy monkey kind of spoiling the effect.

Two girls from the prom committee were on the door, taking the gold-edged tickets printed on parchment, like when you're little and you use tea to stain paper to make it look old. They checked their clipboards and told us where our table was; we'd put our names down for one together: me, Scobie, Birchall, Darnell Hudson, who I was closer to in those days, and Greg Marshall, another guy from the team. I knew Lizzie and Marnie and some of the other girls they hung around with had the table next to ours. Everything was just fitting right into place.

Inside, in the dark, with the pink and purple and red lights that they'd set up, it looked kind of incredible. For once, I was glad that Aggers was a place where people cared about stuff like this, where people had the money to buy metres and metres of fabric and to pay someone to climb a ladder and hang it from a ceiling, over and over.

We headed for the bar. To get there we had to wind our way through all the clothed tables, with their parrots and their monkeys holding namecards, and then across the dancefloor, already starting to fill even though it was still light outside.

I saw her. I saw her caught in a pool of pink light, and in it she was gold. She was Ophelia again. A long, pale dress; not puffy but straight down and pooling round her feet. Tiny straps against her smooth skin. Her hair was wavy and pinned up and falling down, and there were flowers in it.

She looked beautiful.

'Hey,' she said, and up close I could smell the flowers.

We danced. Me and Scobie and Lizzie and Marnie and Birchall and other people, coming and going, moving round us like the lights that fluttered in patterns across the dancefloor. We drank from plastic water bottles smuggled in handbags, and from fancy hip flasks hidden in suit pockets. My mouth felt sticky and I was laughing. Sometimes, when nobody was looking, Lizzie would grab my hand. It was just for a second, just the way she was dancing, but it felt just right. And I knew that it would be the night that I'd ask her to be with me, be together properly. Not a secret. I wanted us to be together all the time, everywhere, me and her.

There were more secret bottles, more hidden hip flasks. I'd had enough, but I was having fun.

I had had too much. But I was having fun.

There was dinner, I know, but I don't remember much, just snatches: perfect white plates, chicken too dry, Scobie flicking his gravy at me and laughing. I remember the rumour that Jorgie Mitchell had thrown up over hers on the other side of the hall, but I don't know if that's a memory I've added later, when I knew for sure it was true (her parents were called to collect her; she threw up over Radclyffe too). We were too happy to eat, too silly to sit, and as soon as we could we were back on the dancefloor, scrumming each other with man hugs and play fighting, all dancing in a circle, arms around each other, heads thrown back as the pink and purple lights shone down on our faces.

I think I remember – although maybe I wish I remember – looking across at Lizzie and smiling. In my head, it's a moment that is longer than any other, everything around us fading away. Just us. I wanted to ask her then and I think I even reached out my hand, might even have started to say 'Let's go –'

But then Marnie grabbed her and tugged her away, laughing, whispering, and they disappeared. And Scobie put a hand on my shoulder, passed me Birchall's dad's hip flask, full of Birchall's dad's whiskey – and that was better, even better, drinking the deputy head's booze.

I don't remember Lauren coming over; one minute it was just us, the boys, and then there she was, her and Maisie and Rochelle Johnson, winding their way into our group, dancing in between us. We were happy, so happy, and nothing could spoil that, and we put our arms round their shoulders, cheered, passed them secret booze bottles and half-empty hip flasks. It didn't matter that they never lowered themselves to speak to us in school, because we weren't in school any more, we were in A Whole New World, a little secret bubble where everyone was smiling, everyone was together.

I don't remember Lauren beginning to single me out; don't remember at what point she began to grind against me, her mass of caramel hair pushed up against my jaw, her hands reaching back to hold my hips. I don't remember the first time she turned her face and her lips grazed my neck, or the second; I just remember becoming aware of it, like a bucket of ice water thrown over my head, and single words bleating an alarm through the pink and purple glow of the whiskey. *Lizzie. Wrong. Stop.*

I pushed Lauren away, gently at first, but she just came back for more, her arm round my neck, her face close to mine, her eyes all heavy-lidded and unfocused.

'Oh, come on, Aiden,' she slurred at me. 'You know you want to.'

I shoved her away hard then, and that's when I noticed that people were looking at us, like they'd been looking at us for a while. Some of them were whispering, some of them were smiling like they were expecting trouble. Scobie was looking at me like he'd been trying to get my attention for ages.

I didn't care about any of them. I looked through all the faces, at everyone dancing, but Lizzie wasn't there. I turned away and started pushing through the crowd, because suddenly I was feeling unsteady on my feet and being drunk wasn't so much fun. I hung around the back of the hall, checking the tables to see where Lizzie and Marnie were. But then I spotted Marnie heading back to our group on her own.

I started panicking. What if Lizzie had seen me with Lauren? What if she'd left?

My phone vibrated in my pocket, and the message was from Lizzie.

Can you meet me outside? she put, and my heart gave a little leap, even though a sicky taste was spreading through my mouth.

I snuck along one side of the hall and found the fire exit. The alarm doesn't work; all the drama students who smoke use it for crafty fags when they're waiting backstage. I headed down the stone steps and into the little alley that runs along the back of the Burford Hall.

I turned the corner and found her sitting there, on the black iron stairs that wind up to the drama studio. Lethal in the winter when there's ice – Hussie spends half her term carefully gritting them because she doesn't trust the caretakers to do it properly. But now it was summer, the air cooling but still soft and warm, and Lizzie was sitting there, gold and pale against the black, her arms wrapped round her knees. She smiled when she saw me coming; moved her feet along to make room for me to sit down. I sat on the step below looking up at her; the white flowers in her hair, the moon fat and creamy behind her.

'Hey,' I said, and she smiled.

'You're drunk,' she said, and I nodded.

'Are you having a good night?' I asked, resting my head against the wall.

She nodded but she wasn't smiling any more. 'I need to talk to you about something,' she said.

I remember: 'I think I'm pregnant.'

I remember: 'What?'

I remember the world tipping and I remember feeling hot, too hot, and I remember thinking that the sicky taste was worse, much worse, and everything was closing in.

I remember: 'You'll have to get rid of it.' The words spilled out but now they don't feel as though they were mine.

I remember her face, shocked like it was slapped, the way she pulled away from me, the way she stood.

I remember realising, remember hearing the words echoed back at me and wanting to rewind, wanting to revise, and I stood up too, but I was drunk, so drunk, and the world was reeling and my mouth wasn't working and so I just grabbed, blindly, grabbed at her hand, tried to stop her leaving, tried to stop, tried to stop, but I slipped, or she slipped, me pulling her, her off-balance, her heel caught in the grating of the step.

I remember her swinging for a second that went on forever, and then I remember her fingers slipped out of mine, and she fell thump thump metallic clang, her head hitting the wall.

I remember her at the bottom, her head in her hand, the flowers crushed, and I remember the way she looked up at me, the way she looked.

She ran.

I ran.

Her footsteps sounded like shots in the dark car park, and she's fast, Lizzie was fast, and I was drunk. I could see her, the little light shape of her, growing smaller and smaller, and then there were other shapes closing in on me, there was a thud at my back and I was flying, sprawling, the still-hot tarmac coming up to meet me.

I lay there, winded, and then I tried to roll over, tried to push myself up. Hands on my arms, hands with fistfuls of my jacket, hauling me up, and then Deacon speaking in the dark beside me.

'You think you can touch my girlfriend?' he said to me, and he spat in my face. 'You think you can disrespect me?'

There is a rage in me I had kept locked down through those twenty months at Aggers. When he hit me, I let him. I let him unlock it, let him set it loose, because it was dark and black and I was drunk and Lizzie was gone. We knocked everything out of each other: air, blood, booze. We fought until they couldn't pull us apart. We fought until his final punch swung through the air, past the moon, and connected with the side of my head.

And then there was only black.

I CAN'T BREATHE. I'm sitting on the bottom step and my head is in my hands and my mind is still back in the Rec car park on a night at the end of June. And I keep thinking. I keep thinking.

What if?

I sat on this step the morning after that too. That was as far as Mum let me get. It was Kevin who picked me up from the hospital, who asked me if I was okay and listened to me list my fractured knuckle, my chipped tooth, my concussion. Kevin who took in my black eye and my fat lip in silence and led me out to the car and he didn't ask, but he listened as the words came spilling out of me anyway – I've hurt someone I care about; I don't think she'll forgive me; I took it out on Deacon. Kevin who put a hand on my shoulder and told me that it would be okay, that he'd make sure it was okay.

He dropped me outside the house, sped off in his car. Leaving me and Mum to it – giving us our space. The worst of it was, I knew I should feel worried, knew I should feel bad, scared of what was coming. And I did. But not about Mum. Not about Deacon. Not about the fact that Selby had been at the hospital and had told Kevin, apologetically, practically tearfully, that the school would have to investigate, that we could both have our sixth form places rescinded.

All I could think about was Lizzie.

I let myself in and Mum was there, in the kitchen doorway, in her dressing gown, arms folded, face bare. Face furious.

'I'm sorry,' I tried, taking a step towards her, but she put up a hand so sharply I shrank back, sank down onto the stairs.

'How could you do this to me again?' she said, and then she started crying.

The crying was the worst.

I look up now at the empty hallway, at the place in the doorway where she stood. I remember later, hearing her crying to Kevin while I was in my room, calling Lizzie. Calling Lizzie and calling and calling and calling. I threw up, at one point.

I think I might throw up now.

She called me, in the end. Two days of me phoning, leaving voicemails, texts, Facebook messages. Nothing, nothing, nothing, nothing. And then, at 11a.m. on the first Monday after the ball, she called.

'I'm not pregnant,' she said, and her voice was small and hard. 'You can stop calling me.'

I want to say that I felt relieved, because that might be normal. I want to say that I felt sad, because that also might be normal. But I can't remember.

I'm scared that I didn't feel anything.

'What?' I said, just like I did on the steps, because I'm an idiot, because I'm useless.

'I made a mistake,' she said, and she hung up.

And now I'm wondering if the mistake she meant was telling me.

The doorbell rings and I jump, the hairs on the back of my neck shooting up. Just for an instant, a sick instant, I *know* it's Lizzie out there.

But it isn't. Of course it isn't.

It's Marnie.

She raises an eyebrow as she takes in my bruised face. 'Can I come in?'

I stand aside to let her past, too exhausted, too caught up in thoughts and memories, to say no. She heads for the kitchen, clicks on the kettle. I sink onto one of the black and chrome bar stools Kevin bought on his last trip to Stockholm.

'What was all that about?' she asks, looking through the cupboards for mugs. 'With Deacon?'

I shrug. 'He hates me. He always has.'

'Aiden.' She turns round to look at me while the kettle burbles its expensive whisper. 'You looked like you wanted to kill him. You looked… *possessed*.'

I feel possessed. My whole body is pulsing with an energy that isn't mine, isn't me.

'He pushed me,' I say. 'I let him get to me.'

'What happened with Lauren? Everyone's saying you started on her.'

I roll my eyes. 'Of course they are. I just yelled at her.'

'Because of the show.'

'Yeah. Kind of.'

'What did you say?'

I think back, and at least have the grace to feel ashamed. 'Nothing smart. Called her a bitch and a slag.'

The kettle clicks off and she turns her back to me and starts making the tea.

'I don't like that word,' she says, still not looking at me.

'I didn't mean it as a compliment,' I say, kind of sulkily.

'I heard what you said to Deacon, too,' she says, bringing a mug over to me. 'About Lauren sleeping around. It's not okay to talk about girls like that, Aiden.'

'I'm sorry,' I say. 'I was just so mad.' I feel about two inches tall again.

She takes a seat at the third bar stool, leaving one between us. 'Yeah, but it's the way you use that as an insult. It pisses me off.' She glances at me and then looks away and sighs. 'It's just – in the summer, people saying stuff like that about Lizzie. Like it made her a bad person, just because she was seeing guys. And now, in the papers, they're making out like she had it coming, and I *hate* that. That's not right.'

I didn't think it was possible, but I feel instantly worse. It's all flooding back again, over and over, the waves crashing down. Lizzie. The photo. Prom.

'Marnie,' I say. 'On prom night, where did you and Lizzie go?'

She frowns. 'When?'

'I don't know, sometime in the middle. After the dinner. You guys disappeared for a bit.'

216

She shrugs. 'We went outside for a while. It was too hot in there.' She smiles a small smile to herself, one which instantly dissolves. 'Lizzie stole a glass of wine from Selby's table so we shared that.'

I try to picture them out in the car park, laughing, their silky shiny dresses against the gravel.

'You left her,' I say softly. 'Why did you leave her?'

She looks at me in surprise. 'She said you were coming out to meet her. She wanted to talk to you.'

I see Lizzie on the steps looking down at me, and my stomach lurches.

'Did she tell you about what?'

She shakes her head, looks at me more closely. 'Is that what this is all about? What did she say to you?'

I shake my head. 'No. Nothing.' My hand twitches instinctively towards my phone. 'I got in that fight with Deacon in the car park, didn't I?'

'Funny how history repeats itself,' she says, darkly, and takes a sip of her tea.

'So, did you just come round to have a go at me?' I get up and take my untouched cup to the sink.

'*No*,' she says, irritated. She gets up too and gets her phone out. 'I need to show you something.'

My heart skips in my chest. 'What?'

She looks up at me, and for a second it looks like she's reconsidering showing me whatever it is.

'I was annoyed about Lauren, too,' she says, lowering her phone for a second. 'Like *really* annoyed. I mean, *I* know how to control my feelings, unlike some of us –'

I let this pass without comment.

'– but I was mad about it. And I wanted to know who'd agreed for her to be on the show. Without even, you know, checking if she *actually was* "Lizzie's best friend".' She makes exaggerated quote marks in the air, and if it wasn't for the situation, I could almost laugh. She's *jealous*.

'I couldn't believe my dad would okay that. So I broke into his office.'

'Seriously?' I'm reminded suddenly of that first time I saw Marnie and Lizzie by the lockers, Marnie yelling about her sexist science teacher.

She waves a hand distractedly. 'Just his office at home. Not, like, the actual *Spoilt in the Suburbs* office.'

'Oh, right,' I say sarcastically. 'Right, well, that's fine then.'

She picks the phone up, and again I see a flicker of something cross her face. 'The thing is,' she says, 'my dad's the exec producer, so he gets cc-ed on everything.'

'Right…'

She sighs. 'And when I was looking through his emails, I found this.'

I have to actually hold my hand out before she finally turns the phone round and gives it to me.

I frown. It's a photo of a screen, so the quality isn't great, and I have to zoom to read the email. It's from a woman – Olive Garner – and the subject line reads CHESKA SUMMERSALL – CONTRACT EXTENSION.

'Olive's one of the producers,' Marnie says. 'She's a total bitch.' I think of the woman with the shiny bob and the clipboard.

The email is short.

Hi guys,
Attached is proposed extension for Cheska. In summary, we're guaranteeing twice the filming time each week, with appropriate payment, and we're also guaranteeing at least two solo scenes for her each episode.
Cheers,
Olive

I glance at Marnie. 'So?'

'Scroll down.'

I do, and I realise that there's part of an email from Cheska left at the bottom.

O!
Brill – thanks. Let me know what they say. This is going to be an amazing storyline! Promise!
Chesk xxx

My heart starts thumping. 'She's surely not talking about Lizzie?'

Marnie's face is grim. 'She must be. What else has got her more airtime?'

'But she sounds so *excited*.'

'That's not the worst bit.'

I raise an eyebrow at her over the top of the phone.

'Scroll back up. Check the date.'

I do, and my stomach lurches. The email was sent on the first of October.

'That's –'

'A week before,' Marnie finishes for me. 'A week *before* Lizzie went missing.'

'So, what are we saying here?' I ask. 'That Cheska knew Lizzie would go missing?'

Marnie looks at me without saying anything.

'That she had something *to do with it*?' The words feel surreal leaving my mouth.

Marnie swallows carefully. 'I don't know. But it doesn't look great, does it?'

We both look down at the phone.

'Okay, put it this way,' Marnie says. 'Cheska needs a new storyline, and she knows Lizzie's acting out, spending a lot of time online... So she makes up the Hal Paterson profile, and lures Lizzie to London –'

'And *what*?' I say. 'She does what with her? With her *sister*? Come on, Marnie... I know Cheska's awful but even she wouldn't do that just to get more time on TV, would she?'

We look at each other and neither of us say anything, because neither of us are sure just how far Cheska *would* go to get more airtime. I think of the way she sat me down on the war memorial and tried to talk me into going on the show. *They'd pay you.* The way the producer said, *We'll do a scene with Aimee, instead.*

I think Cheska would do pretty much anything to stay on TV.

'Come on,' Marnie says softly. 'Let's clean up your face.'

I watch her run warm water into a bowl. She searches in the cupboards and finds a clean, soft cloth, and all the time I'm thinking of Cheska and Lauren on screen. Crying together. Comforting each other. Fake, fake, fake.

My face stings as Marnie dabs at it, water trickling down the neck of my top.

'We need to go to the police,' I say, her hair brushing across my collarbone.

'I know,' she says, her face close to mine, and before I know what I'm doing, I kiss her.

Her lips are full and soft, and as soon as mine touch them, I realise what I've done. I pull away, but she's faster.

'What are you *doing*?' She takes a few steps back, her face furious.

'I'm so sorry,' I say, panicking. 'I wasn't thinking, I didn't mean to – everything's just... I just...'

'Jesus, Aiden.' She turns on her heel.

My head's spinning. *What the hell did I just do?* 'I'm so sorry,' I say, as she pulls on her coat and stuffs her feet in her shoes. 'You were just – and I was thinking of –'

She spins round. 'Don't finish that sentence.'

'Marnie –'

She wrenches the door open.

'Marnie, Cheska's email... the police...'

She glances back over her shoulder. 'Forget it. I'll take care of it, okay?'

And just like that, she's gone.

I SIT ALONE in the kitchen, my phone in front of me. In those ten minutes with Marnie, I'd forgotten about Autumn Thomas and the photo. The photo of baby clothes. *I know what really happened.* My heart bangs against my chest like a trapped bird, and I can't quite catch my breath. *Everything's falling apart.* My hands shake as I type.

Autumn
please

The reply is fast, almost instant.

oh come on
haven't you figured it out yet?
my name isn't Autumn
and neither is the girl's from your English class
(she was OCTOBER, genius)

Oh my god. She was. Of course she was. I can hear Gerber now, calling her name out. And I've forgotten, or I haven't bothered remembering, just because Autumn was nice to me, because I wanted someone to be nice to me.

The panic in my chest becomes something more like rage again.

Who the hell is this?

someone who knows you
The real you
maybe it's time everyone did?

It's like someone's dropped a bucket of icy water over me.

what do you want?

Why don't you come and find out?

My heart's hammering so hard I'm sure I can hear it. It echoes through the empty house like a drumbeat.

where?

get on the train to London
I'll tell you where when you get here

And then, the last instruction:

TELL NO ONE

THE NEWSPAPER ARTICLE spreads over two pages and is written by someone called Jennifer Liao.

I read it carefully, desperate for anything that will keep me in some way distracted on the forty-five minute train journey to London from King's Lyme.

(continued from page 1) Experts were called in from the Met's Computer Science Division in London, and spent three days analysing Lizzie's laptop and the family computer in the Summersall house. They found that Lizzie spent a 'disproportionate' amount of time online, often late at night, on popular social networking sites such as Facebook and Instagram, as well as the site AskMe.com, which attracted attention last year after accusations that it encouraged cyber-bullying. DCI Hunter said that Lizzie's friends list on Facebook had increased 'exponentially' in the last three months, and that 'rather than being individuals from circles she already inhabited, such as school, many of these new friends seem to have been total strangers'.

These findings have led those in charge of the investigation to believe that this is not the first time Lizzie, a talented drama student, has left her home to meet someone she had met online. The investigation has focused on one particular online 'friend', who Hunter said he was '99.9 per cent' sure was the one Lizzie had set out to meet on the evening of the 8th October. All traces of the account have since been deleted, and the experts were called in largely to try and track its creator down. Hunter stated at a press conference a week ago that the main concern of those involved was that 'the person behind this account is not the person depicted in the profile's pictures. They are not the person Lizzie believed they were.'

In light of this, local MP Graham Denton warned of the need for parents to be vigilant of their children's use of the internet. 'People have this idea that only younger children are at risk of grooming,' he said at a party conference on Thursday, 'but that is not the case. We need to allocate more funds into the education of parents and teenagers on the safety measures that should be taken when using social media.'

His comments were echoed in the House of Commons, where the Prime Minister announced that government funding would be allocated to technology companies working on security add-ons for social networks. One, an app called TrueFace, which verifies Facebook users' identities, will launch in the coming days. The Prime Minister confirmed that TrueFace is the first project to receive funding, and said that there would be a 'huge' campaign surrounding it.

Francesca Summersall, older sister of Lizzie, has also been trying to raise awareness of the issues around social networking. Summersall, 20, is one of the stars of locally-filmed reality show *Spoilt in the Suburbs* and a spokesperson for the show said, 'We are dedicated to helping Cheska and her family through this difficult time, and to helping Cheska raise awareness of the potential dangers of online relationships, a cause which is of course now very close to her heart.'

Meanwhile, DCI Hunter stated that police are still following 'several' new leads, and that Lizzie's was 'still very much an open case'.

I lean my head back against the seat and close my eyes as the train rocks through one of the little villages south of King's Lyme. All I can picture is Lizzie, on this train, heading to meet someone who is not the person she thinks they are.

And here I am, doing the same.

The thought doesn't come to me straight away; it isn't a lightbulb moment, not like you see in films. I'm staring out of the window, wondering who Lizzie might have trusted with the truth about us, and then I glance down at the paper again and the first thing to catch my eye is, as usual, Lizzie. My eyes flick over the photograph and its caption.

But then I look again.

Summersall.

Summer.

Autumn.

A new name for a new season – for a new Lizzie? Instantly, a part of me tries to reject it. She wouldn't. She *wouldn't*. But the rest of me keeps thinking. The rest of me keeps seeing.

She'd want to hurt me. I can't blame her for that.

Then I think of Evie, and Lizzie's parents. Could she do this to them? Put them through this? The Lizzie I know wouldn't do that.

But then she's not the Lizzie I know, is she? That's what I keep hearing, that's what I've seen for myself on her Instagram, on her AskMe.

Her AskMe. That's the thing that's been bugging me about the article, too, the mention of that site. Every time it comes up, it doesn't sit right with me. I just don't understand why Lizzie would use it, why she would continue to let people abuse her through it. There's got to be something there. Something I'm missing. I get out my phone and look at the page again, look at Lizzie's answers.

And this time, they don't seem random. They seem deliberate, specific.

Maybe I'm crazy, but they seem like messages.

All the world's a stage, and all the men and women merely players

I am not what I am

I don't want realism. I want magic! Yes, yes, magic! I try to give that to people. I misrepresent things to them. I don't tell the truth, I tell what ought to be truth. And if that is sinful, then let me be damned for it! – don't turn the light on!

After all, a woman's charm is fifty per cent illusion

Maybe I'm being paranoid, but it feels as if they're taunting me. Lizzie telling the world that she is other people, that she can play a part, can mislead. Right here, where anyone could see if they only knew where to look. I think of that lesson in Gerber's classroom, the lesson about *An Inspector Calls*. Lizzie, so serious. *He made her love him. And that's where it all went wrong.* There's a quote from the play here, too, the second question down, after someone's asked her 'Why are you even on here? Are you like 12?':

She kept a rough sort of diary. And she said there that she had to go away and be quiet and remember "just to make it last longer." She felt there'd never be anything as good again for her – so she had to make it last longer.

She had to go away and be quiet. That sounds horribly like a confession. My stomach twists as I remember that in *An Inspector Calls* the dead girl uses two names: she's Daisy Renton and she's Eva Smith. Lizzie Summersall. Autumn Thomas.

Is it going to be Lizzie who meets me? Am I going to get off this train and see her, finally?

The train announcer's voice, soft and gentle. 'We will shortly be arriving at London King's Cross, where this train terminates.'

I guess I'm about to find out.

LIZZIE. I SEE her in the crowd, I see her everywhere. Hats pulled down low over blonde hair, faces in shadow. But each time I get closer, she disappears like smoke, the faces instantly not hers. I make my way out of the station and nobody stops me, nobody is waiting for me, stationary in the stream of passengers.

When I'm outside, I fish out my phone and I send 'Autumn' – and already it's hard not think *Lizzie* – a message. I take a photo looking back at the station, and I type:

> Now what?

I look up after I've sent it, because it's too tense watching and waiting for a reply. From where I am, I can see the pretty red brick buildings of St Pancras and I remember a late-night conversation with Lizzie about it, and about Harry Potter.

> you know that's not King's Cross in Chamber of
> Secrets, right?

it is!

> nope! St Pancras

whaaaaat
aren't they the same?

231

　　　　　　　　　　　　　　sort of but not really

crazy

why'd they do that?

　　　　　　　　　　　　　　looks nicer I guess!

　　　　　　　surprises all the tourists when they show up

i didn't even notice!

I take pictures of it every time we go

　　　　　　　　　　　　　　　　　　haha

　　　　　　　　　they *are* next to each other

exactly :p

I wish I'd sent a picture of it instead of the actual King's Cross. Little in-joke for her.

Stop. You don't know that it's Lizzie.

I watch the people waiting for buses along the edge of the square, and the people walking through the square, around it, heads down. It's only now, coming back, that I fully realise how easy it is to lose yourself in London, how easy it is to disappear into a crowd and never come out again. And the thought doesn't scare me or intimidate me.

It makes me jealous.

My phone buzzes in my hand, and I look back down at it.

Go into the Underground, she types.

Catch the Piccadilly line to Covent Garden. I'll tell
　　you where to go from there.

I get up and head for the entrance to the Tube. It's almost three, so not yet as crazily busy as rush hour, but there's still plenty of people, a lot of them dragging suitcases and bags. I hurry down the steps, already planning ahead, remembering Covent Garden station and wondering where 'Autumn' – *Lizzie* – will want to meet.

I've still got my old Oyster card, in the battered old case Millie, one of my friends here, gave me when we were eleven. It used to have logos all over it – sports stuff, Adidas, Nike – but it's got so faded from being put in and out of pockets that it's just white smudges against the red plastic now. I go to a top-up point and press it against the sensor. Still £4.17 on there, from god knows how long ago, so I turn back round and head for the gates that lead to the Piccadilly line.

On the escalator, I can't help the feeling that I'm on my way somewhere I can't turn back from, like I'm walking to my doom, a prisoner shuffling down Death Row. But I'm not afraid. I feel solid, settled. For the first time in a week, I don't feel like my heart's about to burst out of my chest. Because at least I'm *doing* something, at least there's a chance I'm about to find some answers.

The platform is starting to fill up; three minutes to go until the next westbound train. I head for an emptyish space near the middle and take my place behind the yellow line next to an old man hunched over a paper and a mum with a baby in one of those carriers on her chest. *Baby*. I think of the tiny clothes in the photo. What if Lizzie lied? What if she *didn't* make a mistake? My stomach churns at the thought.

Two minutes on the screen now, and the baby starts to cry. It's a tiny sound, almost lost in the hum of the Underground, more of a mew than a cry, but it cuts through me in a way it never has before. I watch the mum jiggle it back and forth, fanning herself with a magazine.

One minute on the screen now, and Lizzie's quotes start filling my head again.

fifty per cent illusion

all the men and women merely players

The platform is almost full now, people filling the gaps between us, drawing in behind me. Sweat beads on my back. I can't stop a crawling feeling that travels through me, the baby's crying getting louder. But at least the train's coming now; two circles of bright, blueish light appearing around a bend in the blackness of the tunnel, the tracks vibrating.

I am not what I am

My hair lifts away from my face in the manmade breeze, the train roaring down the tunnel, its brakes screeching.

That's when two hands find the centre of my back.

And push.

'AUTUMN THOMAS'

IT'S AMAZING HOW easy it is; how quickly it happens. One minute I'm behind him, the next my hands are on his back and then he's falling, tumbling over the edge of the platform, and my hands are touching nothing but air. The train's thundering up to us, its lights the only thing I see. All I can think – a conscious, clear thought as time around us goes soupy slow – is that this is exactly, this is *all*, I wanted: to see Aiden fall.

And then time snaps back and my hand closes around the thinnest sliver of his jacket and I pull him back, just as the train smacks past us.

AIDEN

THE TRACKS LURCH up at me. Maybe this is the point when I'm supposed to see my life flash in front of my eyes but in reality, when it happens, all I see are the dirty tracks, the dusty concrete and the huge red front of the train, its glaring lights, as it roars towards me. And then someone is pulling me back, the world tipping upright again, and I stumble, my head bobbing back and the ceiling swimming above me. The train pulls in to a stop and the doors open, people pushing past to get off, people pushing past to get on, my heart stamping against my ribs, my lungs heaving.

I can't believe that just happened, I think, and at the same time, I realise that *that just happened*. I wheel around, ready to lay into whoever pushed me.

I wheel around and I see. I finally see who's been tormenting me all along; who 'Autumn Thomas' really is. And the weird thing is that the first thing I think of is Ladlow. I hear his voice in my head, just a couple of days ago, and it all makes sense.

Excellent work, dear Thomas.

Scobie.

Scobie is standing in front of me, panting like he's run a marathon, his glasses slipping down his face.

We stare at each other, neither of us caring about the people passing; only a few of them slowing, wondering if they're about to see a fight.

'You?' I say, and though I mean it like an insult, it comes out as a question.

'Me,' he spits.

I stagger back a little. 'But... why? Why would you do that to me?'

'*Why*?! Don't you think you deserve it, Aiden? After what you did to her?'

The train slides away. The platform is almost empty now; just the last few people straggling towards the exit, the first few new passengers making their way along it.

'You have no idea, do you?' Scobie says, and I notice that his hands are shaking. 'She was so sweet, so kind... And then *you* came along. And you broke her heart.'

Suddenly I realise I'm close to tears. 'Scobie, I –'

'Don't tell me you didn't mean it, Aiden, don't you *dare*. I saw her that night, at the prom. I found her outside the Rec, in bits, because of what you said to her. What you *did*. She told me everything.'

'Everything alright, lads?' One of the station staff has come along the platform to us, a hand on her walkie-talkie.

'Yeah.' My mouth feels dry, my legs like they might give way. 'Yeah, we're fine.'

She looks at us doubtfully. 'You getting on the next train?'

'No,' Scobie says firmly. 'We're going. Come on, Aiden.'

He heads for the stairwell and I follow, dazed, my mind trying to catch up with my legs. 'You saw her that night?'

He gives me a disgusted look. 'You'd abandoned her. You pushed her down the stairs!'

I grab his wrist. 'No. I *didn't*. It was an accident, Scobie. You must know that. *She* must've known that.'

He pulls his hand away. 'You hurt her so much, Aiden. And you've spent this whole time denying any responsibility.'

The woman with the walkie-talkie follows us to the bottom of the steps and so we keep moving, heading for the escalator. But my senses are returning, and with them, anger.

'*Me*? What about you? Did you do it to her as well? Did you set up another profile, make friends with Lizzie too? Found a photo you thought she'd like?'

'What?' He takes a step back, looking genuinely disturbed. 'No. No way. I would never do that to Lizzie.'

'Why should I believe you?'

He looks away in disgust. 'Why would I help you figure out Hal Paterson was a fake if *I* was the one behind it all?'

I look at Scobie. My friend. My best friend, looking back at me as if I'm scum. My best friend who's been lying to me all this time. Who just pushed me in front of a train. Who I've been lying to, too.

'Why did you bring me here?' I ask.

We're clogging up the flow now, standing at the foot of the escalators, people tutting and shooting glares at us as they have to skirt round. Scobie leans closer.

'We're going to find out what happened to her.'

'Me and you?'

'Me and you. You owe her that.'

And because I know he's right, I follow him onto the escalator.

LIZZIE

THE DAY THE phone rang, I was home alone, watching a re-run of *Spoilt in the Suburbs* while I fried a Nutella sandwich in a pan. I was hungover and feeling lonely, I guess, but in that weird way when you know that if someone actually *did* show up, you wouldn't feel like talking to them. I flicked through Facebook while I ate my sandwich. Messages from Lauren, who'd been sick on her new suede boots the night before and – less surprisingly – cheated on Deacon. And from Oli, a guy from the Upper Sixth who I'd been hanging out with at the party. I'd let him kiss me, and I'd gone upstairs with him, but then I got bored. His messages were boring, too – but not as boring as having nobody to message.

So I replied, lying on my front on my bed, laptop and half-eaten sandwich in front of me, the TV on for company. *Spoilt in the Suburbs* was over so I watched some cooking dating show thing and thought about how the girl on it was too pretty for the guy she was making dinner for. I told Oli I was watching a horror film and I was scared, and he said I could hide behind him anytime I wanted.

Predictable.

I rolled onto my back and found my phone under the pillow. I had a text from my mum – they'd be home late, they'd ended up meeting some friends in town for lunch. I saw one from Marnie that I must have opened half-asleep that morning.

Are you okay? it read. **Just got your voicemail. Call me.** Followed by about a million kisses. Which probably meant I'd called her drunk and cried about Aiden. I couldn't help it. I wanted to talk to him all the time and I couldn't, because he'd ruined it.

And then my phone rang. A number I didn't recognise, so I normally wouldn't have picked up. But I suddenly remembered the guy with the pretty eyes I'd met on my way home the night before, so I answered, one hand wandering for the other half of my sandwich.

'Hello?'

'Hi.' His voice so calm, so gentle. 'Lizzie?'

'Yeah.'

'It's Hal.'

Hal. I sat up, my heart thumping. *He called. He actually called.* I'd been waiting for this moment since the beginning of summer.

'Hi.' *Be cool.*

The truth is, there was something special about Hal. He knew how to make me laugh, knew instinctively the things that would annoy me and the way to cheer me up about them. When I had a bad day or a good day, it was Hal I wanted to speak to, Hal I immediately typed a message to. He'd started out as second best to Aiden but he was so much better.

Except for the fact that he wouldn't meet me. He wouldn't call either, and he always had a good reason – his phone was broken or the reception was bad or all of the above – and I couldn't argue with it. But he was there, even late at night or early in the morning, when I wanted, *needed*, to talk. And that was worth way more than the boys with pretty eyes or the ones I kissed in back gardens or bathrooms.

But now he *had* called. Now I was hearing his voice. Without even thinking, I put a hand up and smoothed down my hair.

'How you doing?' he asked.

'I'm good.' Did I sound breathless? I felt breathless.

'Good.' The hint of a smile in his voice. I clicked on his profile picture on Facebook, imagined the corners of his mouth twitching.

'How are you?'

'I'm okay. Listen, I've got the whole day free. Do you want to meet up?'

I got up and started rifling through my wardrobe. 'Umm. Today? I don't know if… In London?'

'Yeah babe.' *Babe*. It went through me, a bolt of the best feeling ever. 'Just a little train ride, right?'

He was quoting my words back to me. I'd said it to him so many times, trying to persuade him to come and see me. I could hardly argue.

'Okay. Yeah, I think I could make it.' I'd already plugged my straighteners in, had half a face of foundation on. 'Where do you want to meet?'

'There's a bar,' he said. 'Up in Angel. It's not too far from King's Cross. The Winchester?'

'Can you send me directions?' I asked, already Googling it.

'Sure, babe,' he said. 'I'll see you soon.'

When we hung up, I looked at myself in the mirror. *This is it*, I thought. *This guy is perfect.*

AIDEN

THE SUN CREEPS out from behind the clouds as we sit in the square, not looking at each other.

'Why didn't you just tell me you knew?' I ask. 'Why pretend to be my friend?'

Scobie scuffs his trainers against the pavement, looks away. 'I was your friend. I *just…* I didn't realise how much it upset her until we got back to school. And you didn't do *anything*. You didn't even care. And then she disappeared, and you just seemed like you wanted to get away from her, put as much distance as you could –'

'That's not *fair*,' I say, hotly. 'I've been trying to find her! It's all I've been thinking about.'

'Only because Marnie asked you!'

I shake my head. 'No. That's not true, Scobie. And what you said, about coming back to school after the summer – I tried so hard, all I wanted was to make it right. But she wouldn't let me, she shut me down. She ignored my calls, my texts, everything. She told me to *leave her alone*. And I didn't want to hurt her any more, so I did.'

He scoffs. 'That's not why. You were a coward, so you took

the easy way out and let her ignore you.'

I'm about to argue, but the words feel weak in my mouth. Because he's right. Her rejections hurt too much, so I just stopped trying. And look what's happened.

'I never knew you cared about her,' I say softly.

He glances at me. 'You never asked.'

I look at the people waiting to cross the road, the sky turning a violent purple behind them, the sun making orange bands across it as it sinks.

'Always,' Scobie says suddenly. 'Even at primary school, I reckon. She was so *kind*. To everyone, you know? And quiet, but not in a shy way, not like me. Just quiet because she didn't need to be loud.'

I nod. I know.

'When we were at Aggers, she didn't pay much attention to me,' he continues, looking out at the sky, at the clock on St Pancras as time ticks by. 'But I didn't mind. I was happy to just be her friend. And I was happy when *you two* made friends.' He shoots me a look. 'I thought you were a decent bloke.'

I close my eyes. I thought so too.

'If I could take it back –'

'Yeah, well, you can't,' he says briskly. 'So you're going to have to make up for it instead.'

I look at him warily. 'How can I do that?'

He gets out his phone, unlocks it, and shows it to me. I take it from him and I need a minute to process what I'm seeing.

'Is this –'

'The Facebook page we made. Yes.'

'But, Scobes, this has like, half a million followers.'

He nods, unsmiling. 'I know.'

I gape at him. 'How did you *do* this?'

He shrugs. 'I got Aimee Burton from *Spoilt in the Suburbs* to tweet the link. And then some guy off that Chelsea programme retweeted her tweet. Then things started getting busier.'

I look back at the page. *You can say that again.* It's packed with posts, people writing places they think they saw Lizzie, people sharing the page on their own newsfeed – I see Aimee Burton's name again: **Guys, please check this out... FIND LIZZIE!** In the comments, hundreds of people have tagged their friends.

'This is incredible,' I say, more to myself than to him.

'Yeah, so, obviously there's too much stuff to sift through,' Scobie says, taking the phone back from me. 'So I decided to be more specific.' He scrolls the page to a post from him, and shows it to me.

Thanks for all your support. Lizzie was seen getting on the 18:06 train on Saturday 8th October. It was a slow train, which means she would have arrived at London King's Cross at 19:03. Were you in the area? Please share your photos – any sighting of Lizzie might help.
PLEASE SHARE

He posted it at 11:36 today. Less than four hours later, it's been shared 10,000 times. It has 236 comments underneath it. My eyes widen.

Photo after photo of King's Cross, from all angles. Crowds and crowds of people; inside the station, outside the station, posing in the foregrounds, weighed down with suitcases. Five posts in a row that feature a hen party, all posing round the bride, bright pink sashes slashed across their bunny girl costumes. Loads and loads of the Harry Potter trolley that's glued to the wall inside the station, people of all ages and races posing with it. **Hope that helps!** people write, and **Thinking of Lizzie!**

I think she's there on the left, maybe? a girl's commented on one. **Could be her just by that door...** someone's put after another.

'This will take hours to go through,' I say.

'Yes,' Scobie says, taking his phone back. 'It did. Thankfully for you, I already have.'

He opens the gallery on his phone. 'I've saved the important ones. You might have to zoom.'

In a folder entitled 'Lizzie KingsX' there are three photos. My heart skips at the thought that three strangers have, without realising, seen Lizzie since she left. My hands feel damp as I open the first. It's one of the Potter shots, a group of lads messing around, pretending to be running at the wall. There's a crowd of people waiting their turn, and I zoom in further and push the photo around the screen, checking each person in turn. It's not until I go round a second time that I see her. She's coming out of the gates from the platforms, so she must have just got off the train.

'No luggage,' Scobie says, from over my shoulder, and he's right. Just Lizzie in a navy coat, skirt, tights and boots, with a yellow handbag no bigger than my fist strung across her body. I'm frozen for a moment, looking at her. She's *almost* looking at the camera, her attention caught by Harry's trolley, and there's a trace of a smile on her face; the beginning or end of one. I think, without meaning to, of our conversation about St Pancras again, and I wonder if she paused outside the station and looked up at the red bricks, at the clock. I wonder if she thought of me.

Scobie reaches over and slides to the next photo, as if to say, *We haven't got all day*.

This one is outside the station, and in the foreground is a group of teenagers, girls and boys, all wearing red hoodies with a logo that's too small to make out in one corner. They're all good-looking and tanned and grinning, with huge, overstuffed backpacks lolling on the floor in front of them. A school group, maybe from somewhere overseas. I zoom in and scan the crowd behind them, and then I see Lizzie over one guy's shoulder. She's heading for the camera, her face determined. I glance behind me, in the direction she'd have been looking.

The row of bus stops.

'And then –' Scobie flicks over to the last photo.

This one is the best quality, the closest shot. It's two guys taking a selfie at a bus stop, one of them kissing the other's cheek, both of them grinning. Behind them is Lizzie, or three-quarters of her face, one corner just blocked by the guy holding the camera, the one on the right. She's turned towards the camera, but not looking at it – looking at something beyond it, her hair blown back from her face.

'A bus,' I say. 'There was a bus coming.'

'I think so,' Scobie says.

I scan the photo, zoomed out this time, but because it's a selfie there isn't much in the frame. It's too close to see which bus stop they're at. I look beyond Scobie, towards the edge of the square. There are three bus stops, and another set on the other side of the road. At least twelve different buses stop here.

'I wrote back to the guy,' Scobie says. 'They didn't see which bus she got on. But they got on the 30, so they were waiting at that stop.' He points to the first one in the row. 'Six different buses stop there.'

'Well, it's something,' I say, although it doesn't feel like much.

Scobie takes his phone and clicks on his inbox. 'There's something else,' he says. 'Some guy sent me a private message – look.'

I scan over it quickly.

hey. saw ur page n it got me thinkin cos it was my bday that night, and we were around kings cross n angel, up the road. anyway, i checked the photos & i think lizzie *might* be in one of em. see what you think – im gonna send to the police too.

I look at the photo he's attached. It's really blurry, like the person who took it was moving, and the bar is really crowded too – a big smudge of faces. But there *is* a blonde girl, caught in profile, a dark bulk which I think is a jacket over one arm.

I zoom in closer, but that just makes the image all pixellated, so I zoom out again and study it. It *could* be Lizzie; the same shaped face, same hair. And then I see it.

'The handbag.'

Scobie nods. 'Yeah. It's the same one, right?'

Small and yellow and strung across her body. 'Yeah.' I look at the photo some more. 'It's got to be her, right?'

He makes a face. 'Maybe. Maybe not. But it's worth checking out.'

'Where is this place?' Before he can answer, I scroll the page down and see him asking this guy that exact thing.

angel, he's replied. **bottom of essex road.**

I look at Scobie. 'And I suppose you know exactly which bus goes there?'

He rolls his eyes at me, as if this is the stupidest question he's ever heard. 'Three of them, actually.'

'And they all go from –'

'That stop, yes.'

On any other day, in any other situation, I would find it funny how Scobie's always one step ahead. But with 'Autumn's' words still fresh in my memory, Scobie's handprints still burning on my back, I'm finding it anything but.

But then I look at Lizzie. I flick back and look at the picture of her at the bus stop, of her coming out of the station. And I *feel* something. I feel as if she's beside me, as if she's whispering right in my ear.

Follow me, she says.

SCOBIE

I SHOULD FEEL bad, but I don't. Then again, maybe I should feel glad. And I don't.

Seeing his face when he turned round and realised should have felt great, but it didn't. Instead I just saw Lizzie on that night, running through the bushes at the back of the Rec car park. Just the moonlight behind her, blood running down her face.

I was out there looking for Aiden. Some people would call that ironic, although it isn't ironic, just a coincidence. Not even a coincidence. A funny little side note: I was out there looking for Aiden, while Lizzie was out there trying to get away from him.

She stopped when she saw me. She was breathing fast and crying.

'What's happened?' I asked. 'Are you okay?' And she fell into my arms and she cried and cried. 'Follow me,' I said, and I led her away and found us a bench. She told me everything.

When I got back, the car park was flashing blue and Aiden and Deacon Honeycutt were being loaded into separate ambulances.

Maybe I would've said something the next day when I went round there, if I'd seen him. But I didn't. His car was on the drive but when I knocked on the door, his stepdad said Aiden and his mum had gone to London for the day. Seemed a funny thing to do – a day trip, when everyone was saying him and Honeycutt were going to get kicked out of sixth form before they'd even started, when Lizzie had told him that she was pregnant. But families are funny, I guess.

So I went to Lizzie's instead. I sat in her room, on the end of her bed, while she stayed tucked up under her duvet. Her eyes were all puffy from crying, but the cut on her head was just a scratch, scabbed up already – it didn't look so bad in the daylight.

But he didn't know that.

She did the test that day. I bought it for her, from the little chemist out by the garage, where I didn't think anyone would know me. Not that it mattered. Nobody in this town knows me.

The test was negative. But he didn't know that either.

I asked if she'd spoken to him, and she shook her head and started crying again. I didn't like that. I did not like that. He'd *hurt* her and then he'd just run away from the whole mess. Lizzie is a good person. A kind person. She didn't deserve to be treated like that. Nobody deserves to be treated like that.

It made me hate him, which is not a feeling I've really felt before. It was interesting.

I left Lizzie's that day and waited for Aiden to call me, but he didn't. The next time I spoke to him was on Facebook, and he told me he was at his dad's. They'd shipped him off to London a week early, and he was going to spend the whole summer there. Which was the normal routine, I guess. But it was all normal. When I saw him the day he got back, he was normal.

He didn't act like someone who might have got a girl pregnant, or had pushed that girl down the stairs, or who had stained the Rec car park with his and another kid's blood (from what I hear, it was mostly Deacon's blood) and who might have lost his place in sixth form for it. He was normal. We played *Call of Duty*. I won. We played *FIFA*. He won. We went and sat by the river. We walked around town. He drove us to McDonalds.

The hate turned to something a bit colder, but a kind of cold that burned. I wanted to push him. I'd watched Lizzie's Instagram pictures get less like her and more like Lauren; I'd watched her change because of him and I wanted to push him more. So I started to think about the ways in which I could get to him. Just in case. I started collecting my own pictures; photos of a pretty girl he *almost* knew. Someone who could sweet-talk her way in.

And then school started, and Lizzie left, and the need to push him got too strong to ignore.

So I did.

But I pulled him back. Pushing him was enough; I don't want actual blood on my hands. And, if I'm honest, I've seen the way he's started cracking since Lizzie disappeared. Aiden's not a bad person, he's just done stupid things. Thoughtless things, yes, cowardly things. But not malicious. I'm not happy about it, but I'm starting to feel sorry for him.

I look at him, rocking with the bus, his face turned towards the window. He looks like a shadow. Big bags under his eyes, his face blank.

Yep, I'm starting to feel sorry for him.

But there's no need to let him know that just yet.

AIDEN

THE BUS IS packed, standing room only, and I'm glad, because I'm not sure I'm ready to sit side by side and make small-talk with Scobie just yet. I keep thinking of how he reeled me in, the lengths he went to in order to make the Autumn Thomas profile real; the photos he must have spent hours stealing. My own stupid stupid stupidity for not checking deeper, even when Scobie himself had shown me exactly how to tell a profile was fake. He must have been laughing at me this whole time, fooling me just by giving her a few more friends, a few more photos. Because I was vain. Because I didn't believe it could ever happen to *me*. I move aside to let a lady with a buggy wedge herself in next to someone's piled-up luggage, and Scobie is shoved aside by two huge guys who carry on their conversation in the middle of the bus, totally unconcerned by all the people crammed up beside them.

How could he do it? How could he sit there with me, on Shark Night, just acting like we were mates?

The bus makes its way up Pentonville Road, stopping and starting with the traffic. I think of Lizzie, caught in a stranger's frame. The photos haven't made her feel more real to me after all; instead, she feels like a ghost. I try to picture her on this road, wondering if the police have taken the last photo seriously; if, right at this moment, they're working through CCTV footage of people packed on a bus just like we are. No luggage, just a tiny handbag. Whatever she thought she was coming into London for, she didn't think she was staying.

And all the time, the thought keeps niggling. *Would Lizzie have done any of this if it wasn't for me?* Scobie blames me. Scobie thinks that this all began that night at the prom. That it all started with me. The lies I've told. The things I've done.

I glance over at him, stuck between an old lady with a huge, overstuffed trolley she's trying to drag past the talking guys to get off at her stop, and two school kids in blazers, both playing on their phones. Scobie's face looks calm, relaxed; nothing like the way it did on the Tube platform, his features all twisted as he yelled at me.

But I get it. He was angry. I would've been too.

Just as I'm about to look away, he glances up. A look passes between us and it feels horribly like we're sizing each other up, like neither of us knows whether we can trust the other. In the window behind him, I see the shops of Upper Street, the groups of smokers spilling out of the pubs, their breath huffing out in clouds.

'This is our stop,' Scobie says, and we force our way out as the doors clap open. The two school kids get off ahead of us. I look down over one's shoulder and see her Facebook inbox open, five different conversations going on. I hope she knows them all. I hope they're all kind to her.

Out on the pavement, the air is so cold it feels like it's biting my face, my hands, the back of my neck. The sky is a sulky grey, the clouds heavy and white. Scobie heads for the traffic lights, Angel station behind us, where a crowd of people wait to cross the road, shopping bags rustling. On the other side I can see a couple of pubs, windows fogged, but when the crossing starts beeping, and we follow the flow of people, Scobie walks past all of these and carries on up the road. We don't speak. We put our heads down against the icy wind, and we walk. We pass some smaller shops, a Tesco Express, and then I see it, on the corner of a side street, just as slushy rain starts falling. The Winchester. A normal, unassuming pub exterior, white and dark red, the doors dark wood. When we get to them, Scobie tugs one open, looks at me, and then walks through. He doesn't worry about the door hitting me on my way in.

THE PUB IS dark inside, warm after the freezing evening. The walls have wood panels and purplish, floral wallpaper; there's a deer's head on one, framed paintings of old-style London on another. The tables and chairs are all mismatched wood, and the room we've walked into, long and thin, bends left where the bar and a dining room are tucked away. It's not as busy as you'd expect it to be, right in the middle of Angel, but a few of the tables have people sitting at them; most of them young and professional-looking, on their way home from work.

Scobie hangs back a bit, looking around him, his phone in his hand. The girl behind the bar comes towards us, smiling, so I say, 'Pint of lemonade, please.'

'Orange juice,' Scobie says, when I glance at him questioningly, and I relay that back to the bartender as if she hasn't just heard for herself. She's young, probably not far off our age, with hair dyed a bright orange colour like a highlighter pen. She's wearing a polo shirt with the pub's name stitched onto the breast, and denim shorts and dark tights, the kind that are thin enough to see through. When

256

she turns around to get Scobie's orange juice from the fridge behind the bar, I see she has Disney characters tattooed on the backs of her calves; Mickey Mouse on one, Goofy on the other.

'What happened to your face, anyway?' Scobie says, not actually looking at me.

'Deacon,' I say, and that's the end of that conversation.

'Anything else?' the bartender asks with a smile.

'That's it, thanks,' I say, trying to give her one of my own, and I pay for the drinks.

'We could sit,' Scobie says, vaguely, and after a few seconds' pause, I head for a table and he drifts after me.

'So this is the big plan?' I ask. 'We come here and… have a drink?'

He shoots me a look. 'It's better than anything you've done.'

That, I can't deny, is true.

We sit and sip in silence, just the ice clinking in our drinks. My stomach knots as I imagine Lizzie sitting here, waiting. But who was she waiting for?

'Why here?' Scobie asks. 'Why would they pick this place?'

I shrug. I have no idea. Up close, it's just a normal, everyday sort of pub. There's a sign for a basement bar that's open until 3 a.m., and I wonder if Lizzie was here that late, if the photo some random guy would later find of her was taken in the early hours of the morning, if Lizzie was here all that time. She was alone in the photo, and I don't know whether to find hope in that or not. Did she leave alone?

The bartender is on our side of the bar now, wiping tables, straightening menus, glancing repeatedly at the clock.

'Well,' Scobie says, as she gets closer, 'here goes.' He necks the rest of his orange juice, and when she's at the table next to ours, he waves her over.

'Excuse me,' he says, 'but we're wondering if you can help us. A friend of ours has gone missing, and we think she was here.'

'Blonde girl?' she asks, and we must both straighten up instantly because she shakes her head and looks at us sadly.

'Police were here about an hour ago,' she says. 'Nobody saw anything. I'm really sorry, it's horrible.'

'No CCTV?' I ask, trying to keep my voice conversational.

She frowns. 'Yeah, it's really weird actually. We have cameras all over the place, but the footage from that night is all messed up or missing. Some kind of fault with it.'

Scobie frowns too. 'What kind of system is it?'

'A really fancy one. All digital, all online, you know.'

'Jen!' Our barmaid jumps and glances nervously back towards the bar, where a shorter, older woman is standing, arms crossed. She's dressed casually in jeans and a hoody, but she's obviously the manager. Jen makes an *oops* face at us and grabs our glasses, hurrying back. We can't hear what the manageress says to her, but from the sheepish look on Jen's face, it seems gossiping on shift isn't encouraged.

We sit in silence, watching people come and go. A group of guys in suits come in and head for the bar. Close behind them are four girls dressed up in tight dresses and huge, shiny high heels. The lights get lowered just slightly and the music goes up a few notches.

'What now?' I ask Scobie, and he turns and looks at me in disgust.

258

'What do you mean, "what now"?'

'We can't just sit here, Scobie. This isn't achieving anything.'

'It's achieving a lot more than just sitting at home.'

I push my chair back. 'I'm going to the toilet.'

But Scobie's gone back to studying the group of guys at the bar, and he just ignores me.

THE TOILETS ARE through a set of wooden doors opposite the bar. While I'm washing my hands, I look at my face in the mirror. More and more these days, I don't recognise myself. My eyes look scared, shadowed with bags like bruises. And then there are the actual bruises. They don't even hurt any more, until I actually look at the swelling, the cut in my lip, and then each one gives a spiteful little twinge.

Why am I doing these things? Why am I here? I'm still washing my hands, the water painfully hot, and I'm imagining Lizzie sitting out there, wondering who she was waiting for. And I'm tired, I'm afraid, I'm remembering Scobie's hands at my back and the train rushing towards me and I'm wishing he'd never pulled me back. Steam is billowing out of the taps and when I finally snatch my hands back, the skin is tight and pink.

'Where did you go?' I whisper, and I wonder if we'll ever know. As I head back towards the bar, my legs feel heavy. In the tiny hallway, I fish out my phone, looking at the time. *Running out*, I think, without meaning to.

And then it starts to ring.

Mum.

I hit the volume down button to mute the call and watch it ring out as I head back into the bar. Scobie's standing waiting for me, looking from his phone to the bar and back again. When I get closer, I realise that he's looking at the photo of Lizzie again, figuring out where she was standing. What she could see. The thought makes me feel sick. The thought of going back to Abbots Grey without knowing makes me feel even sicker.

When my phone finally diverts the call to answerphone, it stops ringing. I breathe a sigh of relief, about to open the internet, but it starts ringing again almost immediately. Mum again. Not a good sign. I have to answer, trying to keep my voice normal as if I've just popped out to pick up milk rather than, oh, just nipped into London to search for my missing ex-sort-of-girlfriend.

'Hey.'

Her voice streams out of the phone at a volume that makes even Scobie, beside me, look up. 'Aiden, where the *hell* are you? Get home now.'

'Sorry, I just had to –'

'I don't care what you *just had to*, I need you home. Now. Immediately.'

'Is everything okay?'

'Is everything *okay*?' She takes a deep breath and is about to launch into a full-on takedown, but then there's the sound of a door opening and a man's voice in the background.

'Mrs Cooper?'

'Just a *minute*.'

The door closes again, and this time, when she speaks, she's almost whispering. 'The police are here, Aiden.'

I feel like someone put the pub around me on mute. I don't hear people talking, don't hear the music, don't hear anything except for the faint buzzing in my ears.

'What?'

'The police are here. To speak to you. Come home now, Aiden, please.'

And it's the please that gets me. While every instinct is screaming at me to run, to get to Dad's or somewhere, anywhere, as far away as possible, it's the please that will put me back on that train. I can't leave Mum to clear up another one of my messes. I hang up and turn to Scobie.

'I've got to go back.'

He looks up from the screen, from the blurred shadow of Lizzie's face. 'What? You can't.'

'I have to. The police are at my house.'

He follows me without another word.

ON THE TRAIN we sit opposite each other on one of the sets of four seats. It's busy going this way; the carriage full of people in business suits commuting back to their fancy country mansions, their tidy little commuter towns. Abbots Grey is just one of many along this belt of railway, and this train stops at each of them, making the journey excruciatingly slow – or at least it seems that way to me. Scobie's face is tight, his mouth twitching as he watches the landscape sail past. He's disappointed. We're leaving without any answers, and Scobie hates not having the answers.

I have one answer, but it isn't enough. I remember myself just a couple of hours ago, on my way into London, thinking that Lizzie might be about to appear and reveal she'd been Autumn all along. *Did I really believe that?*

And then I remember her AskMe page and the weird answers. I take out my phone and look at them again. Properly, this time, without thinking that she might be just minutes away from me, laughing at me.

First up is the one that still makes my heart leap. The question: 'Do you love me?' The username 'aiden k'. The only question on the page she hasn't answered.

Underneath that, a question that's just like most of the others.

haha how can your sister call herself a reality star when she's the fakest slut on tv? The username 'sxxybitch353.' And Lizzie's answer is a quote from *Streetcar*.

I don't want realism. I want magic! Yes, yes, magic! I try to give that to people. I misrepresent things to them. I don't tell the truth, I tell what ought to be truth. And if that is sinful, then let me be damned for it! – don't turn the light on!

I read it, and I remember her in her Blanche outfit, in her spotlight on the stage, while I wait in the wings. The lines are delivered to Hugo Frith, the guy in the year above who played Mitch. He's recently been cast in *Spoilt in the Suburbs*, just a little part, someone's brother who appears at a few parties. The kind of part the producers test all the time, checking out the internet feedback before giving that person more airtime. I hear Lizzie saying the lines to him so clearly it's like she's right next to me, and a shiver goes through me.

Third:

Why are you even on here? Are you like 12?

She kept a rough sort of diary. And she said there that she had to go away and be quiet and remember "just to make it last longer." She felt there'd never be anything as good again for her – so she had to make it last longer.

An Inspector Calls. I think again of that afternoon in Gerber's class. *He made her love him. And that's where it all went wrong.* Is that how she feels about me? I look up and out of the window, at the fields flashing by.

Why wouldn't she? It's true.

I go back to the words and try to put my feelings aside, try to approach it like someone who doesn't know Lizzie would. A diary. Maybe she's leaving clues to her diary. A chill runs through me at the sort of things that might say.

Another question:

you think you're well fit don't you?

Physical beauty is passing. A transitory possession.
But beauty of the mind and richness of the spirit and
tenderness of the heart – and I have all of those things.
But I have been foolish – casting my pearls before swine!

Another Blanche quote, and this one makes me squirm each time. *Casting my pearls before swine.* Maybe, if I'm really generous with myself, I can think that she meant the boys of her summer. The guys I've seen in her photos, in back gardens with beer cans, their arms cast round her like she's furniture. Maybe I can believe she hated all of them: Lauren, Deacon, all of their friends. That they were a waste of her mind, her spirit, her tender heart.

Or maybe I have to admit what I'm sure is the truth. She's talking about me.

r all the Summersall women sluts? bitches be cray

Oh, what a noble mind is here o'erthrown! –
The courtier's, soldier's, scholar's, eye, tongue, sword,
Th'expectancy and rose of the fair state,
The glass of fashion and the mould of form,
Th'observed of all observers, quite, quite down!
And I, of ladies most deject and wretched,
That sucked the honey of his music vows,
Now see that noble and most sovereign reason
Like sweet bells jangled, out of tune and harsh;
That unmatched form and feature of blown youth
Blasted with ecstasy. Oh, woe is me,
T'have seen what I have seen, see what I see!

Her Ophelia monologue. Hamlet and Ophelia: doomed, damned, disastrous Hamlet and Ophelia. If that's how Lizzie sees me and her – I stop that thought immediately, because Ophelia ends up drowned. Ophelia ends up mad and then dead.

I read through the quote over and over, trying to see it just for the words, trying to ignore the memory of Lizzie in her spotlight, her voice saying the lines in my head. But the words aren't much better. *And I, of ladies most dejected and wretched, That sucked the honey of his music vows*. I think of all the things I said to her. All the jokes I told, all the times I listened. I think of her leaning her head against me in the beige and brown light of backstage, I think of her typing to me late at night.

Now see that noble and most sovereign reason like sweet bells jangled, out of tune and harsh. It dawns on me slowly – it's not Ophelia who's mad here.

It's Hamlet.

Scobie glances over at me. 'What are you looking at?'

I hand him the phone, and he frowns. 'Lizzie still had one of these?'

'Apparently.'

'*Why?*'

'I don't know. Her answers are… They don't exactly –' I don't know how to explain what they are. What they mean to me.

King's Lyme is the second to last stop on the train, so by the time we're almost there, the train is much emptier, the two seats beside us vacated. Just as the train begins to slow, Scobie glances up from the screen.

'"Do you love me?" You wrote that?'

Heat shoots up my face. 'No! I didn't even know she had the stupid page until Marnie showed me.'

He looks at it again and shrugs. 'Could've been anyone, I guess. Loads of people thought something was going on with you two. Probably Deacon or Kieron. Or Lauren. That's the kind of thing girls do on here, isn't it?'

'I don't care about that,' I say, irritated. 'It's the other questions that're weird. Her answers.'

He nods slowly, scrolling back and forth through them.

'You think they're about you, don't you?'

I bite my lip. 'Some of them… seem close to home.' I glance at him. 'Do you?'

He shrugs. 'Maybe. But I don't see how that helps us. We already know *you* were a dick to her.'

The train pulls into the platform before I can reply.

As I SPEED out of King's Lyme and onto the dual carriageway, Scobie checks the Facebook page we made to see if anyone else has posted pictures of Lizzie. The car whines as I move up through the gears, and that's the only sound we hear because Scobie and I have fallen back into a cold silence. It's weird; we keep forgetting, keep slipping into our old, comfortable roles. And then we remember. We remember the secrets we've kept from each other, the other selves we've hidden. And I'm tired. Tired of being all these things. Footballer. Actor. Student. Liar. Boyfriend; friend. I've built myself too many identities and now they're imploding.

The police are at my house. The fear that thought strikes in me feels small and faraway, like it belongs to someone else. I knew this moment would come; I feel something that's almost like relief.

'What do you think they want?' Scobie asks, reading my mind in the casual way he does, not even looking up from his phone.

'I don't know,' I say, taking the exit for Abbots Grey, a winding country lane that takes us abruptly away from the grey strip of dual carriageway and into gold and green fields, the light quickly fading. But that isn't true.

Scobie looks up at me, just as we make it to the Welcome sign at the entrance to the town. The last dull rays of daylight flash across the lens of his glasses, hiding his eyes.

'What if they've found her?' he says.

We pull up outside my house and there's the panda car, right outside. It looks so weird, so out of place among the landscaped gardens, the sleek cars and 4x4s, their muted colours. The police car looks like a cartoon, like a picture out of a comic that someone's cut out and stuck onto an estate agent's brochure. When we get out of my car, the neighbourhood seems quiet. So quiet. *Too* quiet.

What if they've found her?

I get out my keys and open the front door and there's a moment's stillness, a moment's silence before the kitchen door opens. My mum comes out, looking terrified, and behind her, Hunter and Mahama. Mahama's face is serious, her mouth a straight line. But Hunter is smiling. It's a smile that doesn't quite reach his eyes.

'Aiden,' he says, as if we're old friends. 'Where have you been?'

SCOBIE

'You're going to have to wait outside,' the male officer, a big guy with a blondish beard and tired, baggy eyes that are a weird shade of grey, says to me. I decide to take him literally, and I sit on the stairs, right outside the closed living room door. Kevin Cooper might have expensive furniture but his doors are thin as anything; I can hear every word they're saying.

'Do you know why we're here, Aiden?' the female officer asks, her voice kind, inviting.

Aiden doesn't answer and in his not answering, I hear his fear. I know what he's thinking. Maybe I'm not the only one who knows about him and Lizzie and the last day of exams. Or the night of the prom.

'We've had a report of an incident today at school. Does that ring any bells?' The other officer doesn't have a kind voice. He sounds the opposite of inviting. *Incident*?

'Look at his face,' Aiden's mum says. 'He's clearly the victim here.'

Oh, his face. I've kind of gotten used to it already.

'That might be the case,' the man says, 'but that isn't the report we have. We have a complaint from the other party involved.'

'*Deacon?*' Finally, Aiden speaks up. 'Deacon called you. That –'

'They have a long-standing, erm, disagreement,' his mum says, cutting over him. 'It's just schoolboy stuff.'

Having seen the results of at least one of these 'disagreements', I feel this to be something of an understatement.

'The fight is a matter for the school in the first instance,' the woman says, 'unless Mr Honeycutt decides to move forward and press charges. The school will want to help you all avoid that course of action.'

'Having said that,' the man says, 'we felt it important to look into this "disagreement" –' he says it in an exaggerated way, like he's making air quotes with his fingers – 'and it's brought up some interesting things, Aiden. Very interesting.'

Aiden has gone very quiet again.

'Do you want to tell us what happened on the night of your Year 11 Leavers' Ball?'

I can hear his heart sink from here.

'Aiden?' his mum prompts, after an uncomfortably long silence.

'We got in a bit of a fight,' he says slowly.

'A *bit* of a fight?' The officer sounds kind of mocking now. 'Kind of a light way to describe something which landed you both in hospital, don't you think?'

So they're still talking about Deacon. Not about Lizzie. Not yet.

'What was the fight about, Aiden?' the woman asks.

'He – erm… he thought I was flirting with his girlfriend.'

'That's –' I hear a few pages of a notebook being flicked through. 'Lauren Choosken.'

271

'Yeah.'

'The same Lauren who just got a part on *Spoilt in the Suburbs*, right?' the male officer chimes in.

'Yeah.' You can tell the word really sticks in Aiden's throat.

'The same show as Lizzie's sister, right?'

'Yes. That's the one.'

'Small town,' the officer says, in a casual voice that's meant to imply he doesn't mean it casually. There's the sound of more pages being shuffled, but even without seeing him I feel that the chances he's actually reading from them at this point are relatively slim. 'Not the first time you've found yourself in this kind of situation, is it, Aiden?'

There's another awkwardly long pause. 'I don't know what you mean,' he says eventually.

'No?' The guy seems to be really enjoying himself now. 'You don't know what I mean? Slipped your mind, has it? The incident at your last school? The one that got you excluded? Permanently?'

Aiden doesn't reply.

'Let me refresh your memory,' the officer says. He's the one doing all the talking now. 'On the evening of June 12th, 2013, you were involved in an altercation with a fellow student, during which you hit him *so hard* that you dislocated his jaw. You had to eventually be restrained by *three* fellow students, and, when questioned later, four separate witnesses described the attack as "unprovoked". That about cover it?'

'What exactly are you trying to say?' Aiden's mum says, trying to sound combative, tough. She doesn't manage it. She just sounds scared. Tired.

272

'Well, it's just that we've got a boy here who clearly has a temper. We've got a missing girl who we're hearing might have rejected him. Interesting, isn't it?'

I have to agree. It *is* interesting.

'Please,' Aiden says. 'It isn't like that.'

There's a moment's silence, and then, in a voice so low I almost don't hear it, the female officer says, 'We know it was you, Aiden.'

'This is ridic–' Aiden's mum starts, but the other officer interrupts. He sounds kind of tired, too.

'We know you're Hal, Aiden.'

What?

'He's what?' His mum says it like she hasn't heard properly, or like she hasn't understood, but it clicks before they can reply, because the next thing she says is almost a whisper. 'Aiden?'

But Aiden doesn't say anything. I lean closer, because surely he *is* going to say something. It's totally illogical for him to be Hal.

Finally, he does speak.

'I'm sorry,' he says, and his voice is very small.

What?

'Oh my god,' his mum says, but already I'm clicking through everything in my mind. The distracted look on his face all the time; the look that, now I think about it, is actually a lot like guilt. The way he's been careful to keep suggesting that Lizzie going missing is nothing to do with the Hal account, that we need to keep looking for other options.

'It's not what you think,' Aiden says, sounding a bit like he's going to cry. But before anyone can actually say what they're thinking, the front door opens behind me.

273

'What's going on in here?' Aiden's stepdad is wearing a suit and Converse, like he always does. He takes one look at me, sitting on the step, and then at the closed door, and then he strides towards it, his face set like stone. He pulls it open, a vein pulsing at his temple.

'Can I help you, officers?' he asks, and he *does* manage to sound combative. And polite at the same time, which is kind of impressive.

'Just having a chat with Aiden here,' the officer says, not sounding concerned.

'In what capacity?' Kevin leans casually against the doorframe but his voice is tight and tense now. 'Because, as you're well aware, you're aren't able to conduct an interview without our legal representative present.'

'Well, Mr Cooper, I suggest you get in touch with your chosen representative,' the officer says, and there's a soft slap as he closes his notebook, and the fancy white sofa squeaks as he gets up. 'Because Aiden here will be accompanying us to the station.'

'No,' Aiden says, and his mum starts crying.

I expect Kevin to argue, or to flat-out refuse to let them take Aiden, but instead he just looks at the two officers and then at Aiden, and all he says is, 'You don't need to cuff him. At least give him that.'

'Kevin –' Aiden starts, but Kevin puts up a hand to stop him.

'Don't say anything. Just go with them, Aiden. I'm right behind you.'

Aiden looks at me as they lead him past. 'I'm sorry,' he says, but I don't reply.

WE SIT IN the lobby of the police station for what seems like days but is in fact two hours and fifty-seven minutes. Aiden's mum cries almost continuously and this makes me feel uncomfortable.

'How could he?' she asks me, but that's a question I'd like to ask him myself. 'I don't understand,' she says, but I think I do. I do understand, and it turns my stomach.

Aiden's stepdad never stops moving. He paces back and forth, making phone calls, sending messages, which is probably in my best interest because I get the impression he's not very keen on me being here. The fancy lawyer he called in the car on the way here turned up about thirty seconds after we did and was ushered in by the officer on duty. After the first hour of waiting, she comes out and speaks to Kevin in a whisper so we can't hear. About seventeen minutes after that, the female police officer, who's now been introduced as DS Mahama, comes and gets Kevin and they disappear back into the interview suite. I straighten up. Something has happened. Something is happening.

'He's my son,' Aiden's mum, totally oblivious, says to me, after blowing her nose for the thirteenth time since we arrived. 'I don't understand why he'd do that to her.'

'He got expelled,' I say. Seeing as we don't actually know yet what it is he has or hasn't done to Lizzie, I decide to get answers on something that is certain.

She looks at me and her eyes narrow. 'That's totally irrelevant.'

'The police don't think so.' I don't either. All this time, I thought I knew all of Aiden's secrets. And now it turns out that prom night was just one of his many lies. I feel like an idiot for even starting to feel sorry for him.

'He's a good boy. He's your friend,' she says in a little voice. 'He wouldn't hurt her.'

I think about this for a while, the clock ticking, the policeman behind the desk flicking through a magazine. I think of the way Aiden looked when he lost his temper with Lauren Choosken this morning. I think of the way Deacon Honeycutt limped past me in town, a week after the prom.

It's not just that. I keep remembering the night last week when he showed up at my house, babbling about Marnie Daniels and the messages they'd found. How he'd made me sit down and try to figure out who was behind the Hal profile. In the car on the way here, I wondered why he'd do that if it was him all along.

But now I see. It wasn't because *he* wanted to know who was behind the profile; it was because he wanted to know who else could figure it out, how easy it would be to trace it back to him. And when he saw how easy it was for me to start to unpick it, he deleted the whole thing.

I've underestimated Aiden this whole time, and that does not make me happy.

After another thirty-three minutes the door opens and Aiden's mum jumps up like she's been electrocuted. The two police officers come out, followed by Kevin; none of them are speaking. Kevin has a grim look and a pale sheen of sweat on his face, but when he sees us standing there, he nods.

And then he stands aside, and lets Aiden past him.

'Aiden,' his mum says, and she sounds half relieved, half upset. I don't say anything, because that's much easier.

'He isn't being charged,' Kevin says, and a kind of smugness sneaks into his voice, like he's just won a new business contract. 'He has a solid alibi.' He turns to the officers as he says that part, as if he's underlining it in their thoughts, too.

'He isn't being charged *yet*,' the officer I now know is DCI Hunter says, stamping out that smugness. 'We'll be requiring your continuing assistance with our investigations, Aiden. There are still a lot of questions we need to ask you, so don't go anywhere. And there's the matter of the assault at the school this morning. We'll be in touch if the victim decides to press charges.'

'He is *not* a victim,' Aiden hisses, but Kevin holds up a hand and he falls instantly silent.

'Thank you, Mr Cooper,' DS Mahama says. 'Mrs Cooper.' She nods to me as they turn and head back into the station, while Kevin ushers us quickly out into the car park.

'But the profile?' Aiden's mum is saying, flapping at her face with a tissue. 'The messages? The guy she was talking to – Hal? Was it Hal? Was that you? Aiden, did you do that?'

'That doesn't matter now,' Kevin says, unlocking the car

and holding the door open for her. 'He made a mistake; we'll stick by him.'

'A mistake?'

I scramble round to the other side of the car and slide into the back seat so I can hear the rest of what she has to say. Nobody pays me any attention. Aiden sits beside me, silent, his mouth set in a straight line. 'He tricked her, that's what they were saying, wasn't it? He pretended to be this Hal person, he talked to her.' His mum won't let it drop.

Kevin starts the engine and reverses, his hand on the back of her headrest as he cranes round to check through the rear windscreen. The tyres screech.

'Aiden, why would you do something like that?' she says in a whisper.

He looks down at his hands. 'I don't know.'

But he does. And so do I. Lizzie rejected him, and he couldn't accept it.

'I just don't understand,' she says again. 'I don't understand how you could do that to someone. *Why* you'd do that to your friend.'

'It doesn't matter,' Kevin says, swiping at the back of his neck with his hand. 'The point is, he isn't responsible for her going missing. They can't blame him for that.'

'But the papers, the news – they all say she went to meet someone she'd been talking to online.'

This is an excellent point. If Lizzie didn't go to meet 'Hal', where did she go?

'Kate, *leave* it,' Kevin says, his voice suddenly hard. 'Aiden feels bad enough about deceiving Lizzie,' he adds, glancing at her.

I look sideways at Aiden. His face is totally blank. He doesn't *look* like he feels bad enough to me.

'And the fight,' his mum says. Apparently she has no intention of leaving it. She's not crying any more, and she's starting to sound pretty angry. This I feel more comfortable with. 'You *promised*, Aiden. You promised not again.'

Kevin indicates and turns off the main road. We're almost back at their house. 'I'll sort it,' he says, brushing at the back of his neck again. 'I'll give Rick Honeycutt a call. There's no need for this to go any further. We can sort it out without the police being involved, same as the last time.'

Aiden lets out a snorty sort of breath and looks out of the window as we drive slowly down their long, quiet street.

'The police *are* involved,' Kate says. 'It's happening again. After everything we went through last time.' Oh. The tears are back.

Kevin swings the car into their curved drive and kills the engine. 'It'll be okay,' he says. 'We'll talk to Deacon. We'll make it right, won't we, Aiden?'

But Aiden doesn't answer, because he's already scrambling out of the car, his own car keys in hand.

'Aiden, where are you going?' Kevin yells, but Aiden's halfway down the drive, the headlights on his car flashing as he clicks the button to unlock it.

Seeing as I've got nowhere else to be, I follow him.

AIDEN

I DRIVE WITHOUT really seeing, without caring. I drive too fast and brake too slowly, forgetting to indicate, not bothering to give way. I see my mum's face in the police station lobby: pale, tear-stained, afraid. Disgusted. I see Hunter and Mahama looking at me from across a desk: cold, practical. Assessing. And I see Lizzie, Lizzie, Lizzie. I see her name in my inbox – *Hal*'s inbox. I remember how excited I felt each time a new message came through, each time I made her type 'lol' and each time she added a kiss. Everything was okay again.

And now everything is falling apart.

'How could you do it?' Scobie says, and I glance at him. His face is furious, the beams of the streetlights passing across the lenses of his glasses and hiding his eyes from me again.

'I missed her,' I say, and I hate myself. 'I *needed* her.'

'So you tricked her.' His voice is flat, emotionless.

And I can't argue. I did deceive her – I won back her trust by lying to her. I want to tell him that I'm sorry, I want to tell *her* that I'm sorry. But above it all, beating through me in an insistent, deafening pulse, is anger. Panic. And that's what keeps my foot on the accelerator, that's what drives me forward.

Deacon Honeycutt's house is tall and pale, with long, narrow windows like a church's. There are fake pillars outside the door and a swooping gravel drive leading up to it. I'm going so fast down it that when I stop, the car skids slightly, gravel spraying up like a wave.

'Really?' Scobie looks at me in disgust. 'After everything, all you care about is Round Two?'

I ignore him and head for the Honeycutts' front door and start hammering the big iron doorknocker, banging on the glass panel with my hand at the same time. I don't care that I look like a maniac. I don't care any more. I don't care.

All the way here, I've been envisaging Deacon's face; imagining landing a fist right in the middle of it. But when he opens the door, I don't do anything. I just stare at him. And he stares at me.

'You went to the police?' I say, and it's almost funny, how betrayed I sound.

He shakes his head. 'Look, I'm not pressing charges. My dad made me report it. I'll get kicked off the team if I've been in another fight. That's all.'

It should make me feel better somehow, but it doesn't. Because I want to argue with him. I want to fight. I want something, *anything*, to take out all these feelings on.

'Look, relax,' he says. 'I'm not gonna do anything. It's over. We're good.'

He's being nice to me and I hate it. And by the look on his face, he hates it too. It's like every word tastes sour in his mouth, but he has to keep on spitting them out anyway.

'"We're good"?' I sneer. 'Right. Were we "good" when you

281

and your mates attacked me the night of the ball? Were we "good" when you called me a rapist?'

He stares right back at me and his mouth moves like a robot's. 'It's all done now. We're good.'

A wild sort of idea flashes in front of me. 'Did Cheska put you up to this?'

He pulls a face, a *WTF*, but before he does, I see his mouth twitch. 'Cheska? Cheska Summersall?'

I pull my ace with glee, jabbing his buttons at random. 'I know you're shagging her. I *saw* you. Maybe I should call Lauren and fill *her* in.'

Finally the fake calm on his face breaks just enough for me to see the panic beginning to surface. 'It's just sex,' he says, like he doesn't care, but his hands have come up into a kind of defensive gesture, an *I didn't mean to*. 'It's nothing.'

'Shame it's not on camera,' I say. 'Imagine the ratings. Poor new girl Lauren gets her boyfriend stolen by poor, grief-stricken Cheska.'

'How'd you think Lauren got on the show in the first place?' he snaps.

'That's how she got on?' Scobie says from behind me, in disbelief. 'Because you gave Cheska sexual favours? That is all kinds of distasteful.'

'No,' Deacon says hotly. Backtracking. 'Nah, I never said that. Forget I said that.'

But I've suddenly remembered the email Marnie showed me. 'Cheska *knew* that Lizzie would go missing,' I say. 'She promised the producers she had a *big* storyline coming up, and they gave her more airtime. That's how *sick* she is. But maybe you knew about that, right? Maybe *you* were *in on it too*?'

He glares at me, horrified. 'Cheska wouldn't do that,' he says.

'Wouldn't she?'

'It certainly *has* benefited her,' Scobie says, considering.

Deacon looks at both of us and then away. 'Nah,' he says. 'That's not it.'

'Oh, really?' I smack the doorframe with the palm of my hand. Hard. The sound reverberates around us. 'So why would she say that then? A week *before* Lizzie disappeared. If she didn't know, why would she say that?'

I stop yelling, because I've suddenly seen an emotion I've never seen on Deacon Honeycutt's face before. He looks *embarrassed*. Ashamed.

'What?' I ask.

He huffs. 'You were right, okay? "Poor new girl Lauren gets her boyfriend stolen by Cheska?" *That*'s the storyline she meant.'

I gape at him. 'It's a set-up? It's for the show?'

He looks away. 'Yeah. Sort of. I mean, Cheska, she's fun. And me and Lauren, we're done.'

'So you didn't cheat on Lauren?'

'Well, yeah, at first.' He shrugs. 'She was mad when she found out, but then we figured it could work for everyone.'

Scobie screws his face up. 'How? I don't understand.'

I do, though. 'Lauren gets a part on the show,' I explain. 'After a couple of episodes, they bring in Deacon, Lauren's lovely boyfriend, and a couple of episodes after that, oh, surprise, Deacon and Cheska hook up. Cheska's got her big storyline,

283

Lauren gets all the sympathy *and* she's on *Spoilt in the Suburbs*, her number one ambition, so everyone's happy.'

Deacon shrugs again. 'Pretty much, yeah. That's how it was supposed to go, anyway.'

'Except then Lizzie goes missing,' I say, and I feel more than a small need to punch him again. 'And the producers decide that's a better storyline.'

'Probably not the best time to introduce a love triangle,' Scobie muses.

'Exactly. But Lauren's already under contract, so they wheel her out as Lizzie's "best friend".'

Deacon rolls his eyes. 'Whatever. I'm just saying – Cheska didn't know nothing about Lizzie. You're way off with that.' His eyes narrow. 'And you can't tell anyone any of that stuff.'

I start to answer but his hand shoots out and he gets a fistful of my t-shirt. 'Listen, Kendrick. I'm doing you a favour by dropping this police thing. You and me both know, I press charges, you're done for. So you do me a favour back and keep your mouth shut about this, yeah?'

My lip curls and my hands bunch into fists, but I know he's right. 'Fine,' I say, and it comes out as a snarl.

'Good.' But he doesn't let go. Instead, he pulls me closer, so we're eye to eye. 'You might have everyone else fooled,' he says, 'but I know you're not the nice guy you want everyone to think you are. I've seen the way you look when you don't know anyone's watching. You're shady, and I don't like you. And if Lizzie figured that out too, well good for her.'

It takes everything I have not to spit in his face. But I don't. Because he's doing me a favour. Because he's right. We watch

284

each other for a second, and then he releases me. 'And I'm telling you – Cheska didn't have anything to do with Lizzie going. She's proper cut-up about it. Leave her *alone*.'

'But –'

'And don't you be sending your step-daddy round here like last time. Making threats like some kind of big man. This is between me and you, Kendrick.'

And he shuts the door in my face.

WE GET BACK in the car, but we don't drive. We just sit and watch as rain starts to spatter the windscreen, the sky growing dark over the tall trees that line the Honeycutts' drive.

'You didn't honestly think Cheska Summersall was behind it, did you?' Scobie asks.

I don't say anything.

'Come on,' he scoffs. 'Can you really imagine Cheska coming up with a scheme that big, tricking Lizzie or convincing Lizzie to help her?'

'Yeah, but she might have known –'

'You really think Lizzie would have trusted Cheska, of all people? Not Marnie? Not, I don't know, *anyone* else?'

'Yeah, okay, Scobie, I get it. It was stupid.'

He shrugs. 'No crazier than some of the things I've been thinking. No crazier than some of the things you've *done*.'

I lean forward slowly and rest my head on the steering wheel, ignoring that. I deserved it. 'Maybe we're thinking too much into it. Maybe she did go to meet some random guy, some other guy she met online…' I don't finish that sentence. I can't finish that sentence.

'Maybe,' Scobie says. 'But I don't think so. Internet perverts don't fold someone's clothes when they accidentally leave them at a crime scene.'

The clothes. I'd forgotten about the clothes.

'You think it's a set-up,' I say, and I can hear myself clinging to the words as they hang between us.

'I think it's meant to look like something it isn't,' he replies, and then, in the same breath, he says, 'An unprovoked attack?'

It takes me a minute to realise that these sentences are independent, and that he was listening back at my house. 'No,' I say. 'It wasn't unprovoked.'

'What did the guy do? Why'd you beat him up?'

I chew my lip. I don't want to think about it. I don't want to remember. 'He hurt a friend of mine,' I say.

I glance at Scobie, who's staring at me in his unrelenting, all-seeing sort of way, and I know I'm not going to get away without telling the story. I lean my head back against the seat rest and I close my eyes.

'At my old school, there was a group of us, right? Me, Ali, Will and Millie. We all lived on the same street, and when we were kids we'd play out together, you know? And then when we went up to secondary school, we still hung out, went to town together on the weekends, that kind of stuff.'

I open an eye and glance at him again, but he's looking out of the window.

'There was this party one night. We were Year 9, it was near the end of the year. Some guy I knew from football had a free house because his parents were out of town, and it got a bit out of control. Furniture getting trashed, people puking on the walls, that kind of thing. But it was funny, you know, because we were all together. We hung out with some other guys from my team, kind of tucked ourselves away in the kitchen, away from all the craziness, and we just sat round playing drinking games, having a laugh.'

I can feel the anger start to throb through me, tightening my temples. I tap my fingers against the steering wheel, trying to focus on the beat instead.

'So you got drunk?' Scobie says.

'Yeah. And the guy – Mikey – he was there. I knew him from football too, not like good mates, but he was alright, you know, funny. He was into Millie, he was pretty obvious about it, but I thought that was cool. I knew him and he always seemed a pretty sound guy. I got chatting to some of the others and I left them to it.'

I squeeze my eyes shut and say the rest in a rush, trying to get it out before I have time to remember.

'She was drunk. She said she needed to lie down. He took her to a bedroom and when she was passed out, he had sex with her.'

'He raped her.' Scobie says it slowly, like he's checking he's understood. Or checking I have. I nod.

'So you went after him.'

Again, I nod.

'That's not what I'd call unprovoked. Surely the police were involved?'

This time, I shake my head. 'She wouldn't tell them.'

'Why not?'

I slam my hand against the wheel. 'She didn't want anyone to know! She was embarrassed. She was so mad at me and the way I handled it.'

Scobie's face creases in confusion. 'But that – but he –'

'I know, okay. I know.'

'That's awful,' Scobie says. 'How could she think that was her fault? She can't still think that, surely?'

'I don't know,' I say, yanking my seatbelt on. 'She wouldn't speak to me after. Ever.' The sour taste is back in my mouth. Berries. The strawberry sweet smell. I turn to Scobie. 'So you have to see that it's not what they're making out. Yeah, I've got a temper, and I hate that about myself. But I would *never* do what they're implying. I would *never* have hurt Lizzie.'

He nods. 'I know that.'

'Okay. Good.'

He gets out his phone again and looks at Facebook. Another 1,000 likes on our page; our message spreading out across the internet. I take out mine and look at Lizzie's AskMe.

'This means something,' I say. 'She left this for me, I know it.'

Scobie glances up. 'Why would she?'

Those three words hurt more than they should. Scobie shows me his Facebook inbox. There are about thirty unread messages.

'More people who've seen her?' I ask, my hands feeling damp and shaky.

'Yeah.' Scobie's phone bleeps plaintively and then the screen goes dark. Battery dead.

'We need to start answering them,' he says, throwing his now-useless phone into the cupholder in disgust. 'We need to start getting answers.'

I start up the car, making an untidy three-point turn in the gravel, and as I drive away, I glance in the rearview mirror and see Deacon Honeycutt in the window, watching us.

I DRIVE BACK to mine as quickly but not quite as carelessly as I drove us away. I'm expecting Kevin and Mum to come running out the second my car turns into the drive, but they don't. Even when I let myself in – nothing. The house is cold and silent, and in the living room the three half-empty cups of coffee from Hunter and Mahama's visit are still on the table.

'They must have gone out looking for you,' Scobie says. 'Where's your laptop?'

'In my room,' I say, but when we get up there, it's nowhere to be seen. 'That's weird,' I say, looking around, pulling back the duvet. I go out into the hall, ready to check downstairs, and see that Kevin's study door is open, his Mac on. This is extremely unusual. 'Come in here,' I call to Scobie.

He follows me into the room, which is large and bright; white desk, white shelves, a big bay window overlooking the garden. It's the one room in the house I'm not supposed to be in, but right now I don't have time to care. 'You get started on here,' I say, pulling out Kevin's huge, black leather desk chair for him – the only thing in here that's *not* white – 'and I'll go grab my laptop.'

291

I jog downstairs and take a quick scout around. I can't see it anywhere, but I figure it doesn't matter, because I can use my phone while Scobie uses the Mac. I pull my phone out of my pocket to check the battery, and it's only then that I notice the little icon at the top of the screen that means a missed call. I swipe down to check it. *Mum.* I hit the Call icon and wait for it to connect. It starts to ring, and an anxious feeling seeps through me.

It's ringing from somewhere beside me. I glance down and see it, halfway under the stairs. My own name flashing back at me. *Aiden.*

I hang up and pick it up. Weird. I guess she could have dropped it if she was in a hurry; she has a habit of leaving it in random places at the best of times.

Where were they hurrying to? The answer is obvious: after me. But then surely they would have caught up to us at Deacon's, or at least passed us on our way back. A strange, loose fear thuds through me, though I don't know where it's coming from. I slide Mum's phone into my pocket along with mine, and jog back upstairs where Scobie is clicking at about three different windows on Kevin's Mac.

'Did the police take my laptop?' I ask.

'Don't think so,' he says, distracted. 'But, Aiden, something weird's going on here.'

'What?'

'The computer. Kevin was totally wiping its memory.'

I look over his shoulder at the screen. The front-most window says 'Full System Reset' above a progress bar. Currently, it's at 64% and is 'Paused'. In another window, Scobie is furiously typing code that might as well be Klingon to me.

'I don't understand.'

'Did you tell him?' he asks, his voice icy. 'Did you tell him before today about being Hal?'

'No! Wait, you think –'

'I think he's got something on here, yeah. I think he caught you out and now he's trying to cover for you.' He hits the return key a little too hard and turns to look at me. 'Question is, what else do you need covering?'

'Nothing! I swear, Scobie, I didn't tell him anything.'

But he's already returned his attention to the files he's clawing back from the hard drive. I watch as he pulls them up, one after another, spreadsheets and tax returns and photographs.

And then a series of screenshots.

Screenshots of a Facebook inbox. *My* Facebook inbox.

Except not mine. It's the inbox for my 'Hal' profile.

I lean forward, my hands gripping the edge of the desk, my stomach turning somersaults. 'I don't – How…? Where did he get these?'

Scobie looks at me, his eyes hard, but he must decide I'm telling the truth. 'You really didn't know?'

'No!' My mind's racing, trying to understand, trying to make sense of it.

Scobie's clicking through more files, and my heart sinks as I recognise each one – my email account. My bank account. The old photo of Sarah Michelle Gellar as Buffy that I have bookmarked.

And there's Mum's stuff too: her work email, her personal one. A Twitter account I didn't even know she had. Her LinkedIn profile.

'Whoa…' Scobie trails off. 'What the –'

'How did he get these?' I ask, my voice flat.

'I mean, it's easy,' Scobie says. 'He's got a master account. He gave you your laptops, right? He must have just logged into both of them remotely. Looking at how many of these there are, he probably had some kind of software running on your computers the whole time, recording what you were doing.'

The thought sends acid lurching up my throat. I think of the laptop he bought me – on my desk, resting on my pillow beside me in bed. Like a snake, coiled, ready to strike.

'So he knew,' I say slowly. 'He knew all along.'

'Looks like it,' Scobie says, opening the screenshot of Hal's inbox again, the chain of messages from Lizzie. 'The question is, what did he do about it?'

And then I remember. The day after the prom, Kevin coming in and sitting on the edge of my bed. I was at my desk, my face still battered and bruised, my arm in a sling. My suitcase was packed beside me, ready for my journey to London the next morning.

'I've spoken to Selby,' he said. 'I've explained the situation, that the Honeycutt kid has been giving you trouble all year. I've told him what a good student you are, how excited you are to be joining sixth form, and he's agreed that, if there's no further police involvement, you'll be able to keep your place. He's a good guy. You're lucky.'

And then he looked past me, at my screen. It was on Lizzie's profile, just like it had been all day. Message after message, unanswered.

'Pretty girl,' he said, and I didn't reply.

'She the one you were talking about? The person you hurt?'

I looked behind me, at her photo, and he took my silence as confirmation. He stood up, put a hand on my shoulder.

'It'll all work out.'

'She's won't reply to my messages,' I said, and my voice was thick, like I might cry.

He squeezed my shoulder once. 'Keep your head down this summer,' he said. 'Go to London, stay out of trouble. Things will turn out okay.'

And all the time, he was looking at her face.

LIZZIE

When I arrived in London, I was suddenly hit by a wave of nerves. Hal and I had talked about everything. *Everything*. It was like when I first met Aiden; I felt like I'd found someone who just *got* me, who just fitted.

So obviously I didn't want to actually meet him. That would ruin everything.

No – that's not true. I did want to meet him, more than anything. I wanted to feel the way I felt when we talked online all the time. I was excited to be able to see him, hear him, touch him. For him to be real. For all the times he'd sent me hugs to actually become real hugs. Real kisses instead of ones made of pixels.

But it was bound to go wrong at some point, like all relationships do. There was bound to be some awkward moment when the conversation dried up, or when he said the wrong thing, or I did, or when he broke my heart and *pushed me down the freaking stairs*, and then the perfect just-the-two-of-us space we'd built together would instantly dissolve, just like it always does. And we'd just be two people again, two people without something special, without a story.

But the butterflies in my tummy were way stronger than the nerves or the doubts. And so, after pacing back and forth in front of King's Cross for ten minutes, I got on the bus. I smoothed down my hair, checked my breath and sat and watched the stops roll by until I got to Angel, where Hal had asked me to meet him.

I missed the pub the first time, too busy looking around and wondering if he was somewhere, watching me. So I had to double-back and by the time I made it to the door, my heart was beating so hard I was sure everyone could hear it.

Inside, it was cool and dark and busy, full of people eating food and drinking beer and craning their necks at the football on the widescreen TVs dotted about the place. I tried to look around without stopping to stare. I tried to remember exactly what the face I'd seen smiling back at me from Facebook each night actually looked like. I couldn't see anyone sitting alone, just people in groups, people laughing, people talking, people looking at each other, watching each other.

But then, through a gap in the crowd, him. Watching me.

Aiden's stepdad.

I was so surprised I looked away. Maybe he hadn't seen me? He probably wouldn't even know who I was, anyway.

But when I glanced back again, he was still watching me. And then he waved me over.

'Lizzie,' he said, standing up as I got near and reaching out to shake my hand, like we were having a business meeting. 'Do you know who I am?'

'Of course, Mr Cooper.' I felt about twelve. 'We met when Aiden and I did *Streetcar*, didn't we?'

'Oh, that's right,' he said, gesturing to the chair opposite his. 'Let me get you a drink.'

'Oh, I –' I looked around. Still no sign of Hal. 'Erm, okay. Sure.'

'Orange juice?'

I glanced up at him, at his clean-shaven, earnest face. Did I dare? 'Maybe with vodka?'

He smiled, just the hint of a wink. 'No problem.'

While he was at the bar, I looked round again, taking my time, making sure I checked in every corner of the bar. No Hal. I got my phone out of my bag and sent him a text: **where u?**

I still didn't even know if I wanted him to show. If I wanted him to be a real person who farted and had faults and couldn't be relied on and would let me down. Or if I wanted him to show up and see me with someone old enough to be my dad, buying me booze like some kind of Cool Guy. What would I do if he actually turned up with Kevin still there?

'Here we go.' Kevin put my drink in front of me, just as my phone vibrated in my lap.

Sorry, the text read. **Something came up**

Tears stung the edges of my eyes so I took a big swig of my drink. A double. *Perfect.*

'Look, I'm really glad I ran into you,' Kevin said, sitting down. 'I know it's not really my place, but –'

I looked up at him, my heart beating faster again.

'You and Aiden. What happened there?'

I looked away again, my face burning. 'Oh, it's – we… It was…' I stopped. There was no real way to explain it.

'No, sorry, it's not my business.' He smiled kindly at me.

298

'But Aiden just hasn't been the same since you guys stopped hanging out. I know he misses you.'

I took another sip of my drink, but suddenly it was hard to swallow. I missed him too. I really did.

'Anyway.' Kevin raised both of his hands, a generous surrender. 'I just wanted to say. Seeing as we happened to meet like this.'

'What *are* you doing here?' I asked, before realising I really didn't want him to ask me the same question. Or maybe I did. Maybe then it would get back to Aiden that I'd moved on; maybe it would make him jealous.

Yeah, I know. I was not exactly a nice person that day.

'Oh, work stuff. One of our clients has an office not far from here,' Kevin said, taking a gulp of his fizzy water. 'Just had a quick drink with their marketing guy.'

'On a Saturday?'

''Fraid so. No rest for the wicked.'

I tried to smile, but I was thinking of the text again. '*Something came up*'. *What does that even mean?*

'Are you okay?'

'Yeah.' Another big, burning mouthful of my drink. 'Yeah, just tired.'

'What are you doing in London? Shopping trip?'

'Yep.' I nodded. It'd be too humiliating to admit the truth. That I'd been stood up by some guy I met online.

'Listen, I'm leaving now. Why don't I give you a lift home?'

And suddenly, I *did* feel tired. Tired of trying to be okay, trying to be happy. Trying to be the perfect girl. Trying to be perfect. I drained the rest of my drink.

'Okay. If you're sure you don't mind.'

'Not at all. Be nice to have some company.' He stood up and held out my coat for me to wiggle on. 'Come on, then.'

Outside it was getting dark. 'My car's parked round here,' Kevin said, turning the collar on his fancy long coat up. He reached into his pockets and pulled on expensive-looking leather gloves. 'Getting cold,' he said.

We turned down a narrow side street and followed it round past a pretty terrace of grand three-storey houses, our footsteps echoing. The pavements were getting that glittery sheen on them under the orange of the streetlights, the frailest of frosts forming like lace.

'Oops, down here,' Kevin said, bumping against me as he tried to turn left while I went to cross the road.

This road was even quieter, the buildings dark and windowless, the pavement lined with black bollards like bodyguards. Shattered glass strewn across the pavement; another kind of glitter. The toe of Kevin's shoe caught a broken bottle and sent it skittering in front of us. It was the kind of surprising cold that cuts right through you. When it's summer, you forget how it ever felt to be cold. And then winter arrives and surprises you. You're cold all the way to the bone.

'Aiden's playing in a match next weekend.' Kevin glanced at me as he fished his keys out of his pocket. He clicked them and a sleek black car up ahead of us flashed its lights. 'Why don't you come?'

'Oh, I –' The cold and the vodka were making my head fuzzy. 'I don't know.'

He was fumbling for his phone, close to me. Close enough to smell the sharp, woody scent of his aftershave, the dry-cleaned wool of his coat.

And then he stopped walking. He put a hand on my shoulder.

'Lizzie,' he said. 'It's not too late. This is fixable.'

But I was noticing the warm way his eyes met mine; how soft his lips looked. I was thinking about how much he reminded me of Aiden, even though he wasn't really his dad. I was thinking about how Aiden had hurt me.

I was always thinking about how Aiden had hurt me. I'm not proud of that.

'It's really over,' I said. But I'm not sure if I was talking to Kevin or to myself.

The hand on my shoulder squeezed a little tighter, and then his fingers smoothed out the fabric of my coat. 'But you could be friends, couldn't you?'

I smiled. 'Is friends enough?'

He smiled back. 'Not always.'

And then I stretched up on tiptoes and I kissed him.

I don't know why I did it. I don't know why I did any of the things I did, except that there was an ache in me that I just couldn't get rid of, no matter what I tried. I missed Aiden; I wanted to hurt Aiden. Hurt him the way he'd hurt me. And so I did these things. I kissed other boys. I kissed his stepdad.

And he kissed me back.

But then he jerked back like he'd been electrocuted, his face twisted in disgust. 'No!' he yelled, and he pushed me away. Hard. I slipped.

There was a moment as I fell when our eyes met and I saw the feelings flash across his. Panic first – and then... Then something cold. Something hardened.

My head hit the bollard with a crack. And then I hit the pavement; a heavy thud.

I was lying looking up at the clear, cold night sky, warmth leaking out from under me. All I could see were the stars; brighter, brighter.

Then gone.

AIDEN

W<small>E BOTH SIT</small> staring at Lizzie's face on the screen. Just like he did that day. Is that when he decided to start spying on me?

'Why would he do all this?' I ask. 'Who *does* something like this?' *And where is he now?* I try and swallow down my anger, try and focus on Lizzie. 'Why didn't he confront me if he knew?'

'Good question,' Scobie says. He's busy reading through the messages from Hal – me – that can be seen in the screenshot. I don't need to. I know them off by heart.

'She gave Hal – *you* – her number enough,' he says thoughtfully, looking at the digits on the screen. *Lets chat babe. I want to hear your voice.* 'So Kevin had access to it. Maybe he called her. Maybe he told her you were Hal all along.'

A fresh lurch of horror goes through me at the thought. I don't want her to know that. I never want her to know that.

'And then what?' I force myself to say. 'She's so angry she hops on a train to London? It doesn't make sense.'

'Maybe she was meeting someone else,' Scobie says doubtfully.

It's the thing I've told myself all along – it *must* be true because I was Hal and she wasn't meeting *me* – but I can't convince myself. Because there's no proof; I've found no evidence that Lizzie ever spoke to any strangers but me. Except –

'Her AskMe page,' I say. 'There's something there, some kind of clue. She wanted me to know something.'

'Oh, for god's sake, Aiden!' Scobie says, red creeping up his face. 'You're delusional! They're just quotes, she wasn't leaving you messages. She hated you! The only clue we have is right here. It's the fact that *the man whose house you live in* was spying on her. Spying on you.'

She hated you. It's like a punch in the face, and I reel from it, speechless. I can't believe it; I won't. The messages are for me. They *mean* something.

'The CCTV,' Scobie says, turning back to the screen. 'At the pub. That seemed weird to me at the time. It sounds like it was hacked. Like someone *wanted* to delete any evidence of Lizzie being there. Of *who* she was there with. Would Kevin know how to do something like that?'

I don't answer. I don't know *what* Kevin is capable of any more. But I think it's pretty clear that Kevin knows what he's doing when it comes to technology.

'Maybe he thinks you killed her,' Scobie says suddenly. 'Maybe he's trying to hide any evidence he knew you were involved.'

I'm numb with fear but the words sting anyway. I feel dangerously close to tears. 'I didn't *kill her*, Scobie. God, you really think I'm capable of that?'

But an idea seems to have seized Scobie, and he's busy searching through directories of code again, his fingers skimming over the keyboard so fast they make me dizzy.

'Maybe *that's* what he was trying to delete,' he says. 'Come on, come on… Be here…'

I push my chair back and dial Kevin again. His phone rings and rings until it diverts to voicemail. He *always* answers his phone. I dial again, stalking the hallway, a buzzing in my ears.

Mum. He was watching her, too. Watching both of us this whole time; so cold, so clinical. Software recording our every move and him locked in his office each night, trawling through our days, checking everything we were saying and doing.

I stop my pacing in front of a framed photo of the two of them on their wedding day. Mum in her smart white dress; not a frilly one – that's not her style, not any more – but one that looks more business-like, more like something you'd wear to the office. She looks beautiful, but now, as I look at the way Kevin has his hand on her waist, the way he smiles at the camera, I suddenly think of the way she *used* to dress – the way she used to wear her kimono from Tokyo over a pair of jeans, the Seventies flares she wore to work with a smart shirt. I think of the Christmases and birthdays when Kevin bought her dresses just like this one, and the hairs on my arms and the back of my neck stand up.

I think about the food he makes us eat. The way he made her take his name.

Control. It's about control.

'Aiden.' Scobie's voice is urgent. One step back inside the door, I know why. He's made the file full-screen and although it's blurred I know immediately what it is.

'Press play,' I say, too frightened to move closer.

Scobie obeys without question, and we watch the fuzzy figures on the screen move jerkily back and forth like a tide.

It's busy; happy hour at The Winchester. People move glasses towards their faces, people turn to one another, wave at friends across the bar.

And then there she is. Just a small blond shape at the bottom of the screen, she skips with the footage until she's right in the middle of the scene. The centre of it.

She stops.

The crowd parts.

Then there he is.

Scobie's hand goes to the mouse, ready to skip it forward.

'Don't,' I say.

The people in the bar move back and forward in front of the table, blocking our view like clouds crossing the sun. I watch the numbers at the bottom of the screen tick on and on, the time passing. I watch him go to the bar, watch him carry their drinks back to the table. I watch her lean closer.

What is he saying to her?

And then they get up. He holds her coat out for her. He *touches* her. There's a thudding in my head, my fists tighten into knots. As they disappear out of shot, I realise the sound I can hear is coming from me; a deep, guttural noise that sounds like a growl. Images flash through my mind – Kevin shaking my hand the first time Mum brought him home to meet me; his hand on my shoulder that day after prom; his outstretched arms, holding out Lizzie's coat to her, shrugging the fabric up over her shoulders.

The growl becomes a roar and the knots of my fists find their place in the centre of the framed awards that litter the study walls, glass tinkling down around me. I aim a foot at a cupboard door and it buckles easily. And it feels good, it feels better, so I pull open drawers, throw things, tear paper, punch holes in walls. I rip the monitor off the desk and I hurl it across the room, turning before it even lands, Scobie scrabbling to get away from me.

Where did they go? I'd be saying if I could make my mouth say words. *What happened to her?*

But I can't. And so I just destroy things.

The drawers in the desk are locked, but that doesn't stop me. I just punch them and pull them and put my foot through them until they're hanging out, broken teeth in a broken mouth, their contents rolling out onto the glass-strewn carpet.

And then something catches the light. A needle. A small glass bottle rolls against my foot.

I stop.

I lean down and pick up the bottle. SODIUM THIOPENTAL, the bottle reads. SEDATIVE.

Sedative.

Scobie has crept closer again, and he crouches to pick up the needle. Sifting through the rest of the drawer's debris, he finds a smashed syringe and my stomach lurches.

I turn on my heel and run down the stairs, phone pressed to my ear again. *Mum. Where has he gone with my mum?*

'Aiden!' Scobie hurries after me. 'We need to call the police. We need to think about what this means. Where would he have taken Lizzie? Where would he go, Aiden?'

I close my eyes. 'I don't *know*, okay?' I throw my phone down, and bang my hand against the radiator. It starts its tapping again and I feel like kicking it.

307

'That's a weird noise,' Scobie says, looking at it.

I shrug wildly. 'Air in the pipes or something. Who the hell cares –'

Scobie takes a step closer to the radiator. 'Trapped air doesn't sound like that. When did it start?'

'I don't know,' I say, exasperated, spinning, because *why* are we talking about Kevin's central heating right now, when we're accusing him of – I can't even start to comprehend what we're accusing him of. 'A week ago, maybe two?'

And then I look at Scobie.

Scobie looks at me.

And we both run for the basement door.

THE BASEMENT HAS two sets of bright, white striplights set into its ceiling, which flicker on as we hurtle down the stairs. There are boxes stacked everywhere and old furniture pushed into corners, ghostly under dustsheets. White metal shelves have been screwed onto the walls with brackets and these are filled with folders and documents boxes, most of them dated from the Nineties – all the newer ones are up in Kevin's office.

The banging is louder down here.

Much louder.

'Where's the boiler?' Scobie yells, but I'm already heading for it, kicking over a stack of old tech journals on my way. I know exactly where it is because two summers ago, Kevin and I tried brewing our own beer, and the boiler cupboard was the warmest place in the house, good for the yeast. It's less of a cupboard, more of a utility room, with shelves for sheets and space for a washer/dryer, but Mum didn't like coming down here all the time because basements creep her out, so she had it moved up to the kitchen. The boiler room is tucked away in the left corner of the basement, under the stairs.

The boiler room door is padlocked. Twice.

'Keys?' Scobie yells, but I don't bother looking. I just pick up a set of hedge clippers and start smashing the locks. I hold the clippers like a baseball bat and I bring them down over my head, again and again, and at some point, I realise I'm yelling, screaming, a noise that sounds like someone else is making it. My hands start to bleed and one of the locks snaps, just a little, just enough. It falls, and I move on to the next one. I know but I don't know that Scobie is somewhere beside me, throwing stuff off the shelves, crying. Maybe it's me who's crying. Maybe it's both of us.

In slow motion, I see it splinter.

One – a chunk of metal flies out.

Two – the curve of the lock snaps in two.

I could reach out and tug it off now but I don't.

Three – the broken lock flies off and hits the wall, taking a chunk of plaster with it.

I drop the clippers to the floor with a clang, and with my bruised and cut hands I try to flick open the plates where the padlocks have been. My hands are shaking and they leave smears of blood on the door and the frame, and Scobie is next to me now, helping, and between us we pull the door open –

And she's there. Lizzie.

Lizzie.

Her hands are cuffed behind her back and she's crouching beside the boiler, bending so that she can clunk the cuffs against the pipe. She's dressed in a filthy t-shirt, a grey cloth bag over her head. When I stumble in and pull it off, she's gagged too. Her face is pale and her hair is dirty. Her eyes are pink and swollen and bruised, and when she blinks against the sudden light and sees it's me, they widen and then she starts to cry. Behind me, Scobie makes a noise that could be a shout or could be retching, then I hear him yelling at my phone, staggering around trying to find a signal.

'Aiden?'

It's a girl's voice, and at first I think it's Lizzie but she's still gagged, still looking up at me, crying, sagging against the arm I've put out to steady her. The sound has come from behind me. I spin round, expecting to see my mum.

But it's Marnie.

Marnie, standing at the bottom of the stairs.

Marnie, holding a knife.

WE STAND AND look at each other, me and Marnie, that long, wide knife from the block upstairs in the kitchen clutched in her hand.

'What are you doing?' I say, and then I think: he would have needed help. To do all this. Someone helped him.

Marnie looks down at the knife in her hand. 'I heard the banging – I thought –'

But then her eyes fall on Lizzie, who has edged herself back into a corner, under the shelves of sheets, shivering. Marnie pushes past me and rips the silver tape off her mouth, the cotton gag spilling out. She pulls Lizzie to her, and then Lizzie is crying, and Marnie is crying.

We're all crying.

I try to get closer, try to reach Lizzie, but when I do, Marnie thrusts the knife at me, her hand shaking. 'Stay away, Aiden. Stay *away*.'

'Marnie –' My voice trembles. 'It wasn't me. It was him, it was Kevin.'

At the sound of his name, she falters. Something dawns on her face, and she looks up at me, tears still spilling down her cheeks. She clutches Lizzie tighter. 'Oh, Aiden.'

'What?' I ask, and I think of the way she suddenly appeared at the bottom of the stairs, the panic on her face. 'Marnie, what is it?'

'Oh, Aiden,' she says again. 'That's why I came. I'm so sorry. There's been an accident.'

The dual carriageway, just outside of town. Over a hundred miles per hour. Straight into the central barrier. I listen to the specifics as they fumble their way out of Marnie's mouth, as she cries and holds Lizzie and, somewhere behind us, Scobie throws up into one of Kevin's box files.

And then I'm running, up the basement stairs, through the house, out onto the pavement, just as an ambulance and a police car screech down the street. I keep running.

Mum.

AT THE HOSPITAL, they fill in the rest of the story. How Kevin's car lurched onto the motorway at just after seven, just after I'd driven to Deacon's house.

He panicked, the newspapers will write in the coming days. *Attempting to leave the country*, they'll speculate. *He lost control of the car*, the police report will conclude. Later, some of the papers will start to wonder if that is actually true, or if he was, as they put it, 'looking for the final escape' and taking my mother with him. The central reservation just before the Abbots Grey exit will remain crushed at the point of impact for three weeks before it is replaced.

But, for now, all they can tell me are the facts. He was driving too fast. The car left the road and hit the barrier, leaving both driver and passenger fighting for their lives. Police wait outside his hospital room. More police crawl through his house, our home, like ants, bagging items, photographing the basement.

I sit in a plastic chair in a hospital corridor, and I think of the man who wanted to be my dad. I think of what he has taken from me.

They lie in separate wards, separate beds, my mum and husband.

The good news, delivered to me at just after four-thirty in the morning, is that she will make it.

The bad news is that he will too.

The most important thing I learn while I'm sitting there is that Lizzie is stable. Lizzie is okay.

It's time to rebuild the things that have been broken.

LIZZIE

THE FIRST, SECOND and third times I try to open my eyes, it's almost impossible. I feel like there's something heavy all over me, like my arms and legs have been turned to stone. My mouth is sticky and cotton-wool dry and my throat feels raw. I manage to lift my eyelids once, twice – a slice of white light, a flash of speckled ceiling tile – and then they crash back down again.

I drift in and out of sleep; there's a constant hushing, a faraway beep. There are voices but the words they say don't often make sense.

Kidney function critical...

... need to get those glucose levels up...

...CT results back... evidence of a cranial bleed... Severe disorientation...

And then I start dreaming. I start remembering. Trays of food pushed towards me. Tape pulled off my mouth, skin on fire. Tape smoothed across my mouth. A needle in my arm. Sleep. Sleep. A face that's not a face – a mask. An animal? Plastic features, grinning mouth. I scream. I sleep. I can't see his face but I know him; I know that I know him. His face. His face looming in front of me. His name out of my reach.

My name out of reach.

Where has my name gone?

I wake again, and this time I can see the needle in my arm. No – a different needle. This needle attaches to a tube, which attaches to a bag that hangs over me. I can see more wires stuck to me with small circles, wires that lead to machines that sketch out the rate at which I'm living.

Am I living?

I start to remember more. I remember that cold, quiet street; I remember his hand on my shoulder. I remember the way the pavement sparkled as we walked, and the terrible sound I made as I met it.

And then nothing.

And then that room. Waking up to total darkness – but no, not darkness. Plastic. All around me, covering me. Fear. Panic. Scrabbling at the plastic, gasping for breath, pushing it away. Screaming. Screaming.

His face. His panic.

You were dead, he said, again and again, as if he could make it true.

Am I dead now?

Sleep. Sleep again.

Lizzie.

'Lizzie.'

I open my eyes for the fourth time and a boy is sitting next to my bed. Holding my hand. I remember his face.

He is the boy who saved me.

'You're awake,' he says, and he squeezes my hand.

'You saved me,' I say. My voice comes out scratchy.

He smiles, but it's a weird smile – it doesn't reach all the way to his eyes.

'We don't have long,' he says, looking over his shoulder at the door. 'Nobody knows I'm here.'

'Are you okay?' He doesn't *look* okay. He's pale, dark shadows under his eyes. He's bruised, too – his eye and his lip puffy and blood-crusted. He can't stop glancing towards the door.

But then he looks at me again. He becomes still.

'Are *you* okay?'

'I don't know.'

'Lizzie, I'm so sorry this happened to you.' He puts his face down towards my hand, rests his forehead against it. I don't know what his name is. How does he know my name? *Is* that my name?

'Shh,' I say. 'Shh. You saved me.'

He looks up at me. 'You remember that?'

'I'm remembering,' I say, although I don't know whether this is true. Whether any of this is true.

His head jerks towards the door. 'Listen.' He wraps our hands in his other hand. 'I shouldn't be here. I just wanted to see you. I wanted to make sure you were okay.'

I nod, even though the dots at the edges of my vision are joining up now, darkness closing in. The boy notices straight away.

'You should sleep,' he says, and he brings my fingers towards his face and kisses them. 'We'll talk soon, okay?'

I'm trying to keep my eyes open but they keep drifting shut. I'm wondering if this is real or if I'm dreaming again. His fingers slip out of mine and I feel as though I'm floating away.

'Wait –' I force myself to open my eyes one more time. 'Were we – are we… friends?'

My eyes are closed and his voice is far away and comes to me just as the dark falls. But I hear it clearly anyway.

'Of course,' he says, his fingers grazing mine again. 'Lizzie, me and you will *always* be friends.'

THINGS COME BACK, but they come back slowly, and sometimes they come back wrong. I can't tell the difference between dream and memory, and I get muddled over people's names, what they mean to me. The doctors tell my parents and the police to be patient; they explain that repressing painful memories is normal in a situation like this. They say this is common, given what I've been through.

Nobody thinks to actually sit down and explain to me what I've been through.

I remember him first. Aiden. I remember his face looking down at me in the basement, but I also remember standing on a stage with him, I remember lying in a meadow and looking up at his face, the sky blue behind him. These thoughts make me feel warm and safe. Happy.

He visits me once more. It's dark outside, and when he's gone, I wonder if I dreamed him. He holds my hand and he tells me I'm getting better, that I'm going to be okay. He tells me that the man who did this to me is going to be punished. He says he will protect me.

And then, one day, I start to remember. Properly. It floods back; it makes me sick. I hold the edge of my bed and I remember everything.

I remember that day, going to London.

I remember who that man is, I remember what he did to me.

I hit the buzzer next to my bed and when the nurse comes running in, I ask for the detective, the one with the scary grey eyes. Hunter.

DCI Hunter sits in a chair beside my bed. He listens to me as I tell him everything; about how Hal called me, how Hal stood me up, and how Kevin was there. How he bought me my drink, how he walked me to his car. How he pushed me. The sound of my head splitting open, the way the stars turned to darkness.

'If Hal had just shown up,' I say, my voice shaking, the thought just occurring to me, 'none of this would've happened.'

'Lizzie,' he says, his voice gentle. 'Hal didn't make that call. Kevin did. There isn't a Hal. There never was.'

I close my eyes, try to process this. I can't make sense of it. 'But why would Kevin call me?'

Hunter sighs. 'He claims he wanted to repair the relationship between you and Aiden.'

I feel sick, remembering the way he put on gloves as he walked, the way he looked at me as I fell. 'He thought he'd killed me.'

'Yes. He claims he panicked. Lizzie, I need to ask you – why did he push you? Did you argue? This is really important. This is what any trial will focus on: whether it was an accident or whether he intended to hurt you.'

'He wrapped me up in plastic,' I say, and I start to cry. 'He hid me in his basement.'

'I know.' He puts an awkward hand on my shoulder.

I stop crying suddenly, what he said before finally sinking in. 'So Hal was never real? It was always Kevin?'

Hunter looks down at the floor. 'No. Not exactly. When Kevin called you, he pretended to be Hal. He knew about your relationship with Hal, he had access to those messages. But he wasn't the one who sent them.'

'Then who was?'

Hunter looks up at me, and then he does a funny thing: he reaches out and holds my hand.

'I'm sorry,' he says. 'This isn't going to be easy to hear.'

Extract from Hertfordshire local newspaper, Abbots Grey Evening News:

Local businessman Kevin Cooper appeared in court today for the third day of his high-profile trial. Cooper, 45, is accused of the abduction of schoolgirl Lizzie Summersall last October.

The court has heard that Summersall was lured to a pub in North London, thinking that she would be meeting a boy she had met online. In fact, the meeting had been arranged by Cooper, whose defence team say was trying to repair the damaged relationship between Summersall and her ex-boyfriend Aiden Kendrick, Cooper's stepson. An altercation followed, during which Summersall sustained a serious head injury.

The prosecution state that Cooper, mistakenly believing Summersall to be dead, then placed her in the boot of his car and drove home to his £2 million home in Abbots Grey where he concealed her body. On discovering Summersall was in fact alive but unconscious, he proceeded to keep her prisoner in a 'calculated and sickening' plot. They pointed to evidence that Cooper's multi-million-pound technology empire had developed security software 'TrueFace' for sites such as Facebook, and suggested that the media attention surrounding Lizzie's disappearance presented 'an ideal business opportunity' for Cooper.

Deborah Grant QC, defending Cooper, said that although he had made a 'monumental error in judgement' when attempting to conceal Summersall's body, it was 'an error made in a moment of pure panic, and a decision which sent him, regrettably, spiralling into a situation far beyond his control'. She said that Cooper was 'an honest man, a good man, who was just trying to protect his family, and, in doing so, made a terrible mistake.' She also accused Miss Summersall, who appeared in court to give evidence after several months of therapy and treatment for memory loss, of being 'a fantasist, an attention-seeker, and an extremely talented actress'.

The trial continues.

Extract from national tabloid newspaper, The Shot:

Lolita Lizzie Made Play For Boyfriend's Dad!

The jury at the trial of internet millionaire Kevin Cooper has heard that the schoolgirl he abducted, Lizzie Summersall, made sexual advances towards him. Cooper's defence team say that Lizzie, 16, attempted to lure him into bed in an attempt to get revenge on her ex-boyfriend and Cooper's stepson, Aiden Kendrick. Summersall had quite the summer, having 'sexual relationships with strangers' and 'getting so drunk she'd forget what she was doing', Deborah Grant, Cooper's lawyer, claimed. She suggests Cooper was trying to defend himself from an intoxicated Summersall when she slipped and knocked herself unconscious.

Comment left on article on online news site, The Daily Verdict:

Frankly, this is disgusting. We're talking about a teenage girl here, and he's a middle-aged man! Of course he wasn't defending himself! FFS. The fact that any jury is even considering that as an argument makes me sick.

Also, helloooo? The clothes? That guy who worked for him has admitted that Cooper got him to dump her

clothes in the park (and he messed it up by folding them, LMAO), and made him sign some non-disclosure agreement and paid him off. Hardly the work of a man in a state of panic, is it? Sounds pretty cool and collected to me.

And what was he actually going to do with her in the end? Why isn't anyone asking that? It's not like he could let her go, could he? She knew it was him, she remembered what happened. So, come on, let's be real, he'd have killed her eventually. Guaranteed.
If he walks free tomorrow, I'm leaving the country. This is a total joke.

Extract from national broadsheet newspaper, The London Post:

Kevin Cooper was today found guilty of kidnapping and perverting the course of justice. He was sentenced to eighteen years imprisonment with a minimum term of twelve years. The jury also found him not guilty of an attempted murder charge. Though the judge said she accepted that Cooper had not initially intended to harm Summersall on the evening of 8th October, she called his actions following the event 'unforgiveable and calculated' and said that she had 'no choice but to deliver a sentence that reflects the serious nature of his crime'.

Stocks in Cooper's multi-million-pound technology empire have plummeted since the trial began. Cooper's wife and stepson were not in court to see the verdict delivered.

AIDEN

I TRY TO move on.

I try to spend time with my mum, helping her unpack our things in our new, smaller house down by the river, down by Scobie's. I try to ignore the constant stares we get, the whispers everywhere we go.

I don't visit Kevin in prison. Neither of us do.

I try to get on with my last year of A Levels. I sit at the back of classrooms, I spend my lunchtimes at home; sometimes with Scobie, sometimes alone.

People wonder why I – we – didn't go back to London, start again. Again. But Mum says she won't hide. She's back in her kimono and her flares, already looking for a job. She's finally starting to smile again.

And so I try.

But at night, the loneliness stretches out in front of me and I ache for the old days, for the bleep of a new message in the darkness of my room.

She didn't come back to school; they say she couldn't face it. She's finishing her A Levels with a private tutor, and then she'll go off to uni, start again somewhere else. She still sees

Marnie, she still sees Lauren. I know, because I hear them talking in class. Not to me obviously. They don't talk to me.

Her privacy settings have all changed; I can't even see her face. I just have the photo I took, the one of her as Blanche, her phone blocking most of her face. Blocked blocked blocked.

I think of all the people I could be. I think of all the faces I could use to win her trust back, to be her friend again. I just want to see her again, to know that she's okay. I think how easy it would be; a simple click of a button. Follow.

But it wouldn't be easy; it wouldn't be real. I know that now.

And so I pick up my phone, and I draft a message, like the hundreds of messages I've started and sent before. I don't even know if this is still her number; I don't even know if she'll read it.

But I have to try.

> Lizzie, I'm so sorry. What I did was unforgiveable.
> And it put you in danger, and I'll never get over
> that. But please. Let me try to make it right.

I press send. I watch and wait. *Delivered*, it says. *15:38*.
The screen is still. The screen is silent.
And then:

...

She starts to write back.

ACKNOWLEDGEMENTS

Thanks – first, foremost and always – to Margaret, Richard and Daniel Cloke. You are my favourite people in the world, and these books just wouldn't happen without your support, encouragement and company. I love you.

And a huge thank you to:

Early readers Hayley Richardson, Ian Ellard and Lizzie Bishop, for all of your feedback and general wonderfulness.

Cathryn Summerhayes and Siobhan O'Neill at WME, for making the tricky stuff fun and the fun stuff better.

And to Emma Matthewson, Rosi Crawley, Georgia Murray, Debbie Hatfield and all at Hot Key, for being brilliant to work with and for giving Aiden, Lizzie, Marnie and Scobie the perfect home. Thank you!

Nicci Cloke

Nicci Cloke is a full-time writer, part-time doer of random jobs. These jobs have included Christmas Elf, cocktail waitress, and childminder. She is also the organiser and host of literary salon Speakeasy. She lives and writes in North London. Follow Nicci on Twitter: @niccicloke

Thank you for choosing a Hot Key book.

If you want to know more about our authors and what we publish, you can find us online.

You can start at our website

www.hotkeybooks.com

And you can also find us on:

We hope to see you soon!